Chapter 1

*A lady is never more vulnerable than when she is trav-
elling, and a refined, lady-like deportment is never
more indispensable than in the quagmire of foreign
lands.*

Lady Lockwell's Handbook of Etiquette

BRIANNIS IAVI HAD NEVER used soap as a weapon before.

Over the course of a short yet illustrious career, she had killed
people with a wide range of both conventional and more innovative tools – among them scalpels, poisoned needles, and on
one memorable occasion, a stuffed swordfish – but the use of
soap had always been limited to her disciplined routine *after*
the deed. In those moments, of course, she applied it gener-
ously. One did not grow up in a surgeon's household without
a firm understanding of hygienic principles and the oozing,
many-coloured consequences an infected wound could have.

Yet on this bright autumn morning, surrounded by the jagged mountain peaks of the Faerie realm, Briannis found herself lathering up in preparation for a kill.

The troubling part was, of course, that she didn't even know if it would work – and if it would, *why*. But the instructions in the letter had been clear, and no better ideas had presented themselves in the two weeks she'd journeyed across this strange, barren land. So soap it was, abundant amounts of it, until the fresh, grassy scent of daisies clung to every inch of her pale skin and she was shivering in the cold mountain air.

Only then did she dress, slowly and meticulously, making sure to give the same treatment to every single weapon in her possession. She slid into her chemise, her stays, her stockings, then paused to rub daisy soap all over the little knife she carried in her left garter. Petticoat, muddy travel dress, a pause to coat the knife from her hidden skirt pocket. Sturdy ankle boots, two more knives. Kidskin gloves, concealing the vial of poison strapped to the inside of her left arm. Pelisse, the fur trim home to the largest dagger she possessed. Finally, she pinned her chestnut curls in place, using several unnecessarily sharp hairpins of the kind that had proven their worth in the past – embedded deep in the eyeballs of her victims.

More weapons than she'd ever needed for any job. Then again, she'd never killed a fae king before.

Not for the first time, she fought a shiver. How had she gotten herself into this situation, again?

The answer to that question included several dozen corpses, a decidedly unflattering reputation, and a midnight arrest that had shocked her very proper landlady to the core. She hurriedly pushed that train of thought aside. Much better to think about the practicalities of the day, now that she had all but reached her destination; it wouldn't do to forget anything today, standing on His Majesty's doorstep.

She neatly folded her blankets, tucking them into the farthest corner of the shallow cave in which she'd spent the night. Her bag came next, carefully tied shut. Upon finding the path the evening before, she had decided to leave her belongings behind for the final leg of the journey; if all went according to plan, she would be back here before nightfall, and she would be faster and more flexible without the weight. Still it made her nervous, leaving her maps and food unguarded. If they were discovered while she was out ... If someone stole them ...

'Stop it, Bri,' she muttered, turning away sharply. 'You'll melt your brain one day.'

Father's wisdom never failed her. She pulled her pelisse a little tighter about herself, ran a last look around the cave, and stepped out into the valley, icy wind catching the flaps of her coat as she found her way along the ravine. Desolate mountains towered over her, shrouded in mist, turning the Faerie realm into a landscape of hazy silhouettes. No birdsong broke the eerie silence. Only the wind howled between the peaks and crags, that ghostly sound that had kept her wide awake during the first restless nights in this place. She barely heard it anymore.

Before her, the narrow path she'd discovered last night emerged from the mist, winding up along the steep slopes.

Towards her destination.

Another shiver ran down her spine.

Sweet divines, this wasn't a place for a proper lady – all sharp ridges and dizzying drops, and who knew what twisted fae traps might be waiting for her up there? Traipsing around the wilderness wasn't her sort of work, either. If the alternative hadn't been the gallows, she would never have taken this job for all the gold and pretty promises in the world. But succeeding was her only path to survival now, and she *could* admittedly use the coin that would come with the victory – so she steeled herself and walked, boots crunching on pebbles as she began her ascent of the mountain.

Or more of a cliff, rather.

Within minutes, she was glad to have left her bag behind. The climb was steep and strenuous enough for just the weight of her slim body, the path dangerously narrow even without a bulging bag on her shoulders. Living on the fourth floor of a creaky canal house had prepared her for the occasional clamber, and twelve days of hiking had made her feel muscles she'd only known from Father's anatomy books – but this was something else entirely, hundreds and hundreds of feet of nothing but verticality.

Soon enough, the fur-trimmed pelisse grew unbearably hot. Every thought fled her mind as physical exertion took over, boots slipping on loose gravel and wind whipping loose curls around her face; she focused only on the effort of moving her feet step after step, keeping her gaze fixed on the treacherous ground. Her breath came in rhythmic little gasps. She counted them, starting over at every hundred – her only way to measure the passing of time.

The sun finally rose above the jagged mountain ridges as she scaled the cliff, and golden light poured into the valley below, washing the ominous mist away. Briannis didn't allow herself more than a single glance down. Later – after the job was done – she'd have time to look and admire. For now, she didn't dare to grant herself a break.

Another bend in the path loomed up. She gripped the rocky outcroppings with gloved hands as she hauled herself around the sharp corner, keeping her gaze deliberately away from the gaping depths to her left. More grey granite emerged above her, knife-like edges jutting into the pale blue sky – but there, peeking over the upper edge of the cliff ...

CURSE
OF THE
THORN
KING

WAYFARER FAE

BOOK 1

LISETTE MARSHALL

ISBN: 9798857396582

Cover design: Maria Spada Designs
Editor: Erin Grey, The Word Faery

www.lisettemarshall.com
www.facebook.com/LisetteMarshallAuthor
www.instagram.com/AuthorLisetteMarshall

To Elsie.
Thank you for the caterpillar facts.

Contents

She stiffened in her place despite all her wiser intentions, panting and hurting, gaping at the destination for which she'd braved two weeks of travels.

Rosethorn Keep.

Only now did she understand how the hellish place had earned its name.

In this barren mountain landscape, where nothing grew but grass and moss and the curious star-shaped flowers she'd spotted along the path once or twice, she hadn't expected the keep to do its moniker justice. But the building that perched atop the cliff like a crown on a king's head was as different from the crude rocks as day from night – a majestic complex of slender towers and pointed spires, every inch of it covered in vines that snaked their way up the turrets and parapets and twisted across gates and sky bridges.

And roses. Hundreds, perhaps thousands of roses, their bright red petals almost aglow in the morning sunlight.

The memory welled up with a pang of recognition. *Wild roses. Pleasure and pain.*

A smile fought its way to her lips, fond and wistful in equal amounts. It was sentimental nonsense, of course, to start thinking about the language of flowers now – she had never been so far removed from the ballrooms of Elidian, where the bouquets and wreaths would be whispering their quiet messages to anyone who knew what to look for. Yet she couldn't help but linger on the thought of her well-thumbed lady's handbook for a brief moment, all those hours she'd spent memorising and analysing, all those hours of preparing for a life that had never been hers in the end.

If she returned to the city with the job done, who knew whether the knowledge might be of use in whatever new existence would be waiting for her?

She closed her eyes, smelling the soap that would have to be her key to victory. *Daisy. Innocence.*

The irony.

With a firm shake of her head, she kicked herself back into motion.

Soon she was panting again, dragging herself these last strides up to the edge of the cliff. With her target in clear sight, she felt even more compelled to keep moving; as she made her way up towards the Keep, she watched the rose-covered walls like a hawk, ready to duck and hide at the first sign of danger. Lady Millicent had said there would be no watchers at the castle – but until this moment, Briannis had taken the assertion with a generous grain of salt. Kings would have people to protect them, wouldn't they?

The battlements *did* seem deserted, though.

She gritted her teeth and climbed. Best not to count it as a lucky break just yet. For all she knew, His Majesty had neglected to hire guards because he was more than capable of fighting off intruders on his own, which meant she still had to get past him.

The rose-framed gates loomed closer and closer, and still she met no resistance. No cry of alarm. No sinister spirits or magic traps. Mouth dry, she took the last heavy steps onto the castle's deserted terrace and stood there for a moment, examined the towering structure as she gathered her breath: high wooden gate, rose-covered battlements, and no sign of defences.

This was too easy.

Unease churned in her gut as she worried her bottom lip, unsure what to do now. Should she just ... walk on? But perhaps she was strutting right into a trap. Perhaps they lay in wait for her behind these granite walls, luring her into a false sense of safety. The lack of opposition was disorienting – she'd expected to know at this point what to avoid, who to outsmart ...

Perhaps it was that damned soap after all, doing what the cryptic note in her cell had promised?

The thought gave her just enough courage to shake off the apprehension and step forward, towards that disconcertingly quiet building. If she was being tricked, there was little she could do about it now. Better to move and hope for the best than to stand there until she would surely be discovered by the creatures inhabiting this place.

Nothing stirred as she wrapped her hands around the handle of the small door carved from the larger gate. She sent a silent prayer to whatever divine spirit might feel protective of murderers, then turned and pushed.

The gate wasn't locked.

Madness, absolute madness ... but when she peered inside with a wildly hammering heart, no monstrous guards waited for her in the lush hall behind, no smirking fae mages, no grim and heavily armed soldiers. Just a pristine velvet carpet and a gurgling fountain embedded in the left wall, the sparkling water inviting her to wash off the sweat and quench her growing thirst.

Briannis slipped inside, holding her breath, and ignored the fountain. It might be poisoned.

Knowing what she did about the fae, it likely would be.

The Keep was eerily quiet, even more so than the mountains outside. When she'd visited the Princeps' palace in Elidian – or, more accurately, when she'd been dragged into it with cuffed hands and chained ankles – the place had bustled with life: servants hurrying around, senators engaging in heated debates, guards stamping through the corridors. This place rather resembled a graveyard. An exceptionally luxurious graveyard, but a graveyard all the same.

A trap? An attempt to make her hold her breath until she suffocated herself?

She tiptoed down the hallway, her hand close to the dagger hidden in her pelisse. Around her, a realm of lush abundance opened up, so very different from the stark world outside that she had to pinch herself: floors inlaid with dark, shimmering quartz and rosy marble, crystal chandeliers dangling from vaulted ceilings. The walls were covered in leaves and a host of blooming flowers, intricately woven together to create dazzling displays of colour across the full length of the corridor.

Briannis prodded the nearest lily, found it real and alive, and hastily darted back, frantically wiping her glove. This *had* to be magic, and she had no desire to fall under the spell of that vile, wife-stealing, mind-clouding power.

Drawing in a deep breath, sucking the intoxicating fragrance of lilies and roses deep into her lungs, she ventured on. The silence seemed to swallow the soft padding of her boots, like a pillow smothering desperate breaths. She was tempted to shout out into that wall of nothingness, just to test if her voice would come out muted, too – but who knew, it might be just what they wanted her to do for whatever twisted reason.

There was no thinking sensibly when it came to fae, Father had taught her. There was just steering clear and hoping for the best.

Past a patch of begonias on the wall, the corridor split before her, left leading to a closed door, right leading into a broad hall. Now she heard something for the very first time, a faint and distant humming – the sound of someone quietly singing to themselves.

The first sign of life. And she'd need to find life before she could make her kill.

Clenching her fingers around her dagger, she slipped into the right corridor.

As she skidded across a wide oakwood floor and then ducked below a doorway covered in more of those damned flowers, the melody grew steadily louder. Quiet steps, then. If she couldn't surprise whoever the singer was, she wouldn't stand a chance; she traded in near-accidents and elegant deaths, not in brutal struggles and head-on charges. *Just* around the corner ...

She paused, peaking through the next doorway. Beyond it was a dining room filled with white-and-blue ceramic displayed on long wooden shelves; at the centre stood a table long enough to seat two dozen guests. But there was no one to be seen – nothing but that persistent, almost droning sound.

Coming from the direction of ... the mirror?

She blinked at the enormous, rectangular frame that hung on the back wall, all ornate silver curls and leaf patterns. Reasonably speaking, she reminded herself, mirrors couldn't sing. Back at home, in the not entirely safe but definitely familiar alleys of Elidian, she would have laughed at the very suggestion of it.

But she stepped forward until she could see herself in the silver surface, and the humming abruptly ceased.

Visitors? a voice purred, except it was not exactly a voice, and it wasn't exactly speaking, either. The sound reverberated through her skull like an echo, a distant memory. *A good day to you, young lady.*

Briannis stared at herself in the mirror, wide-eyed and sweaty, reading the paralysing panic on her own face.

Any questions? the mirror hummed, sounding content. *It's been so long since I've answered any new questions. No, you are not the fairest woman in the world, I'm afraid – not even the top ten, so don't bother asking – but I have no doubt we can find something at which you excel above all others. Floral embroidery? Dancing the cotillion?*

'Where is the king?' Briannis hissed, not daring to raise her voice above that urgent whisper.

The king? The mirror sounded vaguely disappointed. *Well, that is a question, I suppose. In the music room, of course.*

'And where is the music room?'

One question a day, pet. Those are the rules. The humming resumed, and no matter how much Briannis pulled faces at the blasted thing, it would not speak to her again.

That left her with just the one clue. The music room.

Where did one find a music room in a castle as large as a sizeable neighbourhood?

She left the mirror behind, scurrying on through the Keep, aiming for a methodical search and managing little more than a ramble in a growing state of bewilderment. She knew little about the fae, she had to admit, nothing beyond what every Elidian burgher knew, which was that the devils never stayed in one place for long, that their magic could make you hate your dearest friends or fall in love with a clump of mud, and that they stole helpless women and girls and discarded them as they pleased. Fae were disturbers and destroyers. They were fickle and cruel and, although they could not speak direct untruths, liars. They were the opposite of civilisation, and they did not belong in any proper society, hers least of all.

She would never have thought them capable of building *this*.

Rosethorn Keep was a labyrinth, a treasury, a monument to both decadence and dedication. Every room she entered was a new miracle, every door she opened revealed more splendour and strangeness – an abundance vastly different from the grandest mansions of the city, the houses in which nobles and prosperous merchants spent their days. Rather than using gilded candelabras, the candles of Rosethorn Keep balanced on intricately carved deer antlers and levitating chandeliers. Rather than silk wall-coverings, the rooms she passed were lined with more flowers, or with rough quartz, or with strangely luminescent mushrooms shrouding their surroundings in an unnatural blueish glow. And rather than marble floor tiles—

She halted, blinking at the dark stone below her feet. In that smooth surface, the unmistakable shape of a small skeleton lay curled up – a fossil, but what sort of creature was it? A young animal of some kind? Perhaps it was a fossilised embryo? But in that case you would expect to see an egg, and that—

Barbarian child! the voice of Mrs. Bartlett shrieked in her memory.

Oh. Yes. She straightened as hastily as she'd stopped walking. Proper ladies did not care about embryo fossils, and either way, she had a king to kill first.

She walked on.

Through a corridor shaped by a tunnel of branches. Over a mosaic floor so colourful she barely dared to touch it. There were intricate carvings and gleaming jewels. Flowers covered in gold dust and twinkling lights illuminating even the rooms without any windows And everywhere, as if the castle warned her not to forget the truth of its inhabitants, were the sprinkles of magic, turning even the most common of objects into spine-chilling oddities.

She saw hourglasses with the sand running up.

She saw masks changing their expressions, going from wicked grins to theatrical despair in the blink of an eye.

She saw spindles spinning their own wool, she saw knives cutting their own food, and when she stumbled into a high-ceilinged hall with walls covered in Elidian oil paintings, keys were turning themselves in the locks.

It was there, surrounded by picturesque views of the city she knew and loved, that she first heard the unmistakable wail of violins in the distance.

Music room.

She changed course.

Up a broad marble staircase, lined with hovering bronze statues; past a stained-glass window that sparkled in a thousand shades of green; below a ceiling painted like the starry night sky, constellations circling over the plaster. The haunting melody of the violins grew ever louder. A strange song, not beautiful, but captivating, tugging at her heart like a fishline reeling her in. She'd have followed it even without the mirror's clue – a disconcerting notion. Was this how they lured women away from the safety of their homes and families?

Even that thought couldn't convince her to turn and flee. Her future depended on this kill, and she *wouldn't* end up like one of those poor, discarded souls.

The double doors she finally reached were tall pieces of art – smooth ebony wood inlaid with silver symbols she'd never seen before, hands and flowers and suns, arranged in neat lines as if she was looking at some twisted sort of inscription. She drew her knife, took off her pelisse to move more easily, and then hesitated for a last moment, fingertips hovering half an inch from the silverwork. Magic, again, and who knew what touching it might do to her?

But the violins were playing behind that door, accompanied by the sensual tones of a cello she had not noticed from a distance. If she wouldn't find her target here, she wouldn't find him anywhere.

Holding her breath, she pushed open the door.

The room was dimly lit, with candles flickering in every corner, casting long shadows across the flower-covered walls and the smooth oakwood floor. A broad mantelpiece carried a marble bust: a fae portrait, she knew by the horns curling from the sculpted hair. Harps, flutes, and an elegant pianoforte stood unused in the corners. But at the centre of the room, on a low, velvet-covered stage, a quartet of instruments was playing itself, no hands moving the bows as they lured that heart-breaking, blood-curdling melody from the strings.

And sitting on the floor before that stage, his back turned towards her ...

A man.

Although that denotation seemed not enough by far to do the vision justice.

Even sitting cross-legged on an unassuming floor, the king of all fae seemed impossibly tall, with a straight, upright posture that could rival the primmest of society debutantes. A tailored sapphire coat hugged his slender shoulders, the silk embroidered with floral patterns in gold. He wore buckskin breeches and polished black boots, a single signet ring gleaming on his right hand; copper hair flowed freely down his back, the tips reaching nearly to his hips.

That hair – the untamed wildness of it – was the only thing about him that looked fae, dangerous and feral and *other*. The rest of him was far too refined for the creature he had to be, and Briannis found herself frozen in the doorway, staring at his lean back as the strings spun their hypnotising lullaby around her.

Why had no one told her the devil would be *beautiful*?

Then again ... She shook her head, clutching her fingers so tightly around the worn leather of her dagger hilt that it hurt. What else had she expected? All fae were beautiful, that was the danger in them: it was how they seduced you, drove you mad until you forgot your name and all you'd wanted in life.

She *knew* what she wanted, and this straight-backed, copper-haired bastard had nothing to do with it.

So he had to die.

Drawing her knife felt like preparing to cut an exquisite painting to shreds.

But she had no choice – not if the life of her dreams meant a single blasted thing to her. They'd lift all charges against her, she reminded herself as she took a quiet step forward. They'd wipe her criminal records. They'd pay her, enough to buy her own home near the botanical gardens, enough to hire a servant or two and purchase a lady's wardrobe; she would not be the dazzling debutante she'd dreamed of being, she would not have the dukes and marquises falling at her feet, but she would, for the first time in her life, be *respectable*.

Her dagger came up, like a viper about to strike.

Her eyes routinely examined the vulnerable spots, searching for the most promising target. The collar of his coat protected the base of his skull, but nothing except a pristine white cravat covered the side of his throat. That was where she would strike, then, with surgical precision: stab sideways, lodge her knife behind the carotid artery and jugular vein, then yank the blade forward, slashing through the bloodstream. It did not require great strength, as long as you knew what to aim for.

Another step forward. She drew the dagger sideways, slowly, not making a single sound.

As her foot came down, the violins faltered.

The cello soared out of tune.

She had just enough time for a single thought – a single panicked, decidedly improper thought – before the fae king lunged to his feet and spun around. She caught a flash of emerald eyes as he turned in a whirl of wavy copper locks. Of a strong jaw and high cheekbones. Of tight lips twisted in shock.

And then he faced her fully, and sweet divines, she almost ran after all.

The right side of his face was mesmerizingly beautiful, a perfection that made her heart ache even in that fraction of a moment – an eye the colour of lush moss, a strong chin, a straight nose. But the other half was a grotesque, skeletal monstrosity, greyish white skin, a sunken cheek, and a deep-set eye devoid of life and expression ...

Like a corpse's face.

Like someone had already killed him years ago.

She leapt at him before the horror could sink in, dagger aiming a desperate swing at the side of his neck. He didn't move. His good eye remained fixed on her for one bewildered moment, as if he *knew* who she was, as if he knew as well as she did that she shouldn't be here, miles and miles away from home and hearth ...

'Get *back*!' he snarled, his rumbling voice filling the last feet of air between them.

And as if his words were a solid, physical force, something invisible hit her like a fist just below the midriff, slamming the breath from her lungs and sending her tumbling through the air.

Chapter 2

Under no circumstances should a lady be alone with a gentleman with whom she is but slightly acquainted: such a mistake leaves her susceptible to the most severe misconstructions.

Lady Lockwell's Handbook of Etiquette

SHE WOKE UP WITH a disconcerting *snap*.

It was more feeling than sound, something unspeakably deep in her neck – as if her vertebrae had been separated and now abruptly clicked back together. Sensation rushed into her limbs the next moment. A throbbing ache below her midriff and a hard floor beneath her back and ...

Hands.

Hands around the back of her neck.

She stiffened. A soft, impossibly intimate touch – one warm hand cradling her nape. One ice-cold hand brushing along her upper vertebrae, fingers prodding and pressing as if to test the strength of her spine. Warm, cold – alive, dead—

Dead.

With a gasp, her eyes flew open.

He hovered over her, far too close, holding her as she lay sprawled out on the oakwood boards. The nightmarish two halves of his face remained hazy until she blinked two, three times; then they sharpened into view, his gorgeous right side and his decaying left, separated neatly across the middle. Only his hair was the same on both sides, a deep autumn red, flowing over his back and shoulders like a cascading waterfall.

Eyes locked with hers, one dead and cold, the other bright green and hardly any warmer.

Fae eyes.

With a shriek, she shot up from the floor and scrambled backwards – away from that half-dead creature, away from those invasive touches that could have ruined her in an Elidian ballroom. The fae king didn't follow, sitting cross-legged on the floor with just the smallest hint of a smile around his lips. It was not a pleasant smile at all. It looked like sweetness and malice – like a poisoned apple offered to an unsuspecting victim.

'Look at that.' His husky voice dripped with insincerity. 'She's awake.'

What in the world had *happened*? Briannis crawled back until her shoulders bumped into a flower-covered wall; there she froze like a trapped rabbit, thoughts racing past those last conscious seconds again and again. *Get back*, he'd shouted. Just those words. And she'd ... flown.

Magic.

She stared at the red-haired man before her, and he raised a sceptical eyebrow in response – the only eyebrow he had. On his dead side, nothing but the sharp edge of eye socket still showed where the other must have been. Of course it was magic, she told herself with shaky impatience; how else could a corpse be alive? And now she had to get up and *run*, before he could hurt her in whatever unspeakable ways the fae hurt their captives ...

Her legs wouldn't move.

'Struck dumb by the sight of my radiant beauty?' the fae king added, a hint of mockery to his voice. 'Ironic. It's your kind that got me here. One would think you'd be prepared for the fruits of your hard work. What is your name?'

She swallowed heavily, mind still wrestling to catch up. She ought to be polite and compliant ... but could he hurt her with just the knowledge of her name? Should she lie? Tell him she was called Annie Tanner and hope he'd believe it? But who knew what his magic could do, and—

He heaved a sigh, lips twisting into an expression of exaggerated disappointment. 'Tell me your true name.'

Her lips and tongue moved.

She didn't *want* them to move – had never given them the command to move, wanted them to hold *still*, sweet divines help her – and yet they moved, as if an entirely different being had taken control of her body. She spat out the words like unwanted guests – 'Briannis Iavi.'

Her lips slammed themselves shut again.

The sound of her name echoed through the room, having come out too loud and too sudden. She gasped in a breath and started, 'What—'

'Thank you, Miss Iavi.' His smile didn't reach those unnerving fae eyes. 'Honesty from humans is so refreshing. Tell me truthfully if there's anyone with you here.'

'I'm here alone,' she coughed, almost retching as the words forced themselves out. The world spun around her, pieces of the puzzle sliding together. Was she physically incapable of disobeying him? Was that what had happened in that infinitesimal moment of chaos – *get back*, he'd shouted, and so her body had obeyed?

18

But then ...

Oh, sweet mother Eostre have mercy, then he could make her do *anything*.

'Alone?' he repeated, that blasted eyebrow coming up again. 'How extraordinary. No armies?'

'Do I look like the sort of person to work with armies?' Briannis said breathlessly.

One corner of his lips – the living corner, the one not looking like neglected leather – twisted up a fraction. It was not a smile. At best, it was a smirk, and not an amiable one. 'The best murderers rarely look like murderers, Miss Iavi. And you held that knife quite easily.'

She drew in a shivering breath as she glanced at her dagger three strides away – fallen to the floor when she had collided with his first command. The pressure of her fingers had left permanent impressions in the leather hilt. Signs of frequent use. There was little use in denying it.

'I work alone,' she ground out. 'Always have.'

'Hmm.' He tilted his head a fraction. 'Tell me truthfully whether that's the case.'

And there it was again, that nauseating sensation of her body hurrying to obey him, lungs squeezing up air and tongue stirring without her permission. 'It's true.'

'Interesting,' he said slowly, pursing his half-living, half-dead lips as he considered her for a moment. 'In that case, tell me truthfully—'

'Wait,' she blurted out, every muscle stiffening in preparation for what was to come. 'Please, *wait* – can't you just ask questions, please? I promise I'll answer them, I promise I'll be honest, but this is really quite unpleasant and—'

'Human promises,' he said, waving her words aside with a single disdainful flick of his dead fingers – long, white, spidery fingers. 'Last man I knew to promise his wife eternal protection ended up murdering her in cold blood. Apologies for the unpleasantness, but comfort yourself with the knowledge I could make it much, much worse. Tell me truthfully why you're here.'

'To kill you,' she choked, and then, deciding he could hardly command more information from her as long as she kept talking, she rattled on, 'I was arrested and they had too much evidence against me, so this was the only choice I had if I wanted to avoid the gallows – I promise I didn't *want* to take the job, but—'

'How very moving,' he flatly cut in. 'Thank you, Miss Iavi. *They* are His Excellence Lord Cyril and his accomplices, I presume?'

An actual question. Perhaps they were making progress? She jutted her chin up ever so slightly, that old reflex – *Sit up straight, Briannis. A lady doesn't sag like a bag of grain* – as she hurriedly said, 'I didn't meet the Princeps himself, but I was told the order came from him. Most of my instructions came from Lady Millicent – the Mirror Queen. There were a few others as well, but I don't know their names. I could describe them for you, if you wish?'

He merely observed her for a moment, head tilting again in that gesture that made him look not so much curious as predatory. Then, slowly, he said, 'Tell me truthfully whether all you told me in the past minute is true.'

It was even worse this time, as if the command was stronger while it encapsulated more information. The words were torn from somewhere far too deep inside her, coming out with a whiff of bitter gall. 'It's *true*.'

'I'm positively surprised,' he said with a small sneer, elegantly rising to his feet and kicking the dagger on the floor farther away from her. Briannis pulled her knees to her chest in a defensive reflex, feeling a familiar weight bump against her hip as she did so—

The knife in her skirts.

It took an effort not to gasp, the burning gall forgotten. A *weapon*. She still had a *weapon*. Had he really been arrogant enough not to search her at all? Or did he assume his commands would be enough to keep her powerless?

He turned away without apparent suspicion, sauntering around the music stage. If she sneaked after him now ... but no, she would not get a second chance if she failed. She'd have to be cautious and very, very clever here. *A lady is never rash, Briannis.* She would weather this interrogation, wait until he believed himself safe.

And strike.

Her shoulders steeled themselves below her rumpled red dress.

'Tell me truthfully,' the fae king said, throwing a bored glance at the ceiling as he turned at the farthest point of the room, 'what instructions you received to reach me.'

'They gave me maps of the Faerie realm.' There were so many words this time; they hurled over her tongue and tumbled from her lips like prisoners frantic to escape. 'Made by other explorers who'd gone through the gate, they said. They were mostly blank, but they showed a path I could walk to reach the castle, through the valley with the roses, and then the barren valleys with the lakes. Lady Millicent told me I'd have to find a way inside on my own once I'd found this place. She said the Keep wouldn't be guarded. I ... I ...'

She shrieked in a breath, and still her lungs were pressing out air, trying to make her talk and talk and *talk*. Darkness deepened on the edge of her sight. A hand seemed to clench around her throat. Briannis gagged, tried again. 'I—'

'Breathe,' he said.

As if a weight evaporated from her chest, her lungs expanded. She gulped in a mouthful of air, coughed, inhaled again. The red edge on her vision softened; the candles stopped flickering black in the corner of her eyes. When she looked up, blinking moisture from her eyes, the king had paused his sauntering on the other end of the room.

'Thank ... thank you,' she managed to grind out. *Never retaliate rudeness with rudeness.* As long as she had her knives and pins, this was not the moment to lash out at him. 'I'm sorry. If ... if you could just make your questions a little smaller ...'

His one living eye glinted with an unnerving sort of amusement. 'You're being unusually polite for a murderess, Miss Iavi. Is this your usual style, or does my pretty face inspire an unexpected love of decorum in your heart?'

He was *mocking* her, wasn't he? She sat up a little straighter and said, with all the perfectly mannered disapproval she could muster, 'I strive to behave like a well-bred lady, Your Majesty. I find a little courteousness makes one's interactions much more pleasant for all parties involved.'

He looked at her the way she'd seen Lady Templeton look at the stray kitten one of the boys had brought home and hidden beneath his bed for a week – as if he couldn't decide whether he should laugh or drown her in the nearest canal. His voice was perfectly, suspiciously dry. 'How very interesting. Wouldn't you say that driving a knife into someone's guts could also be considered a small slight of manners?'

Not a command this time, and she could have said a prayer of thanks for that small mercy alone. At least she wouldn't have to tell him how much she loathed the life she'd been forced to live for the past years, wouldn't have to admit what future she dreamed of in the quiet moments. Lowering her gaze, she primly muttered, 'Which is why I'm trying not to offend you *twice*, Your Majesty.'

'Oh, don't worry,' he said, a lazy bite to his voice as he swept around and resumed his pacing. 'You have offended me much more than that already. Tell me how you came in.'

'Through the front door?' she blurted, even the forced motions of her lips unable to form a more sensible answer in that moment of confusion. 'It wasn't locked. What do you—'

His sigh as he glanced at her was the exasperated, overly dramatic sigh of a disappointed teacher. 'Miss Iavi, tell me truthfully what measures you took to circumvent the defences of Rosewood Keep and—'

'Defences?' She had already cramped up for what was coming, that tug at her free will she couldn't resist no matter how hard she tried; when it didn't come, she barely felt the relief. Was this a way out – commands she truly *couldn't* obey? 'I'm sorry, Your Majesty, but I don't know what you mean by defences. There were no guards out there, were there? I didn't see anyone. I ...'

Her voice died away.

He stood staring at her with narrowed eyes, the green of his living iris even greener in the dancing candlelight – a stare that made her want to crawl *through* the wall to get away from him. There was something ominous about the sharp lines of his face. As if he might let go of this polished, perfectly dressed exterior any moment and reveal the savage animal inside, the creature that had slammed her into a wall with a word or two, who could make her slit her own throat with another throwaway command.

'You don't know,' he said slowly.

'What ... what don't I know?'

The curve of his lips was almost serpentine, hinting at hidden venom. 'Tell me what you know about the roses, Miss Iavi.'

'They were beautiful?' she choked out. 'There were a lot of them. The Keep is named after them, isn't it?'

'So you don't know.' He let out a laugh, the husky sound of it sliding down her spine and setting every nerve end in her body on edge. 'Tell me truthfully what you used to come in, Miss Iavi.'

'The soap.' It tumbled from her lips by itself. 'Are you talking about the soap?'

His living nostril flared. '*Soap?*'

'The soap I received in my cell, the night before I left on this journey,' she blabbed hastily. Keep talking. As long as she kept talking, he couldn't force the story out of her. 'Someone must have bribed the guards to smuggle it in, I believe? But there was no explanation except a short note that told me to cover myself in soap the morning before I tried to enter the castle – my weapons, too – anything that could be the slightest bit dangerous. I ... Well, I did that. I don't know what it has to do with your defences, but ...'

He didn't move, facing her fully now. Even his dead eye showed a gleam of what might be ... interest? Worry?

Fury?

'That's all I know.' It took all she had not to let her voice rise into a squeak. *A lady composes herself under all circumstances*, but clearly Mrs. Sedgewick had not anticipated the wrath of half-dead fae kings among those circumstances. 'If I did anything wrong, I'm sorry – I'm *sorry*. I just tried to survive. I just—'

'Someone in Elidian,' he interrupted, speaking slowly and emphatically as if talking to a child, 'instructed you to use that soap?'

Briannis nodded. She didn't quite dare to open her mouth.

'There were no other hints? No names? Nothing you haven't told me?'

She shook her head, breath stuttering. He was ... not beautiful; the dead half of his face spoiled every claim to that effect. But as his silky voice grew louder, as his eyes burned

24

even greener, his towering figure in the candlelight turned into something overwhelmingly magnetic – a pull that wouldn't allow her to look away from him, that left her thirsting for every next word he'd speak. When she tried to swallow, her throat was bone dry. When he stepped closer, she no longer even had the sense to shrink away from him.

'Miss Iavi.' His voice carried a smooth, honeyed warning. 'Tell me truthfully what else you know, no matter how insignificant, about the daisy soap you used, the person who gave it to you, or your reasons for using it. *Now.*'

Her lips remained motionless, her mind blank. Did she know anything? It had just *been* there on that desperate morning before her departure – lying with that note in the hay of her cell, making her wonder for a few teary minutes if perhaps the divines were on her side after all. Just that single block of daisy soap, the petals caught forever in the yellow tallow and grease ...

Wait.

'Daisy soap.' She spoke without thinking; the words came over her lips hoarsely. 'How did you know it was daisy soap?'

He faltered.

It was barely noticeable in his motions, in the towering expanse of his lithe body over hers. But that magnetism around him, that force that drew her eyes back to him over and over, weakened in the same moment, the animal inside him sinking back below his skin. A hesitation Briannis could only interpret in one way – a mistake.

For some reason, he hadn't wanted her to know that he knew.

Then his shoulders abruptly loosened, and the skewed smile was back on his face, a hint of malicious amusement dancing in his eyes. 'Perhaps I smelled it?'

She forgot about mistakes.

'Did you *sniff* me?' Her voice soared into a scandalised shriek. 'I was lying unconscious on your floor and you—'

'I had to come closer to you to heal you, Miss Iavi,' he said, lips twitching even on the dead side now. 'I'd just flung you into a wall and broken your neck, you see. Would you prefer for me to just leave you for dead next time?'

'Well,' she said numbly, trying to calm her shuddering breath. *Broken your neck.* That deep, snapping sound as she woke up, his hands stroking up her spine … Sweet divines, what had she gotten herself into? 'I suppose it could be excused under those circumstances, but it's still not very proper to—'

He arched that one copper eyebrow. '*Proper?* Do I need to remind you once again that killing is hardly—'

'So?' she interrupted, pressing her lips shut defiantly as she sat straighter. 'I don't see how one breach of etiquette means we should just throw all appropriate behaviour to the wind, and also, no one will snub *you* for nearly being murdered. Impropriety is an entirely different sort of danger.'

'Ah, that is the issue.' He raked his dead hand through his hair – stark white skin and coppery red locks intertwining as the long strands tumbled over his temples and shoulders. That blasted smirk appeared again, as friendly as a whetted blade. 'Let me reassure you: I wasn't planning to write His Excellence and the Elidian gossip rags about this unfortunate slight of your honour. Does that appease you?'

She shouldn't have flinched. It was the stupidest thing she could do, giving him that leverage over her – but the reflex was there before her thoughts intervened, her body recoiling at the image his words painted. The gossip rags. She knew the power they held, had watched them spread her reputation once before. If they did it again, if the world was to find out the newly returned Miss Iavi had recently lain unconscious on a fae king's floor while he *sniffed* at her …

Her promised life would be in shambles before her first day in it was over.

'You don't look terribly appeased,' he observed, his voice a soft, snarling threat now.

'Please.' She glanced up at him from her humiliating spot on the floor, barely keeping her voice from cracking again. Why did he have to be so *tall*? Even if she were standing, she'd have to look up to meet his eyes – the lowly human, begging at his feet. 'There's nothing else I know about you or that soap. If I swear I won't tell anyone – won't harm you again – can't you just let me—'

The smirk dissolved. 'No.'

'*Please*.' Her blood sang in her ears. 'I'll tell you everything you want to know about the Princeps and Lady Millicent and all of them – I'll tell them whatever you need me to tell them – I'll—'

'Human promises, again,' he interrupted with a scoff. 'Thank you, Miss Iavi, but if I wish to gamble, I can make it more amusing than that. The answer is no.'

'But—'

'And pleading won't help.' He sauntered another step closer, moving with impossible ease – as if he were gliding rather than walking. She had to tilt her head into her neck to look up at him. 'The matter is not that I don't *want* to be rid of you, Miss Iavi. I could think of more welcome company, as a matter of fact. The trouble is that I'm not *able* to let you leave the castle.'

She stared at him.

He quirked up his eyebrow, a crystal-clear challenge for her to shriek again, to burst out crying, to get the vapours like a proper young lady. Between them, his words hovered in the air, sinking in as she sat frozen. *Not able to let you leave.* Nonsensical words, impossible words ...

But he was fae.

Which meant that some way or another, they had to be true.

'I don't understand,' she breathed. 'I walked in. Why couldn't I leave the same way?'

'Those defences you so cleverly avoided.' Another step forward. His hair fluttered around his shoulders and elbows, his boots gleamed in the candlelight. 'They normally become activated when anyone capable of harming me approaches the Keep. Under usual circumstances, they would have kept you out without trouble.'

Oh, sweet mother Eostre have mercy. 'But ... but the soap?'

'Very good, Miss Iavi. The soap.' She thought for a moment he would bite her, so sharp was his voice. 'It contained ingredients that neutralised the defences. However, now that you have attacked me and I have noticed you ...' A one-shouldered shrug. 'They know I am in danger. And in response, they've hermetically locked the castle.'

It took a moment for that to come through.

'Do you mean ...' *No*, her thoughts repeated frantically, like the rhythm of a pounding heart, *no, no, no*. 'Are you saying *neither* of us can go out?'

His living jaw twitched. 'Exactly.'

'But you're the king of this place!' she burst out, and finally her legs regained their strength; shaking, wobbling, she rose, her feet pleading with her to let them take over and run. 'Can't you do *magic*? You're not dependent on your own defences, are you?'

'I wasn't,' he said softly, dangerously, 'before you humans ruined everything.'

She swallowed, pressing herself back against the wall, as far away as she could get from the deadly gleam in his eyes. He stood so close before her now that she could smell the scent that clung to him. The powdery sweetness of flowers, and then there was a whiff of a far more nostalgic fragrance – a smell she'd learned to recognise in the cradle, that reminded her of home even miles away from it ...

Rot. The unsettling sweetness of decay.

You humans.

She gulped in a breath, forcing herself to meet his gaze. 'I ... I don't understand.'

'My powers are waning.' The soft, silky quality of his voice seemed to wrap around her again, the magnetism back in every twist of his lips. 'When I created these safety measures, I wielded much, much more magic than I can currently claim to possess. The roses would have yielded to me then. They don't care much for the force I can unleash on them now, which means they will do what *they* think best for my safety.'

Her thoughts faltered. 'The *roses?*'

'Yes, Miss Iavi. They've wrapped the castle in a shield of thorns, and I recommend you don't try to break through.' The cruel curve of his smile said enough. 'I've seen people try.'

Those flowers – hundreds upon hundreds of them, crawling over the walls of the Keep ... A shiver trailed down her spine. She should have known nothing in this cursed land could ever be truly beautiful, that even nature itself would be deadly and treacherous. Why, *why* had she ever allowed herself to get caught in this rat trap?

And how was she ever going to get out again?

'Is there nothing you can do ...' She grasped the flower-covered wall behind her back, refusing to let her knees buckle or to let him see her shaking hands. 'Is there nothing that could make them retreat?'

'Well,' he said, his voice sweet like poisoned syrup, 'you could die, of course.'

Her heart skipped a beat.

'Danger gone, problem solved. It's that easy.' The chill in his eyes was palpable. 'Has it occurred to you, Miss Iavi, that I don't have many reasons to keep you alive at this point? You seem to have told me everything of use that you knew. You may still be scheming to kill me. It really would be the wisest choice – the wisest choice by *far* – to simply do away with you.'

And how easy it would be for him to dispose of her ... Two words were all he needed. *Kill yourself,* he could say, and she'd have no choice but to draw one of her hidden daggers and slash open her own throat. Briannis held on to the wall for dear life, black spots shimmering across her vision as she gaped at his living eye and desperately tried to come up with words, *any* words, to change the snake's mind behind that half-dead visage.

'Please,' she heard herself say. 'Please ... don't.'

His chuckle reverberated through her, turning her guts inside out. 'Give me a *single* good reason to spare you.'

The silence tightened around them, an absence of words that said more than even a sobbed confession ever could. Such an unnatural quiet, no footsteps in the distance, no muted sound of chatter in the corridors ... Not even the howling wind could be heard between the walls of the castle.

What had the mirror said? *The music room, of course.*

Of course. A self-evidence.

Understanding sparked, and she clung to it with the full force of her despair. *Of course* meant he was here often. Which meant ... *sound,* the cello and the violins and their twisting melody, a haunting imitation of life in this graveyard of a castle.

'I could keep you company,' she whispered.

His face remained motionless – so motionless that for a moment, she wondered if she had spoken the words out loud at all. But he didn't open his mouth to tell her to end herself. He didn't laugh and tell her she'd gone mad. So she *might* have guessed right under the weight of that lifeless silence; it may just be pressing on his shoulders, too.

'I know you don't like me.' She let out a nervous peal of laughter. 'And since you seem to appreciate honesty, I can inform you it's mutual. But we're apparently bound together in this place. We might find out we have some interests in common, if we try a little harder. How do you feel about flower arrangements?'

The magnetism weakened.

He moved back ever so slightly, two rapid blinks the only outward sign of surprise. 'Flower ... arrangements?'

'Yes?' she said, fighting to keep her hands from trembling. 'Or calligraphy. Card games. We could play lawn bowls in one of the larger halls – a carpet would do for grass, and I suppose we can find a few balls in this giant of a castle. How long has it been since you played any game at all, if I may ask?'

'Miss Iavi ...' His lips – one half firm and dark pink, one half thin and pallid – faltered ever so slightly around the shapes of her name. His eyes flicked over her. 'I strongly doubt you'd enjoy the sort of games I like to play.'

The thrill of suggestion in his voice sent shivers down her back; whether it hinted at pain or scandal, she couldn't tell. Didn't matter. Didn't *matter*. All she had to do was stay alive for long enough to drive a knife into his heart, and then she would think again, figure out how to break free and claim the life she'd fought for. If that meant lying and bluffing ... Well, he already believed her a deceitful human, didn't he?

'Who knows?' she said, and forced herself to hold his gaze with all the daring she could muster. 'You'll never know if I'm dead.'

His lips twitched up at one corner, a smile like a snare pulling tight around her. 'Undeniably true.'

'So ...' She drew in a deep breath, tried not to shake. This was it, then. Corpse or captive. 'Are you going to kill me?'

For one long moment, he studied her motionlessly.

Then he said, 'No.'

She was too tense for relief, too busy anticipating the next torturous command he might give. But he stepped back without further elaboration, sending an impassive nod at her sandy dress, her tousled hair.

'You can take up residence in ... shall we say, the Starlit Room?' He glanced at the open doorway; farther down the corridor, she heard another door obediently slam open. 'Go there. Stay there. You'll find everything you need to make yourself presentable.'

Her feet pulled her into motion, eager to obey before he'd even finished his last sentence. In the distance, she heard more doors creak open, guiding her to the room she'd been appointed – the cell she'd been appointed.

The fae king didn't move as she turned and wobbled off, an imbalanced, unnatural gait, as if a puppet master was pulling her strings. It was only as she staggered into the corridor that he spoke again, his voice smooth and languid and heavy with unspoken warnings.

'I'll see you at dinner, Miss Iavi.'

And with that, the door to the music room slammed itself shut behind her.

Chapter 3

At the dinner table, refrain from any conversation that might provoke disgust or distress among those present. Some people will enter into discussions of politics or even describe revolting details of sicknesses during their meals; such behaviour is excessively ill-bred.
Lady Lockwell's Handbook of Etiquette

THE HELLISH LABYRINTH OF the Keep was a blur around her. When at long last she reached a lavish bedroom in shades of indigo and starlight, Briannis all but fell inside, slamming the door behind her and sagging against the smooth wood with a sigh close to a sob.

That bastard.

That *bastard.*

Here she was, back in a cell again after all she'd suffered to get free. Caught by thorns, by walls, by the commands of the twisted creature who had taken her free will and laughed at it ... She reached for the door handle, despite knowing it was hopeless, and found she was unable to touch it, her muscles obeying the fae king even from the other side of the castle. Which meant there would be no sneaking up on him today. No opportunities to leave a sip of poison in his tea and wait for him to rid the world of himself.

By the time he allowed her to leave the room again, his full attention would be upon her, and with it, the cruelty of whatever fate he planned for her.

She'd heard enough stories of the time before the Elidian gates were closed to his people, the women who'd vanish and return ruined and sobbing, or worse, the women who never returned at all. She saw no reason to expect better from the man who ruled them all. *I strongly doubt you'd enjoy the games I like to play …*

Briannis held herself to high standards of civility, but standing in a fae bedroom, at some deadly king's mercy, right in the middle of a rose-covered prison, she had to wrestle down a rare urge to swear out loud.

Then again, swearing wasn't getting her out of this mess.

With a groan, she hauled herself away from the door and strode to the vaulted window in the opposite wall, barely glancing at the plush, night-blue carpet or the iridescent glimmers of the pearly fireplace she passed. Nudging the heavy velvet curtains aside – they shimmered too, catching the light in new angles with every shift of her head – she pressed her face against the cold glass and tried to catch a glimpse of the outside world. Mountains, as far as the eye could see. Shreds of morning mist clinging to the slopes. A pale blue sky, a watery sun, the reflection of a valley lake in the distance.

And just below the window, crawling over the wall like deadly snakes waiting to strike, the rose vines. Their plush, round flowers had the colour of blood.

She should know better, she really should, and yet she found herself yanking at the window's handles without a moment's thought. It swung open with a creaky whine, and for one blissful moment, the cutting mountain air slammed into her face.

Then the thorns swept in.

They flung themselves across the open space of the window in the blink of an eye, weaving a brown-and-green tapestry of sharp spikes and leathery vines. The roses bloomed on them the next moment, buds unfolding to full flowers like welling drops of blood. Within seconds, the wind had been reduced to a weak breeze, the room darkened to a dusky shade.

Briannis staggered back, away from that cursed shield, and tried to keep breathing evenly. No attempts to escape, then. She'd have to kill His Majesty first and hope that, with his death, the flowers protecting him would wither, too.

Don't doubt and fret so much, Bri, Father would say. *You know perfectly well what you're doing.*

Yes. She did. Killing was what she excelled in, no matter how much she despised it; she was the Widowmaker, she firmly reminded herself, the Evening Star, the Butcher of Baker's Lane. The Elidian gossip rags hadn't bestowed all those dramatic monikers upon her just so she could end up in a shallow grave in these evil, barren lands, and she *would* find a weapon and end the king in his sleep if she needed to.

I'll see you at dinner. There might be knives there. Or forks. If push came to shove, she could probably get the job done with a teaspoon.

Heartbeat slowing, she sank down on the edge of the mattress and examined the Starlit Room thoroughly for the first time since her entrance.

It was larger than any room in which she'd lived, larger than Father's living room had been. A bed big enough for five – she blushed and banned that scandalous thought from her mind

– covered in white and indigo blankets. Walls and ceiling in a glittering shade of black, some sort of quartz threaded with sparks of white crystal. A bookcase full of gold-plated tomes. A wardrobe in which one could house a family, built from ebony wood and inlaid with mother-of-pearl that mirrored the broad mantelpiece.

That wardrobe ...

Make yourself presentable.

She threw a glance at her sweaty, muddy travel dress, then veered from the bed and tiptoed to the other side of the room. Inside that monumental piece of furniture – and she couldn't fully suppress a gasp as she threw open the doors – about a dozen gowns were waiting, each of them exquisitely crafted, each of them looking precisely tailored to her measurements. There were stays and chemises. Stockings and lacy bits she didn't quite dare to think about. An extravagant coat, shoes and slippers, all of them exactly the right size.

Magic, dirty magic ... but she couldn't help stretching out a hand and brushing her fingers down the smooth silk of the first dress, savouring the touch. The fabric felt like a distant future. Like a dream come true.

This was how they got the women they stole, she reminded herself as she yanked back her hand – pretty promises, false abundance, fairy tales that were too good to be true. She ought to keep her head clear. The main problem was that none of these dresses contained hidden pockets for knives, the second problem that even if they did, the fae king could easily disarm her with little more than a question. Until she'd solved those troubles, nothing else mattered – not even these gorgeous, glittering creations.

She'd buy her own dresses once she was done.

With the poison from her glove tucked beneath the pillows, the knives from her boots and skirts and garter hidden in various corners of the room, and the sharpened hairpins cautiously arranged at the dressing table, Briannis undressed and slipped into the adjacent bathroom to scrub off two weeks' worth of sweat and sand. As much as she wanted to loathe the glittering tub and the twinkling lights, she couldn't deny it was a relief to get the itchy layer of dried soap off her skin.

By the time she returned to the bedroom, wrapped in a downy bathrobe, the first seedlings of a plan were sprouting in her thoughts.

She was in no hurry to dress; it would be hours until dinnertime, and no one would disturb her in this cell. Instead of the wardrobe, she made for the bookshelves. Any information on the castle might be of use, after all, and who knew when she'd next get a moment to herself?

Most of the books were written in a script she'd never seen before, she found in the minutes of browsing that followed – hundreds of tiny symbols crawling over the pages, hands and suns and ladders and flowers, the same symbols she'd seen on the doors of the music room. She shoved those back onto the shelves without attempting to decipher the mess. But here and there a volume was written in readable, albeit archaic Elidian, and she piled those onto the bed for more thorough research.

There were maps and drawings of the Faerie realm, showing lush, flowering valleys that must have stemmed from the artists' overly fond imaginations rather than the truth of the stark slopes she'd seen. There were long histories full of names she'd never heard before. There were long itineraries describing lands as far as Issi to the south and Karwald to the east, and finally, in a leatherbound book as thick as her fist, she found a series of portraits and a family tree.

It ran back millennia, king after king after king, some of them reigning as long as five hundred years. She traced the lines to the bottom of the page. Until almost two hundred years ago, a certain King Irvath had ruled Faerie; his two children were a daughter who'd died centuries ago and ...

Moridyr III (4256-present)

A name. That was something.

She spent several hours trying to find more, *anything*, about her target – reputation, pastimes, any small weakness. Nothing appeared, not even the shortest footnote. No quick warning that Moridyr III enjoyed disembowelling the women he lured into his bed. No mention of helpful sensitivities to nuts or fears of spiders or anything else she could use. As if he'd made an effort to be invisible – or, just as likely, as if the castle had somehow whisked away any books that could hurt him.

As the hours went by and she made no further attempts to escape, the roses retreated from the window. Sunlight flooded the room again and struck the glitters in the quartz walls, refracting, turning golden, then fiery orange, then rosy red. When dusk began to fall, she finally shoved the last books back onto the shelf and began her dinner preparation.

The gown she picked after much consideration was a mulberry-coloured creation sewn with pearls, the design as elegant as it was lavish. It fit without any adjustments, and so did the silk gloves that came with it. The skirts were loose, most importantly – loose enough for her to slip her garter knife back against her thigh, from where she could smuggle it out during dinner.

Her hair she once again pinned into place with her sharpened pins, and then she waited – not impatiently, but certainly filled with nervous anticipation, practicing answers to the questions she expected.

It didn't stop her heart from stuttering when his knock finally came.

The door swung itself open the next moment, and there he stood – in black this time, as if to confirm his role as the villain in her story, his red hair bound in a simple queue. The smile playing around the edges of his lips was carefully controlled. She almost flinched at the sight of it, almost dropped the fearless composure she'd worked so hard to achieve ... But Mrs. Sedgewick's lessons took over, and she curtsied without thinking, keeping her gaze trained on the floor around his feet.

'Miss Iavi,' he said, and curse that silky voice of his – curse the way every syllable could, without the slightest warning, become the death of her. 'A pleasure to find you here.'

Was he laughing at her behind that little cheerless smirk? It took all she had not to lash out – *Where else could I be, you monster?* – and restrain herself to a murmured, 'Your Majesty'.

He strode into the room without reply, his eyes flicking around the chamber before settling on her. The coat that had seemed black at first glance turned out to be green upon closer inspection – a deep emerald, covered in floral patterns of black lace and set with enamelled buttons. On any other man, it may have looked feminine. But the skull-shape of the dead half of his face took every softness from his appearance, and the knowing smile that twisted his lips looked about as harmless as a drawn dagger.

'Tell me truthfully' – she was almost getting used to the deadly cadence of those words – 'if you carry any weapons on you, Miss Iavi.'

Her lips moved, and this time she was prepared – unable to stay silent, unable to lie, but very well able to *choose* the truths she allowed to slip out in this forced confession. She'd practised. She'd repeated the sentence again and again to herself as the hours slid by. Now it whooshed from her lips without thought, perfectly true yet utterly incomplete – 'I'm wearing sharpened pins in my hair.'

There was a pull to continue, a suggestion of magic itching on her tongue … but she closed her mouth, and nothing else escaped.

Her heart pounded wildly against her ribs as she waited.

'Sharpened *pins*?' The cruel amusement in his voice was palpable. 'You were hoping to end me with two inches of steel, Miss Iavi?'

'They are quite effective in eyeballs,' she demurely informed him, glancing up at him from beneath lowered lashes. The sunken darkness of his dead eye was dull as always, but the twinkle in his living one almost stole her breath – a glint of unnerving intelligence, of deadly curiosity, of ruthless intent. Even more bashfully, she added, 'They do well with poisons, too. No one blinks twice when a clumsy young lady accidentally scratches a man's hand, you see. Not her fault if the wound starts oozing two days later.'

Was it her imagination, or did his eyes narrow for the briefest of moments?

But his words came without hesitation, the command as careless as the last, and far more unexpected. 'Turn around.'

Her feet lurched into motion, almost toppling her in their hurry to please him. With her back towards him, the mulberry dress felt thinner, colder, a mere scrap of cloth – hopelessly inadequate to protect her from the predator behind her, setting his malicious games in motion. 'What are you—'

'If you don't mind?' he interrupted in that tone that strongly advised her not to mind, and then his hands were in her hair.

Hands.

In her *hair*.

She squeaked, managing just barely not to lurch away from him – from that shockingly intimate touch, warm and cold fingers prodding the careful arrangements of her curls to pull out pin after pin. A sleeve brushed over the bare skin of her neck.

A thumb collided with the sensitive rim of her ear. With a gasp, she stammered, 'This is not very ...'

'Proper?' His low drawl curled around her guts, sweet and syrupy. 'I thought you'd realise by now that I'm far from a proper man, Miss Iavi.'

Oh, sweet divines. A shiver broke free at his next sweep through her hair. 'Why don't you let me—'

'And allow those clumsy hands anywhere near a weapon?' he retorted, voice laced with languid amusement as he pulled two more pins from her braided bun. A curl came loose and tumbled down her spine. 'Thank you, Miss Iavi, but I know a warning when I see one. I'll take care of this chore.'

She squeezed her eyes shut as he continued, trying not to feel his nimble ministrations, the fingers grazing her scalp as he took down her hair. *A lady does not enjoy unwanted attentions. A lady composes herself.* But it was impossible to suppress the small shivers that ran down her spine or the goosebumps that rose on her skin no matter how hard she fought them; his touches were unwanted but pleasant, in a twisted, forbidden, invasive way. How dare he turn even her own body against her – how dare he render her so utterly powerless?

He'd pay for it, she promised herself, teeth gritted. He'd know it had cost him in the end.

But she was trembling when he finally stepped away, her hair loose and cascading down her back, and he sounded all too pleased with himself as he said, 'You can turn around now.'

Not a command, and she *almost* felt grateful for it. Eyes cast down, she turned to face him and let her shoulders droop in defeat – please, let him think this was all she had schemed to do. Let him believe he had successfully disarmed her and thwarted her plans for the night. Let him ...

'Dinner, then?' he said with blade-edged sweetness, holding out his living arm.

She almost sagged in relief.

But he was far, far too clever for such stupid mistakes, and her spine stayed tight; she made herself step forward and wrap a gloved hand around his sleeve. *Be meek*, she reminded herself as she allowed him to escort her out of her cell. *Be crushed. Be a diverting little toy, if you must.* Surprise was all she had tonight.

Surprise ... and the dagger resting against her thigh.

She schooled her face into careful gloominess.

The king – she refused to think of him by something as human as a name – guided her down the corridor with long, graceful strides, forcing her to walk just faster than her skirts comfortably allowed. Around them, the castle sparkled, dazzling her. She didn't recognise a single room from her first exploration in the morning, nor the smooth marble floors in colours she'd never seen before, broad stairways flanked by portraits and statues that were equally new to her. Only the walls filled with blooming flowers were a constant, the living, blossoming tapestries covering almost every hall they passed.

Next to her, her host – her captor – pointed out treasures and highlights, his voice so pointedly pleasant that it hovered a mere edge away from mockery. 'A statue of King Caphael II – he reigned about three hundred years before the first walled cities were built in the human realm ... That glass lamp over there is one of the oldest we have – the Issian glassblowers learned the trade from us, of course ... Ah, see that book? Very interesting treatise on taxonomy. I'm afraid the Elidian University is still catching on ...'

And on it went, an unending collection of observations carefully curated to make her feel as small as possible, to remind her that the world she belonged in was little more than a fleeting shadow compared to the grandeur of the castle. Was he trying to get a rise out of her? Hoping she'd crumble at his feet and beg for every crumb of his attentions?

A lady is calm and collected. She clung to her governess's voice like a lifeline.

They finally reached a set of heavy double doors, the dark wood carved with intricate patterns and adorned with silver handles. A glance from the king was enough to make them swing open and reveal the grand dining hall that lay behind.

If she hadn't felt small and lost yet, the sight of the room would have finished the job.

An onslaught of light welcomed them – the lustre of hundreds upon hundreds of candles, hanging from grand chandeliers, lining the walls, standing a silent guard on the long table at the centre of the hall. Flames reflected in delicate glassware and gleaming silverware. Detailed tapestries hung from the walls, depicting what Briannis supposed were scenes from Faerie history, and the vaulted ceiling was inlaid with colourful gems, creating geometric patterns that sparkled wherever she looked.

The table had been set with a feast for kings. Plates full of meat dripping with butter, piles of charred vegetables, and ... Where did those pomegranates come from, here all the way in the north? The smells of roasted meat and fresh bread wafted through the air, and despite her aching nerves, Briannis found her mouth watering. She hadn't eaten since her meagre traveller's breakfast of the morning.

And yet ... she had to keep thinking sensibly. Fairy food – what did the stories say? He might just lock her in this castle forever with a single bite of the wrong dish.

'Sit,' the king said, and her legs kicked into motion, dragging her to the elaborately carved chair he'd indicated at the foot of the long table. Her body plopped her into the seat with too much force, and she winced as her tailbone slammed into the wood.

'Thank you, Miss Iavi.' He sat down at the head with movements so languid they had to be deliberate, tapping long, spidery fingertips together as he examined her from fifteen feet away. Eyes fixed on her, he added, 'For someone who promised me company, you don't appear to be a particularly cheerful presence so far. You're not displeased with the meal, I hope?'

He *was* toying with her – cat and mouse, using her as an amusing little diversion until he would, just as elegantly and lazily, have her slit her own throat and smirk at her as the life rushed from her veins. She kept her gaze lowered and struggled to keep her hands from clenching into fists, from lashing out and snatching the knife from under her skirt – he *would* regret it, she reminded herself. Sooner rather than later, he would regret it.

'I beg your forgiveness, Your Majesty,' she murmured. Her skin was crawling under the scrutiny of his dead and living eye. 'I've been taught a lady should always be guarded in new company, lest she make a fool of herself by letting her hair down with the wrong people. A matter of habit.'

'Ah,' he said, and she could *feel* the tilt of his head more than she saw it on the edge of her vision. 'Of course. Elidian morals. How tiresome. Were you brought up at court?'

She almost let a bitter chuckle escape but held back. 'No, Your Majesty. But my father thought it important that I learn proper manners regardless.'

'He was from Kraaled, I presume? Your father?'

Their very Kraalian name was a giveaway, of course. Briannis nodded, biting down a sting of bitterness at the thought of what he'd say if he saw her here – her proud, gentle father, so sure she'd come far in life, so sure she'd manage what he never had. And instead ...

Instead she traded in death and shared meals with fae. Her heart squeezed.

The king sighed, a deep, dramatic sigh. 'If you insist on buttoning your lips, Miss Iavi, I'll just have to go back to *making* you converse with me. A shame. I understood you preferred natural conversation. How old are you?'

'Twenty-seven,' she forced out, making herself look up a fraction. The sleek monstrosity in emerald and copper examined her as if she was some riddle to solve. 'You?'

That elicited a chuckle from his lips. 'A little over four centuries.'

The books had told her so, and yet it sounded more impossible from his own lips – *he* couldn't lie or exaggerate, after all. Desperate to keep talking, to keep him from forcing her to talk again, she hastily said, 'Is that a common age for fae?'

'It's a common age for those who spend most of their time in Faerie', he said with a little elegant shrug. 'The land slows our aging. If we would spend our entire lives in the human world, we would not grow much older than you.'

'Interesting', she said weakly. 'Is that true for fae only, or ...'

'Oh, no. Humans too.' He smiled like she imagined a spider would smile, trapping flies into its deadly web. 'Which means you may be stuck with me for hundreds of years, Miss Iavi. But enough about me. Are you married?'

Oh no. Oh *no*. She did not like the direction of this interrogation at all, not under the intensity of his gaze, not with hundreds and hundreds of cautionary tales singing in the back of her mind. But lying seemed too much of a risk when he could draw the truth from her with as little as a well-chosen command. 'I'm not.'

'Hmm.' The living side of his mouth twisted into a smile as alluring as it was cruel. 'Interesting, for a lady your age.'

'Assassins don't do well on the marriage mart, Your Majesty,' she said politely.

'Some men might consider your knives an asset.' He nodded at the obscenely voluminous piles of food, and small heaps of it appeared out of nowhere on her plate, slices of tender meat and sprouts drenched in a smoky, caramelised glaze. The smells were heavenly ... but what if it was all evil magic, designed to bind her to this castle for eternity?

She swallowed, picking up knife and fork and cutting off the smallest bite. On the other end of the table, the king had started eating, his motions so hypnotically graceful that it took an effort to drag her gaze back to her own plate.

What if she just pretended to eat? Surely she could stand a few days of hunger, if it meant she would still be able to escape the Keep after finishing her job. Empty fork, pretending to swallow, and—

'Eat,' he said.

Her fork dug itself into her food.

There was no stopping her lips from parting no matter how hard she wrestled, no stopping her hand from shoving a fork-full of soft meat into her mouth. Her jaw chewed mechanically, lips not allowing her to spit out the food. Her tongue moved unaffected by her struggle, pressing the mush of chewed meat into her throat. It slid down her oesophagus like a boulder, every fibre of her recoiling at the sensation of the unwanted substance entering her body; as soon as the magic of the command released her, she gasped for breath, then gagged, clenching her fingers painfully tight around the silverware.

'Now, now, Miss Iavi,' he tutted, and she could *swear* that was laughter below the polished exterior of his voice, 'I did not expect you to find our food that disagreeable?'

'I ... I didn't want ...' She gagged again and reached for her glass with trembling hands; it had filled itself with wine. Even a generous sip didn't wash away the sickening taste left in her mouth. Clenching her jaw, she managed, 'Very few foods are agreeable when forced down one's throat, Your Majesty.'

'The obvious solution,' he said smugly, 'would be to eat of your own volition.'

She closed her eyes, contemplating just how much she could ruin by throwing the glass of wine at him.

'Why do you not want to eat, Miss Iavi?' It could have been a humane question if there had been any concern in the words – anything other than the calculated interest that now hovered below those silky tones. 'Surely you must be hungry, after your long journey. Is there anything else you wish for? Something sweet? Something—'

'I've heard stories,' she ground out through gritted teeth, opening her eyes but training her gaze strictly on her plate. 'About fae food having magical properties. I thought if I ate, it might force me to stay in the Keep forever.'

He laughed – actually *laughed*, a sound like rich, smothering velvet. She flinched at the sound, gripping her glass more tightly. If he came for her ... If he tried to hurt her ...

He didn't get up from his chair.

'I estimated you to be more sensible than that, Miss Iavi,' he said, still chuckling. 'Magical food – what a notion. Do I really give the impression I would gladly burden myself with your company forever? Now take up your fork and—'

'*Stop*,' she burst out.

The word echoed from the walls and high ceiling, too brusque, too unladylike. But the king sank back in his richly decorated chair, gilded wooden curls framing his slender shoulders, as he slowly raised his glass to his lips and smirked.

'Ah. Now that is a little more interesting.'

'Please,' Briannis stammered, lips moving not so much without a thought, but rather with too many thoughts behind them. She had to say whatever would keep him from uttering that next command. Had to keep him entertained. Had to distract him, had to somehow get close enough to stab him – anything, *anything* that saved her from having to spend another torturous day in his presence. But the words that rolled from her tongue were not the lies of a clever intrigante, not the well-aimed flattery that might bring her closer to freedom ... 'Why do you enjoy tormenting me so much?'

He quirked up his one eyebrow. 'You do recall, I hope, that you made an attempt to kill me a few hours ago? That you were trying to appear at dinner with another arsenal of weapons at your disposal, too?'

'Yes, but ...' She gulped in a breath, forcing herself to put down her glass and untangle her fingers from it. Flattery, then. 'Those were hopeless attempts. You know they were. Are you really punishing some weaker creature for the insolence of even *trying* to harm you?'

The venom in his smile was the only answer she could need. 'Does that seem so unlikely to you?'

No. No, truly, it seemed more likely by the heartbeat – but honesty wouldn't get her anywhere in this moment. He'd just laugh at her. If she wanted a chance to strike, she needed to wrestle that blasted control from his claws; she needed him to get distracted, needed him just the smallest bit *lost*.

She, at least, could lie.

'It does,' she said, lowering her hands onto the edge of the table as if deep in thought. 'You don't come across as a man that petty, frankly. Or as a man who allows himself to be ruled by short-sighted emotions like a lust for vengeance.' She laced her fingers together, a wistful look in her eyes. 'I would've expected a more justifiable reason, perhaps. But of course, if I'm wrong ...'

She let her sentence die away. Did that push believability too far? His eyes had narrowed when she bashfully looked up, innocent honesty in every flutter of her lashes – sweet mother Eostre, was this where he burst out laughing again and ordered her to eat and keep eating until her stomach burst and killed her?

But his face had grown colder than she'd ever seen it before, the sneers and smirks gone. The wicked twinkle in his eyes had dulled and mellowed into something ... furious?

'I see,' he said, and while his drawl remained unchanged, the lightness in it had vanished. 'So you *are* fighting back after all, Miss Iavi.'

She stiffened. 'What do you mean?'

'It seemed you insisted on primly simpering your way to the grave,' he said, and there was that twist of his lips again, promising pleasure and pain in equal measure. She shivered. 'But if it turns out you are actually capable of a having a conversation, then by all means, let's have one. You need a more justifiable reason? Let's start with the fact that you're working for the man who is trying to doom my entire people to extinction.'

'The ...' She hesitated, unsure whether this turn of the conversation was more likely to get her any closer to his vital organs. 'The Princeps?'

'Who else?'

'I'm hardly working for him,' she said uncomfortably. 'And either way, he's not *killing* fae. Just trying to keep them from his city, which is pretty reasonable, given that—'

'*His* city?' the king interrupted, and although he spoke slowly, the words carried a sharp enough edge to cut through skin. 'It's *his* city, now?'

Briannis blinked. 'Well, he's ruling it.'

'After he killed the legitimate ruler before him, yes.'

'What?' She let out a small, joyless laugh. 'Of course he didn't – where did you get that idea? He was married to the Princeps' eldest daughter. When they all died in that fae attack, of course he was the one to succeed—'

'Oh, a *fae* attack.' He scoffed, lip curled into a sneer of utter disdain. 'Of course. Should have known that would be the story. Please continue, Miss Iavi – whatever his path to power was, why exactly would His Excellence be keeping us out of the city through which we've travelled for millennia?'

'Your people were tormenting the Elidian civilians!' Briannis said sharply. 'Don't pretend you don't know what they did to the women of the city. Of course they were no longer welcome after stealing hundreds of daughters and wives from their family homes.'

'*Stealing?*' he repeated, lowering his wine to the table with a languid gesture. 'Like one steals a purse of gold?'

'No, I mean ...' An unwelcome blush crept up her cheeks. 'Your people *enchant* women. They forget all about their loved ones and ... and ...'

'Do they now?' He cocked his head aside. 'Who says so? The women themselves?'

'The ones who even make it back to the city,' she snapped. 'I don't even want to *think* about how many others may be lying dead in the marshes, or ...'

'Or may be living happy lives with their new family?' he suggested, voice dripping with acid.

Briannis scoffed. 'Family? After they were unwillingly lured away?'

'Oh, but we already established you only based that assumption on the accounts of those who came back.' A cold chuckle. 'Imagine you're a desperate, frustrated young woman living in the city. Imagine you run into a handsome young man – a young man who tells you stories about faraway lands and the freedom of travelling, who promises you a life not spent scrubbing floors and tiptoeing around your loose-handed husband. Would you need an enchantment to leave at the first invitation to come along?'

'But—'

'And if you left, Miss Iavi, and you soon found you actually hated the long travelling days and the hard beds, and you decided to return home after all, what would you tell the authorities? That you deliberately left your boring husband for a man who did things with his tongue you never even dreamed of? Or would you prefer, possibly, to lay the blame on the people who are already blamed for everything anyway, who—'

'Well, if they don't want to be blamed,' Briannis interrupted heatedly, 'perhaps they should just not go around seducing respectable women, don't you think?'

He canted his head, and the shadows seemed to slide over his skeletal cheek at the movement, emphasising the hollow of his eye, the brittle paleness of his skin. 'And what if some of those women don't *want* to be respectable in the first place?'

She stared at him, speechless. 'Then ... that ...'

'Hadn't occurred to you?' he said sweetly.

Blazes take her, why was *she* the one stumbling over her words when *he* was the one she needed dumbfounded and distracted? With a snappish gesture, she sat up straighter, shook her loose hair down her shoulders, and briskly said, 'These are all details, wouldn't you say? You claimed Lord Cyril was trying to drive you to extinction, and I don't see what a couple of closed gates have to do with *that*.'

He took his time, picking up his wine again, taking a sip, running his tongue along his lip to catch a stray drop. Only then did he say, 'You know, I presume, that the road through Elidian is the only way to get from the human side of the marshes to our side?'

'Well, there are—'

'Other roads, yes, if you wish to drown.' He took another sip. His scrutiny of her never lifted; she could feel his eyes following her over the rim of his glass, sounding for reactions, for signs of weakness. 'There's a reason we created the way through Elidian all those years ago.'

She knew he was waiting for it but couldn't keep her eyes from widening all the same. 'I beg your pardon? Are you saying the *fae* created—'

'Of course we did.' A joyful smile. 'We're wayfarers, Miss Iavi. We need the freedom to leave and enter our lands whenever we damn well feel like it. Our lives depend on it, to be more exact.'

How could he be so coolly collected while he was upending every single thing she thought to know about the place she called home? The spider web of canals, the dykes surrounding the labyrinth of narrow houses, the mills turning their slow rounds on the bastions ... Had *they* built all of that?

Did it matter now?

She clutched her hands together in her lap, feeling the reassuring shape of her dagger against her thigh, and drew in a deep breath. 'Please explain. What does travelling have to do with your lives?'

'The fae are creatures of nature. We're connected to the land.' The words came out on a slow monotone, as if he'd set out the same explanation a thousand times before. 'We need its nearness, need to set foot in Faerie every now and then. If we stay away too long, if that bond is interrupted for too long, both the land and its people suffer.'

She threw a bewildered glance around – abundant opulence blinking at her from all sides. 'Suffer how, exactly?'

'We lose our magic,' he said.

A scoff fell from her lips before she could stop herself. 'I can hardly feel sorry about *that*.'

'And,' he continued, in that same flat, bored voice, as if he had not heard her, 'the land is dying. Our soil dries out. Our harvests shrink every year. Flowers that used to bloom don't even carry buds anymore. Without new souls to reinvigorate the land, the mountains may irrevocably die before the decade is over.'

'And ... and you say that's happening just because Lord Cyril closed the gates?' She paused, shook her head, wrestling the shreds and tangles of thoughts to make sense of them. 'Fertile lands go bad all the same. It doesn't have to be magic. For all you know—'

He slammed his wine back onto the table with too much force, voice abruptly sharpening into a snarl. 'Have you *seen* me, Miss Iavi?'

'What?' she stammered, jolting back. 'I mean, yes, of course, but—'

'This face of mine, rotting away? You've noticed that?' He rose as he spoke, words rolling from his lips louder and louder, echoing from the walls and ceiling. 'What did you think it was – some disease? Poor hygiene? Old age, perhaps?'

'No, but—'

'I *am* Faerie,' he snarled, stepping around the table. Long, skeletal fingers tugged at his cravat, untangling the pristine cloth so fast she barely realised what was about to happen. 'My lineage is bound to this land. If I die, so does Faerie. If Faerie dies, so do I. Right now, it has been dying for *decades*, Miss Iavi, and do you wish to see what it has done to me?'

His buttons sprung open under his swift fingers, coat and waistcoat parting. Briannis knew she had to look away, knew she had to get out of this room before the situation could turn impossibly more inappropriate – but her eyes remained glued to the frantic movements of his fingers, to his fast-approaching nudity with a morbid fascination she wished she could deny.

Two more steps and he yanked apart the white muslin of his shirt, looming over her now. Below that last layer of cloth ...

She was too intrigued to even gasp.

Just like his face, his torso was both dead and alive – one side tanned and muscular, one side white as snow, the skin dried out, the muscles withered to show every individual rib jutting out from his chest. Like a starving man who had died two days ago, except he was still moving ... It was indisputably an ugly sight. Gruesome. Terrifying.

Fascinating.

Old reflexes took over.

She stretched out a hand before the memory of Mrs. Sedgewick could stop her, prodding the grey, dull skin of his stomach – hard, she noted without thinking, trying to recall what Father's handbooks had said. Some sort of magical gangrene? But no, she had taken care of the gangrene patients at times, and they had looked *much* worse – oozing sores, foul-smelling blisters, quite unpleasant even to a girl who'd spent her childhood playing with mummified fingers and preserved organs in jars. This was really quite mild in comparison. His dead skin was hairless – that was interesting – and a few degrees below the expected body temperature ...

'It isn't numb, is it?' she said absently, prodding a little more firmly. 'You do still feel this?'

No answer came.

She looked up, fingertips still pressed against the dead skin just above his navel – looked up and found him gaping down at her, living eye wide with shock, lips parted in an almost-cry.

No more sneers. No more malicious cackles. Despite the dead side of his face, despite the ethereal beauty of the other half, he briefly looked ... human?

'What?' he said.

He was no longer snapping.

'Is it numb?' Briannis repeated, gesturing vaguely at his gaunt stomach. 'I'm trying to diagnose you. Do you have any idea how deep it goes, this curse? Did it affect your vital organs, too? Your heart still appears to be beating, but—'

'You— What?' He was still staring at her as if she was some ghostly apparition – unreasonable, really, given that *he* was the half-dead monster between the two of them. His voice had gone raspy. 'Aren't you supposed to be screaming at this point, Miss Iavi?'

She scoffed. 'I've seen worse. At least you don't seem to be actively rotting.'

He parted his lips again but didn't utter another word, gawking at her with what would have been comical bewilderment under any other circumstances. If he hadn't been capable of killing her with little more than a look. If she hadn't been plotting to dispose of him the moment he was even the slightest bit distracted.

And only then did she remember, in a flash of panicked recollection, that this was exactly the state in which she'd set out to get him.

Chapter 4

Always hold your knife lightly while eating: the article is intended to cut fish or vegetables, not to slaughter a pig!

Lady Lockwell's Handbook of Etiquette

SHE WAS TOUCHING HIM.

She was *touching* him.

The world could have ended as her warm fingertips settled against his stomach, and Moridyr wouldn't have noticed, would have failed to feel or see or smell anything but her firm prodding and her pensive pout and the unmistakable scent of life that clung to her. His skin felt like it might curl out to meet her, to get more of just this. Every starved fibre of his being honed in on the sensation in a moment so blissful it hurt – life, *presence*, a single innocent touch lighting a bonfire in what had been a dark, empty space inside him for far too long ...

He didn't notice her other hand slipping beneath her elegant skirts until the moment she pulled back.

And only then did he see the dagger.

She was faster than his confusion. He had a single moment to wonder where this new weapon had come from, what she was doing, what in hell he'd gotten himself into – and then she lashed out like a viper, a flat blade slicing between his third and fourth rib with alarming precision. He *felt* the sharpened steel entering his body in that moment of paralysis, felt her knife tear skin and dead flesh and embed itself deep into his torso ...

Pain bloomed through him, so fierce he saw red spots before his eyes.

His liver. Thoughts came in staggering bursts as he doubled over with a choked cry, as she nimbly leapt from her chair and darted away from him. She'd hit his *liver*. Pressing one hand flat against the wound, he could feel the warm blood trickle out between his fingers – a pain that made the world spin around him, the sort of injury that would kill a mortal man in mere minutes.

Fuck.

Had she been planning this all along?

That touch, those questions, that glance of compassion ... A flash of fury burned through him, at his own sentimental stupidity more than anything else. He should have *known* those impossible glimpses of empathy weren't genuine. Just a ruse to get to him. Just another strategy from Cyril's deadly little puppet.

The sound of quick footsteps echoed through the hall. Was she running? Was that what he looked like to her – too badly wounded to even wait and confirm the kill?

'Stay,' he ground out.

The footsteps abruptly halted.

Dragging in a breath, he raised his gaze, blinking tears from his eyes. Briannis Iavi stood frozen in the doorway with the bloodied knife clutched in her right hand, watching him with a ruthless sort of sympathy – the way one watched a butchered pig draw its last laborious breaths. He could detect no shame in her eyes. No fear. Nothing but anger and ...

Interest?

He almost laughed. Whatever she may think of herself, if his murderer was a proper woman, he was a fucking frog.

And then his rational thoughts kicked back into motion, because what was he doing standing here, lamenting his condition, thinking of frogs, when he should be using all that swiftness and cleverness to save himself instead?

'Mallow,' he managed to get out, his voice a wheezing moan. 'Mallow flowers. Tell me – *truthfully* – if you know what they look like?'

'I do.' Her words shot through the hall, forced out by his command. More dazedly, she added, 'What ...'

'Wall. Twice left, once right.' He could feel his skin growing colder, the sensation familiar on his left and disconcertingly new on his right. 'Mallow flowers. Get them to me. Five of them. Fast.'

Her expression suggested she was about to ask questions, but her feet didn't allow her to: before her mouth could open, she'd already lurched down the corridor in that unnatural wobbling gait. Moridyr dropped down into the chair she'd just vacated, praying his gasped commands would be coherent enough to make her do his bidding. If she didn't return – if she somehow got out from under the spell ...

Thirty years ago, he could have healed himself in a heartbeat.

Right now, without the support of the flowers, he would be lucky if he could heal a single papercut.

The pool of blood on the floor grew ever larger, warm, sticky wetness gushing out between his fingers in dizzying amounts. On the edge of his sight, the candlelight grew dark. His heart was a frantic drum in his chest. How long had it been now?

Damn her twice over, he *was* going to bleed out in his own dining hall. Over five thousand years of an unbroken lineage, and one little good-mannered assassin ...

Moridyr III, the last king of Faerie.

The sound of footsteps hurried closer. He almost passed out from relief.

And then her lithe silhouette blacked out the last of the candlelight as she appeared before him, throwing five mildly squashed mallow flowers into his lap – tiny, fragile things, and he'd never been so grateful to see them. Fingers trembling, he closed his living fist around them, savouring the moistness of bruised petals against his palm. Heal, please, *heal* ...

The agony dulled below his midriff.

He unfolded his hand and found a last mallow flower sticking to his finger. As it pulverised, the pain softened further, leaving nothing but a faint throbbing behind. The blood had stopped flowing, he noticed through the light-headed haze – it was still dripping to the floor, but more and more slowly, nothing but what had already gathered on his fingers.

It hurt to straighten his spine, but he did it anyway, rage and spite moving him before his thoughts could. Briannis Iavi had staggered back to the nearest wall, the bloodied knife still in her hand. This time it *was* fear contorting the features of her pretty little face.

'What ... How ...' Her eyes had gone wide, shooting from the flower dust on his fingers to the wound that no longer bled. 'That ...'

'That,' he growled, cautiously lowering his hand from his healed wound, 'may have been a mistake, Miss Iavi.'

'*Magic,*' she breathed, and if he'd announced he'd healed himself by sacrificing the lives of several innocent virgins, she couldn't have sounded any more appalled. 'You used *magic* to heal yourself? And to ... to make that flower disappear?'

LISETTE MARSHALL

Fuck. Too close to the truth – *far* too close to the truth. He staggered forward, feeling like his blood-starved mind was running seconds behind, as if his thoughts were wading through muddy water. Now she had to die, didn't she? Did he have any other choice? 'Miss Iavi ...'

'Mallow.' She about gasped the word. '*Healing, survival under tough conditions.* That's what the handbooks say – that's what it means in our flower language – but how—'

'Miss *Iavi!*' he snapped, lengthening his strides.

She barely seemed to notice. Her dagger sagged down, her stunned eyes observing his approach without truly absorbing a thing. 'But then the daisy soap ... *Innocence.* Daisies mean *innocence.* Is that why I could enter the Keep – because that soap made me look innocent and harmless to the thorns? Did you—'

He clamped a hand over her mouth and shoved her back against the wall without further ado, his bloodied fingers smothering the rest of her sentence. She went rigid, that perfect lady's stiffness. Above his larger hand, her nostrils flared – but even so close to the stench of blood, there was no inkling of hysteria in her gaze.

His heart pounded in his ears, his temples, his throat. Now it ought to be very simple. *Kill yourself,* he'd say, and she'd have no choice but to obey – to slash that treacherous little dagger through the creamy expanse of her throat and solve his troubles at once. Two little words. He'd been an eloquent man once, before the Gate closed; his voice was truly his most natural weapon. It should have been an easy kill.

Her warm breath dampened his palm. Even against the dulled nerves of his dead side, he could feel the panicky tension of her lips, the small trembles that betrayed her fear no matter how hard she tried to control herself.

Kill yourself.

His lips didn't move.

60

Wide, clever eyes watched him from half a foot away, waiting for his command – knowing what he could say, what he *should* say. What was he waiting for? She wouldn't stop trying to murder him, and so he had to kill her. She knew a secret his people depended on, and so he had to kill her. She turned the Keep into a thorn-guarded prison by nothing but her presence, and so he had to kill her.

But he looked down before he could help himself. Saw her shaking fingers around her dagger, the goosebumps pebbling her arm, the fast pulse beneath her collarbone. Heard how the castle's silence no longer sounded like the quiet of the grave with her quickened breath to break it, smelled the bitter scent of human fear below the divine fragrance of her body.

Fuck.

Fuck.

Did it matter how hard he tried to deny the truth? He already knew he couldn't do it. Among halls of lifeless art and gold and jewels, she was the most priceless treasure by far – a living, breathing, talking soul.

'Drop your knife,' he said, voice low.

Her fingers flew open, and bloodied steel clattered to the ground. Her breath came even faster against his hand now, small breasts heaving against her dress as she gulped in desperate breath after desperate breath.

'Don't move except to speak.' His pulse was a roar in his ears as he eased his hand from her mouth, leaving smears of blood on her cheeks. 'Try that little trick one more time, Miss Iavi, and I swear to every single soul in Faerie I'll make you regret it. Do I make myself clear?'

She didn't move, as he'd commanded, but she rasped, 'Yes.'

'Good,' he murmured, stepping back. He didn't want to step back. He wanted to feel her, smell her, hear her – soak her into his senses like an intoxicating wine until he was drunk on her presence. Sweet divines, how could he hate her so much and want to devour her at the same time, this prim creature embodying all the human morals he detested, serving all the bastards he loathed? 'Tell me truthfully if you carry more weapons on you.'

'I don't,' she spat – but was that a spark of relief in her eyes?

Wrong question, then. 'Tell me truthfully if you're hiding more knives somewhere.'

This time he'd guessed right; he could see it in the darkening shadows on her face, the defeated tension around her lips. 'In my room.' She choked out the words, unable to keep them in despite her attempts. 'I've hidden them in my room.'

'How many?'

She swallowed. 'Three more.'

Good heavens, he'd been an idiot not to check her immediately this morning, to assume the one knife she'd drawn on him was all she carried. As if it wasn't bad enough that his powers were useless, that any command not to harm him would likely not hold for longer than a handful of hours. Did his wits truly need to abandon him, too?

With a grim chuckle, he said, 'Well, let us go take a look, then.'

No command, and quite as he'd expected, she didn't oblige – remained motionless against the wall, small breasts heaving, jaw clenched. 'Why?'

Moridyr raised his eyebrows. 'Being murdered over dinner is not something I would like to make a daily habit of, Miss Iavi.'

'No, I mean ...' Her cheeks grew nearly as red as the blood still smeared on them. 'I'm wondering why you even care to disarm me. Why you haven't killed me yet. What is it that you want from me?'

If only he knew. He should know so, so much better than this, clinging to the little life he could find in her dagger glares and disapproving frowns – should know so much better than to set himself up to be abandoned all over again. But then again … he didn't want friendship or fondness from her. Nothing he could gain and lose. Nothing that could leave him open and vulnerable and shatter him all over.

All he needed was another living soul – an independent mind. Someone who was not merely another piece of obedient furniture.

So if she stubbornly hated him … well, that was perfect, wasn't it?

'You offered me your company,' he said, and the smile that slid around his lips was the coldest he wielded. 'We haven't even found out yet whether you might enjoy my games after all.'

She flinched a fraction.

Good. No friendship. No fondness. Holding out his arm, the emerald sleeve drenched with blood, he smoothly added, 'Your room, then?'

The noncommittal suggestion was a lie, and they both knew it – he could see it in her tightening lips, her widening pupils. With gritted teeth, she pressed away from the wall, jutted up her chin, and icily said, 'As you wish, Your Majesty.'

He flashed a smile. 'Most grateful, Miss Iavi.'

She ignored his proffered arm and strode out before him with a spine as straight as a broomstick, her steps brisk and determined. As she hurried up the stairs – it appeared she'd memorised the way back to the Starlit Room perfectly – she added in that same pristine tone, 'Were those games of yours the reason everyone else seems to have left this court, by any chance?'

'Incidentally,' Moridyr said, heart twinging despite knowing that was exactly the result she had aimed for, 'no.'

'So where did they go?'

'They were unable to stay as I lost my powers.' He wished he didn't have to speak the words – didn't have to relive those years of knowing that slowly, inevitably, the never-ending symphony of life at Rosethorn Keep would go quiet. But he couldn't lie, and he doubted a refusal to answer would make her shut up on the subject. 'The roses become activated when a threat tries to enter the castle, as you'll recall. Thirty years ago, very few people were a threat to me.'

Her footsteps didn't falter, but he heard the small catch of her breath. 'And now ...'

'Most fae could kill me, if they felt so inclined. Humans too, as we've just established.'

'Oh.' She sounded a little dazed. 'I see. So when your strength started waning, they fled the castle before they would be locked up with you forever?'

They fled. Oh, the hate in her thoughts of him, the worst assumptions she didn't hesitate to make ... He had all but shoved them out of the door. Had resorted to commands with those who'd refused to leave most staunchly, determined to stay loyal to their king and crown. Had seen them go, one by one, until it had been just him and the boy, living through the years in the abundance of their castle ...

And then it had been just him.

For fourteen fucking years.

'I sent them off,' he said, his voice a bored drawl that seemed in no way connected to the painful thudding of his heart. 'Fae are free folk. I had no desire to turn my home into a prison for them.'

Her laugh was bitter. 'Whereas being a prison for humans is perfectly fine with you?'

'You were the one to sneak in,' he pleasantly reminded her. 'Also, you seem to forget that I do happen to like most of *my* people.'

She stiffened for an infinitesimal moment at the top of the stairs, then stamped on through the castle, not bothering to grace his thinly veiled insult with even the shortest of replies.

Which was just as it should be, he had to remind himself as he followed, his eyes clinging to her slender little figure. He didn't need her to *give* him anything. He would just take what he needed, and once she'd lost her use to him, he'd do away with her and be none the worse for it. Simple as that. The only way to make sure he wasn't setting himself up to be broken again.

Just as it should be.

She reached her room without looking back even once, slipping inside and slamming the door shut behind her in a clear unspoken message. Moridyr waited. Inside, he could hear the sound of drawers opening and shutting; it wasn't long before she reappeared, still covered in his blood, now carrying three small knives in one gloved hand. How had she smuggled them in – her boots? Her garters?

Something heated inside him at the thought of prying her weapons from those slender legs he'd glimpsed below her skirts, the intimacy of the vision as much of a temptation as the simple appeal of soft, warm skin.

'These are all the knives I had with me,' she declared as she dropped them at his feet, gaze flicking up over his bared, blood-smeared torso as she lifted her chin to defiantly meet his gaze. 'Anything else, Your Majesty?'

Everything. He wanted *everything* else.

Touch me, he almost said, the command burning on his tongue, *hold me, want me, look at me again as if you don't see a corpse in my place.* And she would. Everything within Rosethorn Keep obeyed him, the magic of his bloodline tied into every inch of his home; she would never be able to refuse. The need for her touch built in his body like an itching pain, burning below his skin, aching for warmth and pressure and softness ...

'Tell me truthfully if these are all your knives,' he managed.

She scoffed. 'These are all the knives I brought with me. I had to leave the others I owned behind in the city.'

The city – his mind spun with the memory all of a sudden, his last journey to the south, the last time he'd laid eyes upon the rows and rows of red gabled roofs. *Tell me about Elidian,* he wanted to burst out, *tell me about the lights, the balls, the music. Tell me if they still sell the same foods at the markets – tell me about the smells, the textures. Tell me about the flowers blooming in the glasshouses, about the thud of books on wood in the university halls. Tell me about the ridiculous wigs and the dazzling dresses, the senate hall rumours, the sordid gossip.*

Tell me about life.

What was he thinking? He couldn't get sentimental here, couldn't make himself vulnerable for those clever dagger eyes to see. Briannis Iavi was not a friend to comfort him. Well-bred and deadly, clever and desperate, she was nothing but an intriguing puzzle for him to solve, a present to unwrap layer by layer – nothing but shallow amusement and simple entertainment.

Hell, he *deserved* some harmless fun after thirty years of isolation, after fourteen years of perfect, quiet solitude. Why was his own mind playing tricks on him, trying to turn this game into something meaningful?

'Anything else?' she repeated, her voice strung tight, and only then did he realise he'd been staring at her for several heartbeats too long.

'Not for now.' He stepped back, feeling like a predator giving up on the sweetest, juiciest prey. His torso was still throbbing with pain. His mind was a whirlpool. He needed a drink, a nap, and another handful of mallow flowers before he could trust himself anywhere near her again. 'But I'll see you at break-fast tomorrow morning for a second attempt at pleasant companionship. Don't commit any murders in the meantime, Miss Iavi.'

He didn't wait for her reaction – relief or apprehension or whatever else it might be. He didn't dare risk a single word more falling from her lips.

Instead, he turned on his heel and fled.

Chapter 5

*On no occasion, regardless of the provocation, should
one repay rudeness with rudeness. Nothing serves as a
stronger reprimand to incivility than flawless courtesy.*
Lady Lockwell's Handbook of Etiquette

EVEN WITH HER BEDROOM door locked behind her, the heavy
bronze key turned and turned until it couldn't move any further, Briannis felt like she couldn't breathe deep enough to get
the air she needed.

She paced the glittering room for what felt like forever, unable to sit down, the sickeningly beautiful fae dress fluttering
uselessly around her legs. Her mind spun, too many images
and impressions to string a single coherent thought together.
Flower magic. Dying fae. Breakfast. Tomorrow morning.

A second attempt at pleasant companionship.

After she'd cut straight through his liver. After he'd *survived*
the wound. After he had been a hair's breadth removed from
killing her instead – she was sure he had been, had caught

that forbidding glimpse of finality in his good eye as he'd held her against the wall. He'd been ready to speak the word, end this deadly dance with a single simple command, and wipe his hands clean of her.

And instead, he'd spared her.

For his blasted *games*.

She did not want to think about what those might entail but couldn't stop herself from doing it anyway.

It was the look he'd given her moments before he blessedly left her alone – that heated glance of need, the raw desire emanating even from the sunken depths of his dead eye. For all his pretty stories of women following fae of their own accord, he had been locked in solitary confinement for what might be decades, and he hated her to pieces. If he wanted her, if he wanted *anyone* ... She'd known men to violate women for less.

I am not a proper man, Miss Iavi.

She whimpered, grinding to a halt in the middle of her star-flecked bedroom.

What to do? The leathery rose vines crawled over the window again as if they sensed her need to escape, warning her off. Her knives were gone, and while she had managed to choose her words carefully and hide her last vial of poison, she doubted she'd be able to use it before breakfast. His last command would probably stop her even if she found an opportunity to try.

Could she hide?

She drew in a deep breath, considering that option. He hadn't ordered her to stay in her room this time. And as long as she was nowhere to be found, he couldn't command her to return to him and play his games, either.

Hiding would give her the time she needed to tip a spoonful of foxglove into his tea at an opportune moment and wait for him to do away with himself.

She was too glad to have come up with a semblance of a plan, *any* plan, to question herself any longer. No time to lose, then. Divines knew when the beast would change his mind and decide to bother her in her bedroom after all. With quick, agitated motions, she shot into the pale pink coat from the wardrobe, snatched her vial from beneath her pillow, and slid the poison into the slim pockets – her last key to find her way back home, and for a moment, the breath caught in her throat as she tiptoed towards the locked door. If she lost it ...

The lustre of the Elidian senate dome flashed before her mind's eye. The broad canals, the stepped gables. The summer evenings in the Arragher gardens with their exotic fish ponds and their extravagant wine fountains, and the crisp winter mornings when even the marshes outside the city ramparts froze over ... They felt an eternity away from her already, as if the beauty of the city had existed only in a fleeting dream.

Keep your head clear, Bri. You're as good as your own best idea.

Father. She abruptly released the air from her lungs, gripping the heavy key and turning it. If for no other reason, she would return to the place where he'd envisioned their perfect life.

That thought at least grounded her as she slipped into the corridor.

A quick glance around confirmed that no fae kings were lying in wait for her – a small blessing. Arms wrapped tightly around herself, she hurried away from her bedroom, in the opposite direction from where her captor had gone. How far should she go before settling in some dark corner and risking a nap? It wouldn't help her to get lost, which meant she probably shouldn't wander off too much: in the candlelit darkness of night, every gilded, bejewelled corridor looked like the next. Better to crawl away in any of the myriad bedrooms and start moving again when the daylight woke her in the morning.

She risked opening a few doors but disqualified most of them for her purposes. Some had no window – she might accidentally sleep in and be found before she could move on. Some were mostly empty – she would be noticed with a single glance. Some turned out not to be bedrooms at all, but rather passages to other corridors or halls or stairwells – how could *anyone* ever find their way in this bewildering hell of a castle?

The next door she tried was locked.

It was so unexpected she didn't register the fact on her first try, yanking at the handle a second time before she realised the door *couldn't* be opened.

But nothing else in this castle was locked.

She'd been wandering around for hours this morning, trying every single door she came across, and all of them had opened easily for her – no secrets in a place where thieves would never be able to enter. And yet this door – she tugged at it a third time, just to be sure – had been firmly sealed.

Presumably, that meant she'd be wise to walk on and pretend she'd never noticed.

But then again ... She knelt, pressing her eye against the keyhole in an attempt to see the room behind. Unfortunately, all she saw was darkness. If His Majesty was more desperate to protect this room than any of the others, who knew what he was hiding inside under the cover of night? A weakness? A weapon? Something she could use to find her way out of this ornate prison? If only she'd known anything about lockpicks ...

She threw a look down the corridor, hoping a sturdy crowbar would magically appear. To her displeasure, although not to her surprise, it didn't. But a slender silver candlestick glimmered temptingly at her from a long side table covered in sculptures that seemed carved from pure rubies, and if she could just wedge the thin end between door and frame, wouldn't that be enough?

She inched half a step towards it, eyes shooting from door to side table and back again. A risk, of course, but—

'I suggest you don't,' a bored voice said behind her.

She shrieked and whirled around.

He stood leaning against the silk- and leaf-covered wall of a dusky side passage she could have *sworn* was empty when she'd passed it, green eye sparkling in the candlelight, dead side even more lifeless in the shadows. His red hair hung loose again, cascading over an impeccable new coat – this one a deep royal purple, adorned with an intricate pattern of ivy leaves stitched in gold thread.

If not for her hammering heart trying to choke the air from her lungs, she could have thought him beautiful.

'Do what?' she squeaked.

'Destroy any part of a magical castle.' He didn't move, sending her that smile that wasn't a smile at all but rather a sly, seductive trap, daring her to challenge him, to defy him. 'These doors will fight back if needed. I strongly recommend respecting their locks.'

The hairs prickled on the back of her neck. 'I just wanted ...'

'To explore the Keep?' he suggested with that lethal little tilt of his head. 'Of course, Miss Iavi. A most noble endeavour, especially minutes to midnight.'

'And what are *you* doing here, minutes to midnight?' she snapped without thinking. The poison burned in her pocket, her only way home, her very last hope. 'If you were looking for me in my room, I would very much like to know why you were setting foot in there in the first place, given that—'

'The Keep was getting fretful,' he interrupted blandly. 'Then it occurred to me I hadn't ordered you to stay in your room this time.'

It occurred to me. Did he really want her to believe he had honestly forgotten to take that simple precaution? Briannis almost scoffed. He was fae, for goodness' sake – he schemed like he breathed. Had he deliberately given her that freedom to see what she'd do with it? Had this been a trap, an attempt to make her reveal her next line of attack?

'Ah,' she said, schooling her face into a mask of cold disapproval.

'You look offended by the notion.' Now he moved away from the wall, prowling towards her with a dancer's deadly elegance. She couldn't help her gaze flicking down to his newly tied cravat, to the silk hiding that breathtaking contrast of beauty and death. 'Don't worry, I have no desire to lock you up unless I need to. You'd be a worthless companion, holed away in a bedroom. But you *will* stay out of this one room.'

One room. Just this door, looking no more intriguing than the dozens of others she'd passed so far – a black rose carved into the wood, the handle dull from use.

'What's in it?' she heard herself say.

'Who knows?' The mockery in his voice was thick as butter. 'Forbidden flowers, perhaps? A captive princess? The maimed bodies of my dead wives? The entire point, Miss Iavi, is that you are not supposed to find out.'

She swallowed hard. 'You could make that point in more reassuring ways.'

'Yes,' he said dryly, 'but what would be the fun in that?'

'Is that all you fae care about? Having *fun*?' She almost spat out the words. 'Never mind about kindness and duty and responsibility to others? Never mind about … about …'

He was still sauntering closer, languid step after languid step, voice lazy like a long summer morning. 'Respectability, again? You're getting predictable, my dear.'

'And I'm not *your dear*!'

His laughter was low and syrupy, utterly unaffected by her fury. Or at least it *seemed* unaffected – she staggered back a step, heart pounding, mind spinning. They'd been here before, hadn't they? He was toying with her again like he had over dinner, cat and mouse, using her fury for his own entertainment. But the end of that conversation ...

As easily as he'd recovered, as smoothly as he had slid back into this display of venomous grace, his control *had* snapped in the moments before she'd stabbed him, while he was snarling at her and stripping himself of his clothes.

So how much of his silky composure was an act? And how much of it was armour, a flimsy shield to hide the far more dangerous beast below?

With him prowling closer and closer, she wasn't sure she wanted to know.

'Please,' she got out between shallow breaths. 'I was just curious. Unable to sleep. I'll go back to my room if you want me to. You ... you should probably sleep, too, shouldn't you?'

'Oh, yes,' he easily agreed, slowing his steps. 'I definitely should. I have a stab wound to recover from, just to name one thing.'

'Very unfortunate.' Her voice caught. That look was back in his eye again – not so much hungry but hankering, like a starving man craving a meal he couldn't have. A look that should disgust and terrify her. A look that *certainly* shouldn't send little shivers of excitement up her guts, the thrill of new discoveries to make – *a lady does not enjoy unwanted attentions.* 'Do ... do I see you at breakfast, then?'

'I'm very sorry, Miss Iavi,' he muttered as those burning eyes slid over her, passing the loose strands of her hair, the bare skin at her collar, her gloved hands. He was barely two steps away from her now, and the corridor seemed to narrow around them, seemed to shrink to the caress of his soft voice and the memory of his body below the purple silk. 'You cannot start wandering around my home in the depth of night and then vanish on me without explanations. What were you doing here?'

Her legs swayed beneath her. 'I already told you ...'

'Curious and unable to sleep,' he finished with a slow nod, pronouncing the words with utmost care. Too much care. She could taste the disbelief in every syllable. 'I know what you told me. I also know that you're a murderess and capable of lying. It's what makes humans so fiendishly dangerous, truly.'

He was calling *her* dangerous – this creature drenched in death and trickery? She felt like her wits were sprinting away from her, wise enough not to stay in the presence of those piercing eyes, that razor-sharp tongue. But her eyes lingered, unable to look away from him, drinking in every inch of his sculpted jaw, his jutting cheekbones ...

This had to be some fae enchantment warping her thoughts. There was no chance she'd look at that skull side of his face with her own eyes and lose her words at the sight, not revulsion but ... admiration?

Grasping for sense, she stammered, 'If you're worried I was looking for a new way to kill you – well, you ordered me not to attempt any murders tonight. I wouldn't have been capable of it even if I'd wanted to.'

'I know.' Again that quick examination sliding down her body, setting the skin below his gaze on fire. 'Tell me truthfully why you—'

'Oh, for goodness' sake! I was trying to hide, if you must know!' She staggered a last step away and met the wall, still not nearly enough space between them. Back to wall – the way she'd been standing in the dining hall, his cold hand pressed over her lips, his heated breath brushing her face. 'I figured I'd rather sleep in a linen closet and avoid you than ... than ...'

'Than have breakfast with me?' He breathed a chuckle, lips twisting into a smile that made her guts twist with it. 'An ill-informed choice. The Keep serves a delicious morning meal.'

'That was *not* the source of my worries,' she snapped through gritted teeth. 'As you know very well, *Your Majesty*.'

'Perhaps I do have an inkling,' he admitted, looking amused at the title she'd just flung like an offense into his face. 'I'm gathering you would prefer not to play my games after all, then? Such a shame. They're not entirely volitional, I'm afraid.'

Briannis wondered if it would be possible to hold her breath until she fainted. If she just dropped lifelessly to the floor, he couldn't force her to wake up, could he?

Could he?

She dragged in a shivery breath, just to be sure, and managed, 'What are you planning to do to me?'

His good eye narrowed, and although he didn't move, it felt like he was leaning even closer, prying even deeper. 'You seem to be afraid of something.'

'I'd prefer not to tell,' she said weakly. 'I might give you ideas.'

'You seem convinced I'm striving to make your stay as unpleasant as inhumanly possible, Miss Iavi,' he purred, and she almost pressed herself *through* the wall in her hopeless attempt to put a few more inches between the two of them – between her clammy skin and the lure of his magic pulling at her, transforming his eyes into green and black jewels, turning his dead skin to pale alabaster in the candlelight. 'Who knows, you might just amuse yourself well enough. You didn't seem to mind our little rendezvous at dinner, after all.'

'I ... I don't know what you're ...'

He chuckled. 'Oh, you do.'

Tanned skin, muscular ridges, and then the endlessly fascinating contrast of his jutting ribs ... Her breath went shallow. Why, *why* had she touched him – why had she let that shameful, ridiculous part of her take over, those instincts she'd trained so very hard to unlearn, to bury beneath good, sensible manners?

'You have no idea,' she breathed. 'You know absolutely nothing about me.'

'I know that most truly respectable ladies aren't interested in magical gangrene,' he said sweetly, and the way he examined her, watching every gesture and expression, made her feel like *she* was the one stripped bare between the two of them. 'Most respectable ladies don't become assassins, either. So who says you aren't interested in the way of the fae as well?'

'I do! I say I'm not!' She tore her gaze away from him, aiming it at the crystal-covered ceiling to avoid the snakelike challenge in his eyes. Sucking in a deep breath, she shakily added, 'I never *wanted* to be an assassin, you know.'

'And yet you're suspiciously good at it. You hit me straight in the liver with your first stab.' From the corner of her eye, she saw him cock his head to one side. 'Most people don't develop such skill in an art they do not enjoy.'

She shook her head, blinking back those stupid, stupid tears burning behind her eyes. 'My father was a surgeon. I saw a lot.'

'And that is all?' he said softly. Such a dangerous question, treacherously gentle, seeping through her defences like water soaking into dry soil until she could barely distinguish his words from her own thoughts. 'You're trying to tell me you don't take any satisfaction from it, figuring out the fastest, cleverest way to end someone? That it's not an intriguing puzzle to you, the way my half-death is an intriguing puzzle to you? That you—'

'No!' She shot away from the wall, past him, backing away from that voice digging into shadows she barely knew herself. Shadows she didn't *want* to know herself. All those hours spent in cosy teahouses, observing houses and their inhabitants across the street ... All those visits to quaint ladies' shops, buying wigs and glasses and ridiculous hats to hide her true identity from accidental witnesses ... Her voice rose to a shrill shriek as she added, 'I didn't enjoy *any* part of it! You're wrong, do you hear me? You're *wrong!*'

He merely turned, eyes bright as they followed her in the candlelight. A faint, knowing smile lingered around his lips, twisting the dead part of his mouth into something almost lively.

It wasn't a hunter's smile. Rather, a victor's smile.

'Respectable ladies,' he said, such infinite patience in his coaxing voice, 'don't shout at kings either, Miss Iavi.'

She could have punched him – could have punched that blasted self-satisfied smile from his blasted charismatic face – but punching was not something respectable ladies did, either. With effort, she unclenched her gloved hands and lowered them, feeling the reassuring bulge of her vial in her pocket.

Her poison. She sucked in a cooling breath. She had to keep her head clear now – she still had her foxglove. His taunting and needling didn't mean anything, not if he would be the one to die in the end.

And he *was* wrong. She knew who she wanted to be, didn't she? Not an assassin. Not a cursed king's plaything.

'You,' she said pointedly, and she said it with all the haughtiness she could muster, all the well-bred disdain Mrs. Sedgewick would have displayed at a vulgar drunk or a misbehaving servant, 'are upsetting me with this nonsense. And with your sneaking after me, too. If it's all the same to you, I would like to return to my bedroom now.'

He merely quirked up his one coppery eyebrow a fraction.

And how was it that that measly gesture turned his macabre, maimed face into something almost graceful – into a mask of dangerous elegance that made her heart stutter in fear and fascination at once? It was playful, that expression. It was – oh, sweet mother Eostre help her – an *invitation*.

'Alone!' she snapped, cheeks flaring red-hot as she stumbled farther back.

'Very well,' he said in a voice that could have been dripping with honey. 'I look forward to continuing our conversation tomorrow, Miss Iavi. And I hope you sleep well in the meantime, of course.'

'I'd wish you a good night,' she said, jutting up her chin so she could glare at him down her nose, 'but I don't think you deserve it.'

She heard him laugh behind her as she stalked off.

Merciful divines, she might throw herself to the roses if she had to stand this for another day – his impertinence, his lewdness, and worst of all that inexplicable yet undeniable charm playing tricks on the safe and structured essence of her life. It had to be magic. It had to be some tricky enchantment. Hadn't everyone warned her all her life? Fae *were* dangerous, and if she wasn't very, very careful ...

No. She would *not* give in to him. She would *not* let him drive her insane. She just needed to find yet another way to handle him.

Hiding wouldn't do, in a castle that could track her every movement. Attacking would be rash and unwise, with only one attempt left and no plan to guarantee success. And clinging to her manners, to the safe and sensible person she wanted to be, wasn't working, no matter what Mrs. Sedgewick had imprinted on her all those years ago. There was no correcting this devil. All the good manners in the world wouldn't inspire him to behave like a proper gentleman in return, because he *knew* what manners were, and he spat on them.

Which indisputably left her vulnerable to his thoroughly unmannered games.

So if she was very, very honest for a moment, there was only a single card she had left to play – unladylike behaviour.

She would not be so vulnerable if she could, for just a few days, be someone else entirely. A woman he couldn't strip bare, because it wasn't her at all.

Someone had given her that daisy soap, Briannis reminded herself. Someone had believed she could do it. She still had her poison, she still had most of her wits about her ... so she still stood a chance. Abandoning a few of her principles for the remainder of her stay was not too high a price to pay, not if the gossip rags would never find out, not if it meant she could escape with her life and collect her reward at home. Just a few days.

Until she found his weakness. Until she could finally complete her job and escape this hell of a place.

She turned the key in her bedroom's lock with far more composure this time.

Chapter 6

One should always maintain a respectable distance from gentlemen; in her dealings with the other sex, a lady's commitment to modesty serves as a hallmark of her refinement.

Lady Lockwell's Handbook of Etiquette

THE ROSES TWISTED OVER the high windows of the breakfast room, stealing most of the sunlight that might otherwise have flooded the mahogany floorboards.

Briannis's hands were clammy as she stepped in, piles of buttery buns and plates full of fresh fruit confirming that the castle doors swinging open around her had indeed led her to the correct destination in the labyrinthine building. She forced herself not to stall, not to fidget or show any signs of nervousness. *A lady is calm and composed.* What had her governesses prepared her for, if not for this moment, for this mission?

The king was already there, of course. What else would he be doing, if not waiting for another opportunity to torment her? He was seated at the other side of the round breakfast table, elegantly sipping steaming hot tea from a porcelain cup so fragile that it was nearly translucent. As she made her way to join him at the centre of the room, he lowered his cup slowly, almost theatrically.

'Miss Iavi.'

She curtsied. 'Your Majesty.'

'Before you sit down,' he said pleasantly, with a grand inviting gesture at the elegant padded chairs, 'be so kind as to tell me truthfully whether you carry any weapons on you.'

Thank every holy name in the world that she'd left her poison in her room. She fought to keep any sliver of smugness from her voice as the words tore out. 'I don't.'

'Excellent.' He took another sip of tea. 'Please sit down.'

She was prepared for the nauseating sensation of her body obeying, and was momentarily brought off balance when her muscles didn't jump into motion. *Please.* That little word – enough to soften the command to a request.

Best not to tempt him to take it back. She sat down, pursing her lips at the ridiculous collection of meats and cheeses and jam in seven different colours – breakfast for a large family, and a rich one at that. This was probably not the moment to inform her host she rarely ate more than a few pieces of fruit in the mornings.

She gingerly picked a bun from the nearest pile and picked up a dark red jam – blackberries, if she had to guess, although who knew what other fruits might be found in this incomprehensible land? The silver spoon in the jam jar stirred before she touched it, and she almost squeaked as it scooped up and floated towards her plate all by itself.

Somehow, she managed to keep her face straight. The king would be amused by her shock, and she didn't feel like doing him such favours.

It was only after the spoon had covered her bread in purple-red sweetness that he spoke up, voice still equally smooth and pleasant. 'You are quiet this morning, Miss Iavi.'

'I thought I'd let you do the talking,' she retorted equally pleasantly, smiling her blandest smile at him across the table. 'It seems to be a favourite pastime of yours, and I would hate to wound your tender feelings by limiting your time with the beloved sound of your own voice.'

She could hear Mrs. Sedgewick shriek out in horror in the back of her mind.

But ... was it working? He was just a little slower to reply, and the smile he returned to her after that blink of hesitation was just a little less vicious than before. His voice, though, was still thick with mockery. 'Your selflessness certainly does you credit, Miss Iavi.'

Obvious scorn, but she wouldn't let herself be shocked by his outrageous lack of decorum; her reaction would only amuse him, after all. So she shook her poor governess aside – *A lady distances herself from ill-mannered company immediately* – and retorted in an equally insincere tone, 'I do my best to be of service, Your Majesty. Humble attempts, but I hope they may please you all the same.'

She took a small bite of bread, savouring the sweet and tart flavours that danced across her tongue, and watched the king's eyes widen ever so slightly on the other side of the table. A small victory, but it *was* a victory, and for the very first time in this castle, she felt as if she might regain the slightest control of herself.

He hesitated just a moment too long, then said, 'I believe I can conclude you slept soundly, Miss Iavi?'

'Oh, quite.' She looked at him cheerfully, triumph heating the blood in her veins. 'Some time to think can make all the difference, wouldn't you say? I spent several hours contemplating you, as a matter of fact.'

He reached for a small basket filled with braided white bread. 'You flatter me.'

'Oh, that was not my intention at all,' she assured him without thinking. It was rather unnerving how easily she turned into this un-Briannis-like version of herself – sharp-edged rather than soft and comfortable. 'It's your curse I've been pondering. You didn't answer my question yesterday, you see – is it numb, the dying part of you? Or does it ever hurt?'

The question hung merrily in the air above their abundant breakfast, shameless and unforgivably intrusive.

His mouth twisted into a pensive scowl as he observed her, and for a moment, Briannis feared she had gone too far. But the expression flattened before she could apologise, morphed into a look of what seemed to be ... interest?

'And why would you want to know, Miss Iavi?'

She had her answer prepared, had practiced it in case the question came with a command attached. 'My father was a surgeon. I learned a lot about the workings of bodies when I was younger, and I thought I might be able to help you.'

Amusement flared in his eyes. 'Must I bring to your attention the fact that you were trying to kill me a mere twelve hours ago?'

'I'm grateful for the reminder,' she said sweetly. 'My fickle human mind had forgotten. Mortals. You know how we are. Would you pass me the tea, please?'

'Liars,' he said dryly.

'I beg your pardon?'

'That's what you mortals are. Liars.' But he did hand her the teapot, floral porcelain matching his own fragile cup. 'Please tell me why I would trust your noble intentions a single night after you were declaring me and my people wicked, women-stealing scum of the earth.'

'My father would have said even scum of the earth deserves adequate care,' she said, pouring herself a cup and choosing her words with utmost caution, 'but I have to admit that has little to do with my motivations. I've come to the conclusion that under the circumstances of this moment, it would be ridiculous to make another attempt on your life. We're locked in together, and you could make my time here extremely unpleasant. So I'm hoping I might persuade you not to do so. As I said, I thought I'd try to be of service.'

Until he lowered those smooth shields of unbothered rudeness. Until he trusted her enough to make mistakes, to make himself vulnerable ... but it seemed wiser not to speak that part out loud.

He took a sip of tea without answering. His eyes found her over the gilded rim of his cup, emerald green and coal black watching her closely as she bit off another mouthful of bread and blackberry. Only after she swallowed did he say, 'Tell me truthfully whether those are, indeed, your motivations.'

'They are.'

She hadn't lied. She had merely been ... selective.

He lowered his cup back onto its saucer, so slowly she didn't hear the tingling of porcelain against porcelain. With a sigh, he leaned back in his chair, interlaced his long, slender fingers, and said, 'It does hurt, yes.'

His voice had lost that familiar poisonous quality, the faint mockery that lay below every word he'd spoken so far. Instead, the confession came out with a distant, off-handed air about it, as if he was admitting to having forgotten his glasses in his bedroom.

A small thrill prickled up her spine. She suspected that same carelessness signalled the exact opposite of its face value – meaningful honesty.

That was progress.

That was another victory.

'What hurts, exactly?' she said, and she was back in Father's practice, dutifully scribbling down notes while he peered at his patients over his oakwood desk, the smell of cloves and wormwood clinging to every inch of the room. 'And does it do so continuously? Or in stings? Would you describe the pain as burning, chafing, something else?'

'I ...' He faltered – *faltered* – as he narrowed his eyes at her, thoughts visibly whirring even behind his dead eye. She suppressed a triumphant grin. There – that would teach him. He couldn't provoke and pry if *he* was the one at the centre of the conversation for a change, could he?

'Your Majesty?' she said sweetly.

'It's the zone between living and dead that aches the most,' he said sharply – such beautiful, unfiltered sharpness, the cat fallen prey to the mouse's teeth. 'Where the living nerves still feel the tear and dryness of the dead part. I've tried every single flower I can think of, but none of them ease the pain in the slightest. I live with it now, and most of the time, it is ... ' Another small hesitation. 'Manageable.'

'But unpleasant?'

His lip curled up slightly. 'Quite, yes.'

'Have you tried other methods?' It was a struggle to remind herself this was not the *actual* aim of the conversation – that her questions were a ruse, nothing but a tool to hide the truth of her intentions. It was so very easy, even after all this time, to be swept up in the fascination she'd worked so hard to let go. 'Not magic but just ... medicine?'

'I'm not a healer, Miss Iavi,' he said tersely, and was it her imagination, or did those words come out a fraction defensive?

'Well, you should be happy you didn't yet kill me, then.' She smiled that sunny smile at him again, knowing that her smugness made it come out a tad saucy but unable to care. She would start caring again when she was back home among civilised society. Here, witnessed only by a man who would soon be dead ... What was the harm in letting go a little?

It was so easy to not be herself – so uncannily easy.

'We'll see how much you're truly able to do,' he said, and although she could tell he was aiming for an unimpressed sneer, it fell short by several marks. How much did he hate it, having to ask a lowly, lying human for help? How much did the wounds hurt for him even to allow such humiliation? 'What do you suggest?'

She shrugged. 'Research.'

'*Research*,' he repeated, sounding like she'd suggested regular baths in moonlight and perhaps some happy thoughts as a remedy.

'I suppose you've heard of it?' she said, all but rolling her eyes at him. 'Trying things. Trying more things. Starting over because it's all rubbish. Trying even more. Father also yelled a lot in the process, but I think that may be an optional element.'

He looked torn between laughter and annoyance. 'Thank you, Miss Iavi, I happen to have heard of it even in this uneducated hamlet. I was rather wondering *what* exactly you were planning to research in the first place.'

'Common plants. Without magic.' She put down her half-eaten roll, no longer hungry at all with a puzzle to focus on. 'We could see if oils help to soften the dead skin – some hydration might assuage the tearing pain between the hard dead area and the softer living skin. And what about comfrey? It's very effective for tissue repair. Or ...'

'The tissue in this case is dead,' he said flatly.

'Most corpses aren't still walking around,' she retorted. 'And you bled profusely when I stabbed you on the left, if my fickle human mind recalls correctly. There still has to be *some* life in you even on that side.'

He parted his lips, shut them, parted them again. 'Yes, but ...'

'But you feel like a fool for not thinking of it yourself?' she suggested dryly.

'Miss *Iavi*.' His hand came to his heart in mock outrage, a spark of amusement returning to his good eye. 'Where in the world have your manners gone?'

'I have declared them useless for the occasion,' she informed him, rising from her chair. 'Unless you insist I prioritise etiquette over your wellbeing, of course, Your Majesty. Do we have beeswax in this castle? I presume it could ... oh.'

A small glass jar of beeswax pellets had appeared between the cheese and butter in the middle of the breakfast table.

'You appear to have won over the Keep,' he said, examining the jar warily.

'Well, that certainly makes matters easier.' She shoved her plate aside, tapping impatient fingers against the edge of the table. 'Almond oil. And let us try lavender oil – oh, that's too much to ask? Just lavender, then, please.'

The purple flowers appeared next to the other ingredients with a faint shimmer. She stretched out a hand to pick them up, then hesitated, memory lingering on realisations she had not yet dared to give much thought or consideration so far.

'Lavender,' she said slowly. '*Peace and serenity*, according to the flower language I learned.'

Something reminiscent of his old, vicious mask settled back over his features. 'Is it?'

'What is its magical meaning?'

'If I were to use it on you' – he was drawing out the words in what might be hesitation or simple theatrics – 'you would sleep. For a long time. Possibly forever.'

She blinked. 'Peace, indeed.'

His face remained impassive. 'I'm glad one of us at least feels clever about your little discovery.'

'So I was right? The Elidian flower language is based on fae magic?' She gathered the rest of her ingredients and muttered a request for mortar and pestle under her breath. The requested tools appeared immediately. 'That doesn't seem to make a lot of sense.'

'It has made it easier to hide the true value of the flowers,' he said, still speaking unnervingly slowly, as if he wasn't sure what to make of her interest.

'Why would you—'

He sighed like a long-suffering teacher. 'You are cleverer than that, Miss Iavi.'

'You ... you've been deliberately hiding that you need flowers to perform magic.' Something clicked in her mind. 'Are you afraid if humans knew, they would make it impossible for your people to get their hands on flowers?'

'Cyril closed the gate knowing damn well what it would do to us,' he said, eyebrow slightly raised. 'It's not a matter of being afraid. I know for a fact he'd sell his daughters to figure out this secret, and his ignorance is the only thing that allows fae in the human world some chance of survival at this moment.'

She swallowed, turning back to her new mortar and pestle to hide her clashing thoughts. *They used to come into the city with their wagons covered in flowers*, Father had told her years and years ago. *They would set up their camp in the parks and gardens and no matter how hard we tried, we couldn't get them to leave ...*

It would only have taken a single furious father or spurned lover to burn the flower patches to the ground. With it, those damned magic powers.

Which would have kept the women of the city safe ... but somehow that argument no longer sounded as perfectly righteous to her as it had done a day ago.

'So you hid it in plain sight,' she said, grinding the lavender flowers to a fragrant paste, 'and now every well-educated young woman in Elidian is unwittingly an expert on the theory of fae magic?'

He smiled, and there was a glimmer of familiar sly arrogance in the expression. 'Quite amusing, isn't it?'

'You and your amusement,' she said, the sting falling just short of convincing.

A chuckle was his only reply.

She turned back to her salve in silence, melting her wax over the table candles, using an empty little bowl to mix in the oil – feeling strangely at home with instruments and ingredients she hadn't held for a decade. On the other side of the table, the king was silent, watching her without encouragement, but without any sneers and nettling questions, either.

Was it really that easy to declaw him? Stop taking his bait, utter a few words of sympathy, and gone was the villainous façade?

She added in her lavender, and then some comfrey just for good measure – few things that couldn't be fixed with comfrey, Father always said. The result was a brownish ointment that, thankfully, smelled better than it looked.

'There you go,' she announced, shoving the bowl towards him. 'I suggest we start by applying a thin layer on the dead skin once a day, then evaluate in a few days if you notice any difference. Then we can alter the formula or chuck the whole idea out of the window and start over again, if necessary. Anything else?'

He frowned at the salve – a long, lingering look, not unlike a chess player studying his pieces before making his one brilliant, reckless move.

Then he looked up at her.

Smiled.

And said, 'I could use your assistance applying it, Miss Iavi.'

Deliberate bait, positioned for her to gasp in shock and outrage – now that she understood the game he was playing, it was so obvious she almost burst out laughing. Yesterday she *would* have gasped. She would have told him to behave, would have haughtily glared at him, would have done everything to entertain him and place the power back in his hands.

Like that little mouse, trying to flee those merciless claws.

But she was a mouse with teeth, to the blazes with it, and she would *not* do him the satisfaction of shrinking back after everything she'd achieved this morning. She glanced at her hands. *Barbaric child*, Mrs. Bartlett shrieked in her memory ... But once again her only witness would soon be dead, and hadn't she decided to do away with manners for today?

Once she was back in Elidian, she would slide back into the formalities as if none of this had ever happened.

For now, she had a king to tame.

'But of course, Your Majesty,' she said, honeyed voice mirroring his own. 'Shall we start with your face?'

And seeing him freeze in surprise for just the blink of an eye – sweet divines, it was worth every glare and disapproving frown bubbling up in her memory.

He recovered quickly. 'I'll gladly leave the decisions to the healer between us. Please proceed in whatever way you think best.'

She wondered, rounding the table to where he sat lounging in his chair, what he would do if she were to grab the butter knife from the table and plant it deep into his living eye. But no, he too had had a night to think. She couldn't assume he hadn't put some new defences into place, and she shouldn't anger him again until she knew exactly what she was doing.

So she snatched the salve from the table and said, 'Close your eyes.'

'Don't try to stab me,' he murmured as he obeyed, and as much as he sounded amused by his own command, she knew it would limit her movements all the same. The butter knife would have to wait, then.

'But I do have permission to hurt you?' she said as she bent over him.

He pulled a face, skull skin drawing tight. 'Isn't that what you healers do?'

She laughed – she couldn't help herself – and dipped her fingers into the fat, fragrant substance she'd mixed. One last moment she hesitated, hand hovering half an inch away from his face. Then she shook her head, reminded herself she had already touched him in far more intimate places, and brushed a smudge of salve over the borderline on his forehead.

He hissed a sharp breath.

Startled, she pulled back. 'If that's already painful ...'

'It's not,' he said tightly. 'Please go on.'

She frowned but obeyed, scooping up a next dollop. The salve was still a little warm on her fingertips as she rubbed it cautiously over his forehead, the edge of his eye socket, the bridge of his nose. His breath went shallow as she worked, eyes squeezed shut as if to keep out harsh sunlight – all the signs of agonising pain, and yet he couldn't have lied when he told her it wasn't hurting.

'Still all right to continue?' she muttered, pausing.

He let out a rough breath. 'Please.'

The weight behind that single word – an *actual* plea, not just a royal command disguised as a request – made her falter with her fingers already on their way to his face again. And abruptly she understood. It wasn't pain. It wasn't pain at all.

Rather ... the opposite.

Decades of solitude. How long had it been since he'd allowed anyone to take care of his hurting, dying body?

It shouldn't make her feel anything, that thought, and certainly not *sympathy*. But sweet divines, he looked so unexpectedly vulnerable as he waited for her hand to return, eyes closed and head tipped back, every ugly inch of dead flesh bared to her inspection. So unexpectedly powerless. As if it wasn't the salve he needed, not the wax and herbs, but rather ...

Her?

A small and most unwelcome thrill ran through her.

If not for his command, she could have killed him five times over in this quiet moment. And yet, watching his maimed face, she didn't find her thoughts straying towards the butter knives or the forks or the napkins that would probably fit perfectly around his throat.

Instead, she found her fingers itching to just ... touch him?

Just brush a thumb over that sharp edge of his cheekbone. Just cup her palm around his chin. Just trail her fingers down the line of his jaw.

Her heart was hammering wildly, her hands unmoving in the cold air between them. What was she *thinking*?

'Miss Iavi?' he said quietly.

'Apologies,' she blurted out, biting those ridiculous urges away as she bent over again. 'Some straying thoughts.'

He didn't reply but let out a small sigh as she smeared the salve on his cheek, then moved down to his lips, massaging beeswax and oil deep into every inch of his face as she worked.

Was it taking effect already? The skin seemed to bloom a little pinker under her ministrations, blood flowing back to the surface. If he kept this up for a few weeks, who knew if ...

No. Stop it. He didn't have a few more weeks. She couldn't give him a few more weeks.

And that thought *definitely* shouldn't make her heart twinge.

But he was so strangely beautiful under her hands, long lashes that lay curled against his living cheek, the cascade of coppery hair over his temples and shoulders, the firm curve of half his mouth. And even his dead side ... Watching him from so close, exposed and unguarded under her fingers, it was hard to remember why she'd ever been frightened of him. He looked fragile. Like a bruised flower, like a wounded animal. Like someone she ought to handle with care.

A small shiver ran through him when she finally reached his jaw, and it took all she had to dutifully take care of the last inches of skin, pull back her hand, and shove her salve back onto the table.

'I'm finished.' Her voice came out a little breathless, but at least it didn't shake. 'How much does it hurt now?'

He slowly blinked open his eyes.

Their gazes locked.

Sweet divines, she should be running – but her feet had taken root where she stood, her legs unmoving as if he had commanded them still. If his body was a bruised flower, then his eyes were the petals that had been torn apart and trampled on – a despondency in that one green iris that made her heart crack and ache, that made her want to wrap her arms around him and press him close until the darkness lifted. A cruel villain, she'd thought. A beast, she'd guessed.

But the man sitting before her was neither.

A few kind words. A simple medicine. Now what on earth was *happening*?

'I have to go,' she stammered even as every muscle and tendon in her body screamed the opposite. 'There's enough salve left. You can do the rest yourself if you want. Let me know if it makes any difference and I can—'

His hand shot forward.

Strong, living fingers closed around her bare wrist, the pressure just firm enough to be commanding, to make her stiffen as every sensible part of her mind cried out in alarm. Warmth radiated up from the spot where his palm lay pressed to her pulse. She could feel the echo of it in her lower belly, somehow – could feel his touch sizzling in her veins, a sensation that should have her tear away and flee and protect herself from this madness.

She stood paralysed, unable to take her gaze off him.

'Could you ...' His lips twitched as he hesitated, eyes pleading with her not to laugh, not to lash out. 'Could you stay?'

'I ...' she started hopelessly.

'Help me do the rest. *Please*,' he added hurriedly as her hand jerked into motion. 'Sorry. I'm sorry. It's been ... so long. If you don't mind ... if you ...'

She drew in a desperate breath. 'But I *should* mind.'

'Yes,' he said, sounding numb. 'Yes, I suppose you should.'

Neither of them moved, the presence, the visceral *awareness* of him turning the air in her lungs to molasses. The hand on her wrist shook a little. She felt like she was falling – tumbling into some bottomless abyss and flailing down, down, down.

'If I refuse,' she whispered, 'will you make me do it?'

He went motionless for a moment – perfectly, lethally still.

Then the fingers around her wrist abruptly let go.

'No,' he said, in a hoarse, husky voice that made her heart flutter senselessly. 'No. I may be a man of many vices, but there are lines I won't cross. You're free to go.'

And that should be a relief, shouldn't it?

So why was there none of that lightness, none of that sudden release of the tightness on her chest; why was she still not running? She felt light-headed, as if she'd drunk too much of the sparkling wine from the Arragher fountains, as if she'd gone outside the city on a hot summer's day and inhaled the poisonous marsh fumes for hours. *You're free to go.* He was fae. He couldn't lie. He wouldn't restrain her, no matter how wounded that plea in his eyes.

And he was so damnably beautiful.

'Take off your coat and shirt,' she heard herself say.

He was fast, yet there was none of yesterday's sharp fury in his motions – staggering, almost clumsy fingers untangling his cravat, unbuttoning his silvery coat and pristine white shirt. He wore a string of small flowers by his throat that hadn't been there yesterday. Fragile petals, white at the heart and pink at the outer edges ... Eglantines?

It had to be some sort of defence, but she couldn't recall their meaning right now and couldn't get her mind to try harder. Her eyes were drawn instead to the body that revealed itself as he stripped off his shirt – strong shoulder on one side, angular, withered bone on the other side. Slender muscles down his stomach, mirrored by the hollowness of decaying guts. A small trail of coppery hair that started down his navel on his right side, and no trace of it on his left.

Only when his shirt finally hit the floor did she pick up her makeshift bowl of salve and say, 'Get up and turn around.'

He obeyed as if her commands held magic, too.

She brushed his long hair over his shoulders and tried not to feel the silky softness of it, tried not to imagine running her fingers through the strands and losing herself in the sensation. He stood straight as a pillar before her, the right half of his back lithe yet muscular, the left half pale and gaunt as she'd known it would be. His left shoulder blade was a sharply drawn triangle beneath taut skin, the edges jutting out so far she wondered if she could pry her fingers underneath the bone.

Gently, she dipped her hands into the salve and rubbed them until they were slick with the warm concoction. Then, steeling herself, she swiftly pressed her palms to the dead side of his body.

The sound that escaped him lay a hair's breadth removed from a moan.

His skin was cold to the touch. She drew slow lines from shoulder to hip, following his spine, following the razor edge of his shoulder blade, and tried not to notice the subtle twitches of his hands, the way his breath caught and released in short gasps with every time her hands found their way back to his body. By the time every inch of his back had been covered in a generous layer of beeswax, a fiery warmth had taken over her cheeks, skin burning with a nonsensical need to ... to hold him?

To be held. To be touched.

This truly ought to be the end of it. And yet she found herself reaching out for the salve once more, heard herself ask him to turn back and face her.

He obeyed without words, meeting her gaze with dazed, half-lidded eyes. The eyes of a man completely at her mercy – a man who had relinquished all control and handed himself over to her with nothing but those fragile eglantine flowers to protect him.

It was in that moment that she realised, with a pang as liberating as it was concerning, that he was not the only one enjoying himself.

What if they don't want to be respectable, he had said, and for the very first time, Briannis could summon up a sliver of understanding for the poor, misguided souls. Respectability was constant work. It was exhausting. Whereas *this* ...

She brushed a first fingerful of salve over his collarbone and revelled in the thinly veiled gasp that escaped him.

On she went, rubbing the fragrant mixture into the deep ridges of his ribs, feeling the rise and fall of his shallow breath underneath her touch. And down, over the hard hollowness of his stomach, until his fists tightened with need. And down, past his navel, feeling like she was crossing boundaries that shouldn't be crossed ... but he never made a sound to stop her, merely watched her as she worked, eyes following the path of her hands as they moved over his skin.

Another inch down she moved.

Breathing the scent of beeswax and lavender and sweet decay, fixing her eyes on his dry, pallid abdomen, she massaged her thumbs over the last strip of skin his breeches left bare. His breath had started to shake now, and she couldn't tell if it was from pain or something else entirely. She leaned in closer, fingers still working the salve into his skin, feeling the heat emanating from the living half of his body.

He ceased breathing entirely.

She looked up without thinking and found his face alarmingly close, lips parted ever so slightly, even the leathery half of his mouth touched by a hint of pink. His green eye sparkled with inhuman fire. His black eye had become a bottomless abyss, pulling her closer – inviting her to dive in and never emerge again.

Her fingers stilled on his abdomen. Her heartbeat thundered in her ears, pulsing heated blood into every inch of her skin.

'Oh,' she breathed.

There was that look in his eyes again, starved and ravenous, a night that could swallow the light of a thousand suns. 'Miss Iavi ...'

He faltered. Time seemed to slow as they stood motionless, gazes intertwined in what could be heady anticipation or apprehension – something in the air that came close, very close, to the pressure of a lightning bolt about to strike.

'You may want to leave,' he added, barely even moving his lips. His voice was low and raspy, little more than a growl; the words came out with laboured breaths. 'Before I no longer let you.'

For one impossible moment she believed she didn't care.

She almost opened her mouth to tell him she wasn't a coward fleeing his games again. That the shame and infamy seemed a most reasonable price to pay for whatever awaited on the other side of his warning – whatever made his gaze cling to her with such thrilling intensity.

Then good sense kicked in.

She was going to *kill* him, for goodness' sake; she'd come here to disarm him, not to throw away her honour and innocence for a man who would be dead within days. What was she planning to do – return to Elidian alone with a swelling womb?

What would she tell the Princeps? The Mirror Queen? The blasted *neighbours*?

She yanked back her hands as if she'd burned herself, stumbling away from him. Half-naked – *much* too half-naked for anyone's sanity – he was fully a creature of nightmares. And yet those eyes, those desolate eyes ...

'Thank you,' she forced out, 'for the warning, Your Majesty.'

'Go,' he said through gritted teeth.

For the very first time, she didn't mind the command, didn't mind the magic jerking her feet into motion and carrying her out of the room in that unnatural wobbling way; in that moment, it may just have been the only power capable of saving her from herself.

Chapter 7

A handbook on manners need not concern itself with the perpetually unmannered: I will therefore refrain from reiterating the horrific tales of fae trickery we all know, and merely advise my dear readers to employ every available means to evade these deceitful creatures.

Lady Lockwell's Handbook of Etiquette

IT TOOK SEVERAL HANDFULS of cold water to the face before Briannis trusted herself to think clearly again.

She stumbled from the bathroom to the bed and threw herself inelegantly into the downy blankets and pillows, face pressed into the smothering warmth – unable to produce a single sensible conclusion except for the undeniable, deeply troubling fact that she was a fool. Surprise him, she'd thought an hour ago. Make him stop toying with her. Make him reveal whatever he was hiding beneath the thorny smiles and the shameless cruelty.

What she hadn't realised – what she *should* have realised – was that if she made him stop being a vicious villain, he would become ... someone else.

Someone she might not want to kill.

Her hand slid below the pillow on which she'd slept, fingers finding the vial she'd hidden there for the night. Even in that safe little hollow, the glass was cold. Two teaspoons of death – it took an effort not to gag.

Those helpless eyes, pleading with her to stay.

Those trembling fists, trying so hard not to reach for her.

He was *hurting*. He'd spoken the words, unable to lie, and so she had no choice but to assume it was true: this broken shadow of a man she'd glimpsed was the king of Faerie in his most genuine state, the victim she'd come here to kill. The one person whose beating heart stood between her and the life of her dreams.

This wasn't her sort of work, for goodness' sake. She killed swiftly and coldly. The men she targeted – they were always men, somehow – were swindlers and blackmailers, rapists and abusers. She was a desperate lady's weapon, sent out to smother the rumour of a daughter's ruination or settle thorny inheritance issues. She'd never been asked to kill a man whose greatest crime was merely existing.

And yet ... what else could she do?

Stay here?

She let out a bleak laugh into the warm mattress. She didn't trust him *that* much, the dying king of thorns. He may be broken, but the divines knew broken men could be monsters of their own; a single courteous warning to get out of his way could hardly be called proof of his noble character. If she stopped thinking about the haunting look in his eyes, the hard fact was that she knew hardly anything about him.

There was still that forbidden room, after all. *The maimed bodies of my dead wives.* A suggestion spoken in jest, but what if it was true?

What if the truth was even worse?

Father had warned her so many times that fae could make your head spin until you no longer knew what was true. Well, her head *was* spinning. If nothing in the world seemed certain anymore, shouldn't she cling to wisdom she'd heard from so many others rather than to the smooth trickery of one annoyingly sharp-eyed fae king?

Don't trust them. Don't fall for their promises. They'll do anything to get you under their spell.

She couldn't stay here.

And if she ever wanted to see her home again ...

It was easier to think of Elidian than to imagine how that flaming green eye would soon go dull and empty. She turned to her back and closed her eyes, allowing herself to feel homesick for the first time since she'd started her journey two weeks ago.

The almost comically narrow house on Tanner Street, built in the time homeowners were still taxed by the street-facing width of their property, and designed according to the principles of good Elidian frugality. Miss White's teashop around the corner, where she no longer even had to place her order after years of loyal weekly visits. The echoing corridors of the University, where she attended the weekly lectures for young ladies on every Fourth Day evening, listening breathlessly as professors set out their most recent thoughts on everything from Karwaldian heraldry to the many applications of glass lenses.

And it was almost Oak Month ... Which meant it was almost Liberation Day. Which meant she would miss the festivities this year, the street performers and the extravagant balls, the Nightingale Theatre and Sobgoblet Theatre competing for the

rights to the most popular plays. The picnics and the prome-
nades and of course the legendary party in the gardens of Arragher Manor – that party that made her remember every year
again what she was fighting for.

She didn't need wine fountains. She didn't need exotic flowers and towering wigs and room-high portraits of her own silk-
and velvet-clad appearance. But every kill, every bag of coin she
received in return, brought her just a little closer to an existence
in which people like the Duke of Arragher knew her name.

Like Father had wanted.

Like she'd promised him in his last days, as he lay withering
away in the tattered blankets of the only hospital she'd been
able to afford.

Just one kill. Her fingers found the vial again, stroking the icy
glass. Did it matter who the prospective victim was? A single
life in return for the promise that had made Father smile even
while he drew his last laboured breaths. If she just clung to that
image, to the way he'd squeezed her hand and whispered he
was proud of her, she could forget any look the fae king had
given her.

But she'd have to be fast.

If she had to spend another tense meal with him, if she –
divines help her – got persuaded to take care of his wounds another time, who knew if she would recover her sanity a second
time? Better not to take the risk. Truly, it was best if they simply
never met again.

Two teaspoons of death. If she was clever, she might be free
to leave the Keep before nightfall.

Moridyr smelled beeswax and lavender wherever he walked.

It was like being slapped over the head with a memory over and over again, except this memory didn't exist purely in his mind; instead, it was his body that reacted eagerly to every whiff of lavender he inhaled, his starved senses reliving the morning over and over again. He breathed and felt small, warm hands circling his back. Breathed again and felt a thumb rub slow circles over his aching cheek.

Beeswax and lavender and fingers trailing down his abdomen, touching him in places where only his own hands had been for decades.

Go.

Perhaps he shouldn't have been so fucking gallant.

He wandered aimlessly around the Keep for hours, looking for something to do and concluding time and time again that the only thing he wanted was to turn straight around and make his way to the Starlit Room. Pull her into his arms. Smother her protests with his lips. Find out if he could get her to swear with his face between her thighs.

A small groan escaped him as he rubbed his eyes and inhaled another lungful of that damned fragrance. *She* was supposed to be the captive between the two of them. How had he ended up in her snare instead?

I do my best to be of service.

With that cheeky, cheerful smile on her dainty face. With that obvious challenge in her eyes. He *had* tried to get under her skin last night, that much was true – but he hadn't expected her to one-up him and just shed the whole damn skin the next morning.

Humans. Liars.

But he had the nagging suspicion her transformation hadn't been a lie at all – rather, that she'd been way too sincere for the comfort of them both this morning.

He rounded another corner and found himself in Mirror Hall, a room he'd have visited hours ago if this had been an ordinary morning. There were plenty of pressing questions to ask, after all. What else Cyril was planning, now that he'd become bold enough to send assassins to the Keep. How many others might be coming this way. Who had smuggled that piece of daisy soap into the Iron Hold – if it was the one person who knew of the roses' weakness, the one person Moridyr trusted more than anyone else in the world.

But the words he heard leaving his lips were, 'How do I convince Briannis Iavi not to kill me, if I prefer not to command her?'

The mirror didn't have eyes, but Moridyr was quite sure it would have rolled them if it had been capable of it. *Are you just looking for an excuse to fuck her?*

'Counter-questions are not answers,' Moridyr said, glaring at the reflecting silver. 'We've talked about this.'

You have talked about it, the mirror corrected. *At great length.*

He raised an eyebrow, not in the mood to let himself be pulled into the game the looking glass was so fond of playing – stringing along a conversation until its user accidentally asked a second question, which would be promptly answered, thereby forfeiting the right to an answer for the rest of the day.

Fine, the mirror grumbled after a small stretch of silence. *Cyril promised her a house and enough money to live a comfortable lady's life. He's not planning to ever give it to her, of course, or to even let her return to the city alive, but that won't stop her from killing for the promise. I suppose if you tell her it's all a bag of moonshine, she might refrain from slitting your kingly throat.*

Moridyr shouldn't have been shocked. Hell, he'd known the sly bastard to do much, much worse. But he could see his own eyes widen in the silver surface, and his curse came out with more feeling than any of those he'd uttered in the last ten years at least.

Not what you wanted to hear? the mirror said gleefully. *I suppose you could also fuck her and hope she'll stay for the precious quarter-dead brood you could produce together, if that's more in line with your wishes.*

'Go to hell,' Moridyr muttered, leaving a cackling mirror behind as he strode on.

Cyril's fucking promises.

He felt sick, as if the mere mention of Elidian's usurper Princeps and his broken oaths was enough to remind his guts of that cursed day thirty years ago, the betrayals, the bloodbath. *A lady's life.* Of course Briannis Iavi, determined to be a paragon of propriety, would not be able to resist that temptation. What was a single, women-stealing life to the sum of her hopes and dreams?

Should he tell her?

She might believe him, with the mirror's confirmation. She might even agree to keep him alive. She might – his heart clenched with some emotion he wasn't eager to name – *stay.* For lack of a better alternative, out of resigned necessity ... but did it matter why she would be here, whether she would have chosen the Keep as her home of her own volition, as long as the result was the same in the end?

It did not, he firmly told himself.

Which meant he should tell her before she accidentally succeeded in killing him and ended both their lives over a baseless dream.

Where was she? He turned his attention to the Keep, allowing the awareness of every floor and wall and window to seep into his conscious thoughts – *there*, the unmistakable weight of something new and alive moving through his home, vibrations of her presence spreading through wood and stone like water ripples. The breakfast room – what in the world was she doing there?

Was she looking for him?

It was only then, as he turned and hurried for the nearest stairwell, that he allowed himself to admit he'd expected her to avoid him for the remainder of the week, if not the year. The jump of his heart at this evidence of the opposite was ... troubling.

Just a game, he tried to remind himself – but there had been absolutely nothing playful about those firm hands on his skin, about the heated blush on her cheeks, about that fire burning in her brown eyes. The scent of lavender still wafted around him, muddying his thoughts.

Breakfast room first. He'd think again when he'd found her.

But when he strode into that round room two minutes later, with jittery limbs and yearning skin, the petite figure of his would-be murderer was nowhere to be seen, and only a fresh pot of tea stood steaming at the centre of the table. Only as he muttered a curse and stepped toward it did he catch sight of the note she'd left next to it.

I thought we should have tea. I'm looking for you. If you find this, please stay here so we don't miss each other.

It wasn't signed. He figured she hadn't seen a need to do so; there were no others he could have suspected of writing it.

With a muffled curse, he sank into his usual chair, smelling lavender and beeswax again. Was he deluding himself, or did the tearing ache between his shoulder blades truly hurt a little less than it would on most days?

Where was she now?

The Whispering Hall, another quick scan of the castle's state told him. It would take a while until she'd be back in the breakfast room, then. He sighed, reached for the pot of tea, and poured himself a first cup – the Keep could serve them more if they needed it, and he could at least keep himself properly hydrated while he waited. It was one thing he'd learned would assuage the constant, itching ache.

The Keep was feeling unusually tense, he noted absently as he brought the porcelain to his lips. Was it still getting used to the foreign presence wandering through its halls?

He swallowed a first mouthful of scorching tea. It slid down his throat with comforting spiced warmth – ginger, orange, and ... something else.

What was the something else?

He took a second sip and a third, emptying most of his cup. An unfamiliar flavour, almost bitter – not unlike grapefruit, but more syrupy, more ...

A faint flutter at his throat interrupted his musings.

His throat.

His *throat*.

He grabbed for the small string of eglantines he wore beneath his cravat – for the spot, at least, where the eglantines had been when he'd put his shirt and coat back on mere hours ago. But as he felt beneath the linen with frantic fingers, the softness of the flowers was nowhere to be found. Nothing but some powdery dust. Nothing but the empty string, damning evidence of a catastrophe averted.

Five eglantines, gone at once. *Five* of them.

Moridyr stared at his almost-empty cup, the ginger tea with the strange aftertaste, and felt the realisation rise in him like bile.

'Fuck,' he said out loud.

Around him, the Keep was silent. Ominously silent, as if even the walls were reproaching him for his carelessness, for not having thought beyond the obvious danger of knives and daggers. Five eglantines – she must have put enough poison in that teapot to kill a horse.

And if she had ...

'*Fuck*,' he said again, and then he was running.

It didn't matter, he tried to convince himself as he sprinted down the corridor and leapt down a flight of stairs, landing with a speed that almost broke his dead ankle – it didn't *matter*. Hadn't he saved her life once before already? Hadn't he warned her he would make her regret a second attempt? Didn't it make her a heartless vixen at the very least, to poison his tea mere hours after she'd so thoroughly, so lovingly tended his wounds?

Shouldn't he be glad to be rid of her?

But his limbs paid no heed to sensible objections, to any sense of self-preservation; he barged through a half-closed door in a storm of lavender, yanked a handful of mallow flowers from the wall before hurtling down the corridor and storming into the next room. The Whispering Hall. A distance of mere minutes – he'd chased the boy through the castle often enough to know – but how many times over could she already be dead in that time?

Five eglantines, and humans were so gods-damned fragile.

There, *finally*, were the silver-plated doors; he slammed them open with his living hand, clutching the mallow in his dead fingers like a drowning man. Silvery marble and fireflies and rusting willow branches and ...

'Fuck.'

It seemed his tongue had no other words left.

She must have collapsed in the middle of the room the moment the poison settled in his stomach – limbs sprawling, hair half-loose, face as pale as his dead side. With four long strides, he was at her side – 'Miss Iavi?'

No reaction came but her rapid, shallow breath.

'Miss Iavi – *Briannis*.' Her name felt strangely intimate on his tongue. He fell to his knees, shook her shoulder. No reaction.

She still breathed – small, strangely vulnerable gasps – but her eyelids didn't so much as flutter.

He chucked the mallow onto the floor; the flowers were useless as long as he had no idea *what* he was supposed to heal. What had she used? Holding his breath, he pried open one eyelid. A numb, unseeing brown eye stared back at him, looking nothing like the eyes that had watched him with all that gods-damned tenderness this morning, the eyes that had looked at him with *want* ...

Stop. Focus. The pupil was not dilated. No belladonna, then.

That left just about a hundred other options.

With a curse, he pressed his fingers to the artery below her jaw. Her pulse was an irregular flutter, rapid heartbeats followed by seconds of nothing at all.

Wolfbane or foxglove? He needed more than some mallow for that.

'Don't die,' he snapped at her motionless face and strode out, thoughts whirling, limbs buzzing with senseless panic. He doubted the command alone would be enough to keep her alive – not anymore, not after all these years – but perhaps the magic would keep her breathing just a little longer while he looked for the support he needed. Water lily would have been best, but it bloomed only on the inner courtyard, too far for this emergency. Swallow-wort – would that work? *Cure for the heart.* If he combined it with the mallow, it might just take effect in the physical sense ...

Where was the damn plant growing again?

Not in the first wall he passed, which was all begonias and tansies and thornapples – helpful to get rid of enemies but not nearly so helpful to heal them. Only three corridors away did he catch sight of the star-shaped black flowers, blooming quietly between rows of hawthorn and sage.

He yanked them off the wall so violently he nearly tore the full plant with them.

It doesn't matter, he repeated to himself time and time again, the words all but drowned out by the wild rush of blood in his ears. *If she dies, it's because she tried to kill you, and that means it wouldn't matter.* But he almost sank to his knees with relief when he returned to the Whispering Hall and found her still breathing, an unhealthy rash forming over her face.

Foxglove, he grimly concluded. Some nerve, to kill a flower king with flowers. If not for the eglantines ...

Moridyr III, the last king of Faerie.

He doubted she'd be following his example, crouching over him in panic, employing every skill she possessed to save him.

Gritting his teeth, he picked up the mallow flowers again, squishing them in his fist with the swallow-wort. He focused his attention on her faltering, fluttering heart – *heal*.

Her pulse steadied ever so slightly.

But no matter how many flowers he used, no matter how many times he shook her and begged her and repeated her name like some unholy prayer, she didn't regain consciousness.

He carried her to his own bedroom in the end, her body limp and clammy in his arms. The royal wing was the part of the Keep he knew best. The part of the Keep in which he could find every flower he needed with his eyes shut if need be, where he held what little remained of his pathetic magic within arm's reach.

And for all that he wanted to deny it, he could not stand to have her anywhere else.

She looked small and fragile against the stark white pillows; her cheeks were almost equally pale. He used more flowers. He wiped the cold sweat from her brow and loosened her dress and took the remaining pins from her hair. He told himself that he was an idiot, that he was setting himself up to end either dead or abandoned. Then he went on and wasted another handful of flowers on his idiocy, unable to stop moving, unable to do nothing while she lay in his bed and might be slipping from his fingers.

It wasn't that he *needed* her, he reassured himself. He would not be that much of a fool, to ever need anyone again.

It was just that he *wanted* her, with burning, agonising ferocity.

It was just that if she died, she would never look at him in that spellbound way again, as if he was something magnificent and fascinating rather than a half-decaying corpse. It was just that he wasn't ready to never feel her hands on his body again. It was just that he'd felt her breath on his face that morning, heated and dazed, and didn't want to wonder for another fourteen years of silent isolation what might have happened if he hadn't told her to go.

The afternoon bled into the evening. The evening bled into the night.

She'd started shivering, then, and no matter how many blankets or warm bottles he tucked in around her, nothing seemed to keep her warm. Just before midnight, she vomited. He cleaned out the mess, peeled off her ruined dress, wiped the sweat from her feverish skin again. Her eyes still didn't open.

'Briannis,' he whispered for what had to be the hundredth time. 'Stay with me. Please.'

She didn't respond.

He still smelled of lavender, and while every fragrant inhalation felt like a kick in the teeth, he couldn't bring himself to wash it off.

In the end, when his own eyes began to burn from the long hours of staring at her lifeless face, he stripped off his coat and boots and lay down beside her, close enough to feel the violent shudders wracking her small body. He clung to those shudders as he dozed off and jolted from his sleep again and again, keeping watch through the darkest of night.

As long as she was moving, she might still wake up.

As long as she was moving, she might stay.

Chapter 8

There exists a misconception among certain young ladies that wicked deeds will go unpunished as long as they are performed in secret; this is always a grave mistake.

Lady Lockwell's Handbook of Etiquette

REALITY RETURNED TO BRIANNIS in shreds of wakefulness, some of them so strange she thought they must be dreams.

She was in a bed – a grand canopy bed she hadn't seen before, the posts intricately carved with patterns of flowers and delicate vines. Around her, gossamer fabric hung down from the canopy, woven with shimmering threads that caught the light in ever-changing glimmers. Golden sunrays filtered through the rose vines covering the window, brushing over the flower-covered walls and ornate wardrobe on the other side of the room, and when she turned her head to follow the path of the light, her gaze found a number of gold leaf-covered doors, a table cut from a giant tree trunk, a levitating chandelier hovering just beneath the ceiling.

Only then did it dawn on her – the fae king's bedroom.

She was in his *bed*.

She wasn't sure what shocked her more: the fact itself, or the equally concerning realisation that part of her seemed not at all discontent with the conclusion. Scrambling up in the blankets, she threw a more frantic look around. The other side of the enormous bed had obviously been slept in – another observation that should have called for vapours and smelling salts – but the room's primary occupant himself was nowhere to be seen.

How in the world had she ended up here?

Foxglove. Tea. She remembered that. Her note, her flight to the other side of the castle, and then all of a sudden her heart had broken into some mad gallop and she'd collapsed, world going dark in an instant ...

Had she accidentally poisoned herself? But that did not make sense. She hadn't come anywhere near that tea – had barely been able to *look* at the warm brew after she'd stirred in her poison and left it there for him to take. A heart attack? But she was twenty-seven years of age, for goodness' sake. Women in their twenties did not have heart attacks, did they?

She swallowed heavily, tasting bile in the back of throat. Her skin was clammy, as if she'd slept through a blistering fever.

Footsteps interrupted her frantic attempts to diagnose herself.

She had one moment to realise she was wearing nothing but her flimsy chemise, that her hair was down and her legs would be fully bared the moment she stepped out of bed – and then one of the side doors opened and the king of Faerie strode into the room, dressed in boots, breeches, and a half-buttoned white shirt, no coat or cravat to be seen. His sleeves had rolled up to reveal one muscular forearm and one thinner, skeletal one, the radius and ulna bones drawn clearly beneath the white skin. His hair, unbrushed and ruffled, had been bound into a simple queue. Even the living half of his face was pale, dark circles beneath his eye that mirrored the hollow of his eye-socket on the other side.

He wore the look of a man with a long night behind him and an even longer day ahead.

Two steps into the room and he ground to an abrupt halt, stiffening where he stood. 'Bri— Miss Iavi?'

There was a rawness to his voice, a sense of unguarded intensity – and strangest of all, a hoarse, unmistakable trace of relief.

She blinked at him, feeling like she'd slept through two full months of developments. He was holding a piece of damp cloth and a full jug. As if he'd been about to dab the sweat off her brow and feed her small sips of water. Had he spent his night nursing her back to health – had she vomited all over his bed?

Had he just almost called her by her first name?

And then her gaze travelled back up to his neck, to his face, and she noted the one other piece of his attire he was missing.

The eglantines.

Eglantine. I wound to heal. Now she recalled their meaning, and pieces of the puzzle abruptly slid into place. So it *had* been a defensive spell, but not in the way she'd thought – it didn't prevent attempts at assassination but rather healed them instantly, averting the damage onto the killer's shoulders. That moment her heart had rattled out of control was the moment the poison had settled into his stomach. A mouthful of concentrated foxglove.

She should be very, very dead.

And instead ...

'You saved me?' she croaked.

A small pause. Then, slowly, he said, 'So it appears.'

The words came out uncertainly, as if he had not thought the situation through to this point yet and was as unsure what to make of it as she was. His gaze did not swerve away from her barely dressed presence. There was that look in his eyes again, bleeding flowers and snapped stems, the hurt that had gotten her heart all tangled up at that blasted breakfast – the look that had driven her to poison him before she could do anything she would regret.

He'd trusted her with his pain, that look said.

And then she'd gone forth and tried to kill him yet again.

'I ...' she started breathlessly, grasping for words as guilt set its nails into her guts. He'd *saved* her. After her third attempt. After her betrayal. 'I didn't want to hurt you, I swear. I—'

'Ah,' he interrupted, and something sharpened in his countenance as he resumed his steps, sinking into the plush chair by the bed. Gone was the vulnerability, the relief. An echo of that familiar sardonic smile slid across his features, cold and composed. 'It was an accident, then? But of course, Miss Iavi. Did you clumsily stumble your way into all three attempts, or only this last one?'

She couldn't tell whether the mockery in his voice was born from anger or disappointment or something far more dangerous. Feeling even smaller, she whispered, 'That ... that's not what I meant.'

He quirked up an icy eyebrow.

'I didn't *want* to kill you. I'd prefer to keep you alive, really. I ... I could come up with some lie to tell Lady Millicent.' The words tumbled over her lips as if he'd commanded them out. 'But I want to go home – I *need* to go home – and I couldn't think of another way to get out of here. That's all, I swear. I ... I'm sorry. I truly am.'

She expected him to command her to confirm she'd spoken the truth – almost *hoped* he would at least allow her that opportunity to prove herself honest. But the only cold words leaving his lips were, 'I see.'

'I'm sorry,' she breathed again.

This was wrong – this was all wrong – the guarded reserve of his expression, the bitter lines drawing themselves around his lips once more. The cruel amusement from the first days had vanished. And somehow it was *worse* to see him like this, not so much murderous but rather dull and lifeless – as if he had decided she was not even worth the effort of his games and schemes anymore.

He'd joked with her at breakfast. Really, genuinely joked. Like a friend would do. And now ...

Who had thought she could start missing that dangerous twinkle in his eyes?

'Please,' she managed, unsure what the next word would be, what she even *could* say to somehow melt that frigid mask from his face again. 'Please, I—'

'You should drink something,' he interrupted tersely, nodding at the glass on her nightstand. 'Dehydration isn't going to help you.'

He could so easily have turned that into a friendly remark, into any acknowledgement of those softer moments between them. *I know I'm not the healer here ...* But he didn't even look at her as she picked up the glass with shaking hands, green eye staring grimly into the distance while she drank.

Perhaps she should be glad of it. She was trembling so much that half of the water ended up in her blankets and chemise instead.

Still, she managed to swallow three large gulps – enough to soften the aftertaste of her stomach contents. Lowering the glass, she again started, 'I—'

'Excellent,' he cut her off, turning away from her as he rose. 'The bathroom is over there, in case you wish to wash yourself. I'd be careful with food, if I were you, but if you're hungry—'

'Why?' she blurted out.

He froze, muslin-clad back towards her. 'I beg your pardon?'

'Why did you save me?' She started pulling the silk and satin blankets aside, disentangling her own legs. He was so damnably tall standing, and with her stomach churning and aching, sitting in bed like an invalid made her feel too feeble for this conversation. 'You threatened to make me regret it if I ever tried again. You'd have been perfectly justified in letting me reap the fruits of my own stupid labours. So why do I find myself in your bed under your gentle care instead if you don't even want to *look* at me?'

For a moment, he remained motionless – had she gone too far? But he turned before she could apologise, his lips a thin line, his expression inscrutable. The dark eye socket and the hollow paleness of his dead cheek looked like warnings. Like nauseating reminders of what might have been if he'd made the mistake of trusting her and her pretty promises.

Coldly, impassively, he said, 'You know exactly why, Miss Iavi.'

Decades of silence. Decades of captivity. Better to watch every bite of food he ate and lock his doors at night than to go back to that existence, to a silence only broken by his own echoing steps and the haunting songs of the violins.

Better to hate a living woman than to hate a corpse.

'Just how long ...' Her voice cracked. 'Just how long have you been all by yourself in this place?'

His bitter smile didn't reach his eyes. 'Long enough that I've considered leaving the Keep at times.'

He spoke the words the way he'd admitted to the constant ache of his dead skin: detached, disinterested, a remark barely worthy of being spoken out loud. It was that off-handedness, more than anything, that delayed the landing in her mind, the full realisation of just what he'd said – *leave*?

He could have *left*?

'Wait. What?' She blinked at the roses, blooming blood-red before the window. 'Are you saying ... are you saying you could just have walked out of the door if you wanted? That you have been able to walk out whenever you wanted all these years?'

His eyebrow crept up. 'As long as no one is alarming the roses, why wouldn't I be able to?'

She stared at him.

'Is this news to you, Miss Iavi?'

Her poison-drenched mind was spinning, trying to stitch what little she knew of this world together. 'I just assumed ... if you were able to leave ... there are still a few others in Faerie, aren't there? Why haven't you gone out and found them? You wouldn't have been so lonely if—'

'What makes you think I'm not perfectly aware?' he interrupted sharply.

'But ...'

'I could have left the Keep and found company.' His gaze slid up to the ceiling as he spoke, avoiding her eyes in a gesture almost convincingly close to boredom. 'The roses wouldn't have stopped me. But family tradition dictates at least one member of my bloodline has to be at the Keep at all times—'

'Why?' Briannis said hoarsely.

'Safest place in the world.' He shrugged, a barbed smile at the corners of his lips. 'Assuming we survive unexpected visits from assassins, staying here is the only way to make sure the bloodline and therefore the magic of Faerie endure. I'm the last one left. With humans hunting down my people, I wasn't going to take the risk.'

She forgot how to breathe for a moment.

His people, again. Like the servants he'd sent away before they'd be locked up with him. Like the wayfarer fae out there, surviving by the grace of his connection to the land. If not for their safety and wellbeing, where could he have been instead? Miles away from Faerie, living a quiet life in the woods of Karwald or the Pavellan countryside?

'I called you *selfish*,' she whispered, shame clogging her throat.

His smile was a blade-edge. 'You did.'

'I ... I had no idea. Truly no idea.' What *had* she known, arriving here two nights ago? Nothing but hearsay and reputation, and *she* of all people should have known how reputation was like quicksand, drawing you in deeper the harder you struggled to get free. 'Sweet divines, I'm so sorry. I—'

'Very touching,' he said, a sneer to his voice. 'A shame your apologies and belated guilt aren't going to save a single dying fae child. Now if you don't mind ...' He turned again, shoulders tight below the muslin of his shirt. 'I have some work to do.'

Did he, really? Or was he just impatient to get away from her self-pity and her insufferable blubbering?

She watched him walk out with long, stiff strides, long red hair brushing over the folds of his shirt, tips almost reaching the line of his dark breeches. He didn't look over his shoulder even once. His dead hand lingered on the door for a last moment as he stepped into the corridor, the grey of his fingers even more poignant against the rich golden decorations on the wood. Then he let go.

The door started falling shut.

'I could help!' she heard herself blurt out.

His foot moved so fast she didn't see it happening until his boot bumped against the closing door, nudging it back open just in time. It was all that betrayed he'd even heard her. He didn't turn. Didn't even take his living hand from his pocket.

Just stood there – waiting.

'Once I get back to Elidian,' she said desperately, speaking too fast. 'I could try to improve things, couldn't I? Could try to open the gates again. I'm pretty good at sneaking around. And I wasn't planning to continue killing once I have my reward, but if there's anyone you'd rather see gone from the face of the earth, I could—'

'And I am to believe,' he interrupted, unmoving, 'that you would actually *keep* that promise for longer than two steps beyond these walls, Miss Iavi?'

Her mouth fell shut.

Liars. That's what you mortals are. But she hadn't *wanted* to betray his trust, had done it only to find her way back home – so if home was where her promise would bring her ...

'Command me,' she said hoarsely. 'You could make me keep it.'

He sighed but turned around now, eyes narrowed as he leaned against the doorpost and folded his arms. 'My commands don't hold power outside the Keep. You'd be free to betray me and my secrets to Cyril the moment you stepped out the door.'

Oh, divines help her. 'Well, then command me to tell you the truth and I can tell you I truly don't want to betray—'

'Wishes can change.'

She didn't know what was worse – to feel so utterly powerless to change his mind or to know he was *right* to distrust her. 'Then what do you want to do? Keep me prisoner here forever?'

For a moment he seemed to hesitate, lips faltering on words she couldn't possibly guess from the blankness of his expression. Then, with a sharp shake of his head, he moved away from the wall, stalking three steps into the room.

'Well?' she said, voice rising.

'The roses aren't budging,' he said, lips a thin line as he met her gaze. 'As long as they're keeping the castle closed, it doesn't matter what anyone thinks about your return to Elidian. You're not going anyway.'

'Fine' – that was a lie – 'but what if we could outsmart the roses?'

His eyebrow flew up. '*We?*'

'Well, as I said, if I can help you ...'

'*If.*' There were centuries of bitter life lessons in that one word. 'That's the trouble we're currently running into, Miss Iavi.'

'Yes, but ... Listen, I'm not a bad person!' She swung her legs out of bed, needing to feel the firm reassurance of the floor beneath her feet – the reminder that she was still here, that she was still *her*, that a fae king's justified doubts did not change anything about that. 'I know I kill for a living and I know I made a mistake, and I know you have probably been disappointed in people more often than I have lived days in my life, but I'm *trying*. I truly and honestly am. I saw you as an opponent and an obstacle for too long, and I understand now that I was wrong – so if I'm trying to work *with* you, if I'm genuinely trying to make up for the hurt I caused you, will you please, *please* not slam that door in my face?'

She fell silent, breathing heavily. The king didn't move for a good three heartbeats, the look in his eyes wavering between distrust and dreams, temptation and common sense.

'Your Majesty ...' she started helplessly.

He drew in a sharp breath, turned, and stalked to the rose-covered windows, eyes firmly fixed on the mountains outside. His tone was curt to the point of snappish. 'You spent the night in my bed, for hell's sake. Just call me Moridyr.'

Forty-eight hours ago she would vehemently have objected that she hadn't really spent the night in his bed, not in *that* way at least, and that in any case there was no familiarity to be taken from the business of killing and accidentally being killed in return. Now, she shrugged off the suggestion in that dangerous little sentence with barely half a thought. 'As you wish, but Moridyr—'

'I should tell you there's a chance you won't be able to return,' he interrupted, voice tight. 'Even if we worked together, that doesn't mean—'

'Are you saying you don't even want me to *try*?' She shot to her feet, staggering half a step forward on wobbly, uncertain legs. 'That you just want me to give up and throw the rest of my life away? That's my *home* we're talking about – the only place I've ever been home in my life – and you can't just decide—'

Her knees gave way.

He whirled around before she could cry out, shot forward faster than she could blink. Strong arms locked around her waist and pulled her back to her feet, and then she stood pressed against his tall body, breathless and flustered, knees shaking like twigs in the wind.

The world seemed to freeze around her.

Through the flimsy fabric of her chemise, his warmth was both comforting and deeply disconcerting, the cage of his arms both safe and prison-like. Her senses drank in every sensation with greedy hunger – the press of his chest against hers, the lingering scent of beeswax and lavender, the cold shock of his dead hand against the small of her back. He was so tall. So unexpectedly strong. And he should *not* be holding her like this – she should not *allow* him to hold her like this.

She stood frozen.

'Moridyr,' she breathed. Her voice broke. 'Please.'

'Would it truly be that bad?' he muttered, and for the first time since she'd awoken, there was a hint of humanity in his quiet words, a crack in that jaundiced shield. Warm breath brushed past her scalp. His arms didn't let go. 'If you ended up here with no way to leave?'

'The Keep isn't my home.' Her scoff came out sounding too close to a sob. 'It will never be my home. I'm *human*. I don't belong here with your people.'

Something unexpectedly helpless gleamed in his living eye as he looked down to meet her gaze. Too close, again – much too close, and she couldn't bring herself to struggle, to push away from his warm, solid embrace. *A lady does not enjoy unwanted attention* ... But this was not Mrs. Sedgewick's Briannis. This was the Keep's Briannis, and she was pleading with a fae king, negotiating an alliance that would have to determine where she lived the rest of her life. She'd think about manners if she returned home.

When she returned home.

'I'm not sure I could forgive you for it,' she added, an edge sneaking into her voice. 'For forcing me to stay here while I could be living the life of my dreams in the city. Is that really the sort of company you want for the rest of your days – a resentful prisoner?'

She'd won – whatever sore spot she'd hit, she knew the moment his shoulders sagged that it had been enough. His heart skipped a beat below her palm. His jaw tightened as he curtly said, 'You know it isn't.'

'So then ...'

He hesitated as she let the words die off, secrets and schemes in every silent twist of his lips. She had the eerie feeling he was working out five dozen potential scenarios in those few silent moments, testing every word she'd spoken against circumstances she couldn't even imagine yet – a mind of centuries, knowing the twists and turns of history from its own experience.

'I strongly recommend you don't break my trust again,' he finally said, the words slow yet unmistakably ominous. 'I can be weak-hearted once, but I won't be a fool twice. And with the fate of Faerie in my hands, I won't hesitate to go back on any agreement we made if you even give the vague impression you may be intending to hurt my people.'

'Of course.' She didn't dare to breathe. 'I won't. I promise I won't. And I know what you want to say about human promises, but I promise I'll prove you wrong about those, too – so will you help me, then? To get back home and help you?'

'I suppose we can try.' There was a grim quality to his voice, as if those words were a surrender to the temptation of some unforgivable crime. 'On one condition.'

Relief swept over her with so much force that she found herself *grinning* at him – a broad, utterly unladylike grin of the sort she felt stretching her temples. He'd *trust* her. He'd *help*. Was there any condition she wouldn't agree to for that prize? 'I have to stop trying to kill you?'

'Oh, I took that to be an implied part of the plan.' Suddenly that familiar lopsided smirk crept back onto his face, living side of his lips curling up in a mirthless expression that made the breath stop dead in her lungs. 'No, my one condition is that you'll forget about manners for the rest of your stay. I don't want to hear another word about them, in fact. If we can agree on that little point, we do have a deal.'

'I beg your pardon?' She let out a breathless laugh, glancing down at her hands on his chest. His arms didn't loosen around her. 'Isn't this unmannered enough for your taste? I'm standing here in my underwear!'

'Don't worry,' he murmured, smirk growing dangerously sweet. 'I very much noticed.'

Torturous heat sizzled through her. 'You're *outrageous*!'

'I am, and *outrageous* isn't going to be an argument in this household, Miss Iavi.' The curve of his lips was unsettlingly beautiful, green eye coming back to life with a gleam of unspoken challenges. 'Neither is *improper* or *scandalous* or any of those meaningless phrases the Elidian matrons are so fond of scattering around. A simple "I don't want this" will suffice to stop me at any time. Unless you *do* want something, of course, in which case I would suggest you make matters easy and just don't try to stop me at all.'

She felt like a fish on land, gaping at him. 'You ... what?'

'For example,' he continued, and somehow he seemed even closer now, the heat of his breath stroking her cheek like a seductive caress, 'I'm currently feeling quite tempted to kiss you. Do you have any opinions on that proposition, by any chance?'

The room started tilting around her.

Her hands lay numbly against his chest, perfectly poised to shove him away from her. Opinions – he wanted her *opinions*? *You're being ridiculous*, she ought to say. *I just about killed you. You are furious with me. I want you to leave me alone.* A few words; it should be so straightforward to speak them out loud. But if she did ...

He'd listen.

He'd step back.

He ... he *wouldn't* kiss her.

'What?' she heard herself say again.

'I'm about to kiss you,' he pleasantly repeated, as if he'd suggested nothing more outrageous than a chaperoned turn around the dancefloor. His face was so close the two halves seemed to blur before her eyes. 'I spent a very long day regretting I didn't do it yesterday, and I intend to make up for the oversight in a moment or two. Unless you don't want me to, of course. I eagerly await your disapproval, in that case.'

She swallowed hard. 'You're ... you're not making sense. You don't even *like* me.'

'I don't?' he said dryly.

'I tried to kill you! Three times in a row!'

'Yes,' he agreed, voice lowering, 'and the third time was by far the most vexing of them, because I was just starting to grow significantly fonder of you. I'm still a little vexed, truth be told, but something tells me the taste of your pretty little mouth may solve most of that issue. Anything else I need to clarify before you can consider the proposal?'

Sweet divines, what was happening? And far more importantly, why wasn't she screaming and running away yet? 'But ... I ...'

He waited, watching her, unmoving.

Through thin layers of linen and buckskin, she could feel the ridges of his ribs, the hard plane of his stomach, and – her heart skipped a beat – the rigid bulge of that part she knew from Father's handbooks but had never seen in the flesh, feeling much more imposing than it had ever seemed sketched in ink and charcoal. Her head was turning inside out. Pressed flush against him, the sensation of his nearness was overwhelming, sucking her deeper and deeper into the mire of her own unacceptable desires ...

Although he'd probably tell her *unacceptable* didn't have a place in this household, either.

She was grasping at straws, sinking faster the harder she tried to find sense. She'd been here before. She'd stood on this precipice in the breakfast room, too, a mere twitch away from giving in – but she must have had a reason to resist then, and why couldn't she think of it now?

Why couldn't she think of *anything* under the intensity of his gaze?

'This ...' she breathed dazedly. 'This is why I had to kill you.'

His eyebrow rose a fraction. 'Because you don't want me to kiss you?'

'No.' A shiver ran through her. 'Because you make me want it. It's ... maddening.'

'We're not in the city, my darling little menace.' He lowered his head ever so slightly, forehead bumping against hers with feathery weight. His voice was a siren's song, the husky sound of it slithering down her spine, pooling in places she barely dared to think about. 'There's no one here to judge you or gossip about you. So if there are no consequences anyway, if you plan to go back home and forget everything that's happened to you here ... why wouldn't you let yourself be who you want to be as long as the insanity lasts?'

Who she wanted to be.

This ... this wasn't who she wanted to be, was it?

But she was too far gone to think, too far gone to make sense of the fire burning beneath her skin. His nose brushed past hers as he lowered his face, and the breath evaporated in her throat. His living hand tightened on her spine. Cold, cautious fingers came up to brush along her jaw, nudging her chin upward ever so slightly.

In the last inch between their parted lips, her shallow gasps mingled with his straining breath.

'I ...' Her voice came out on a squeak. 'I might still taste of vomit.'

'I might taste of rot,' he murmured, a chuckle lacing the words. 'I'm afraid there's only one way to find out.'

'Oh.' She sucked in a shuddering breath. 'Yes. Research?'

'Research,' he muttered and kissed her.

His lips were warm. Cold. Warm again. They brushed over hers gently at first, as if she might shatter at the touch; then he deepened the kiss, coaxing, seducing, urging her mouth to open with a flick of his tongue.

She gasped – she couldn't help herself.

He pushed forward, and then his tongue slid *into* her and he was *kissing* her and all she could do was cling to him for dear life and pray her knees wouldn't buckle from the sheer heady bliss of it. She had never felt anything like this. His kiss was gentleness and urgency, tenderness and ferocity, a dizzying mixture that drove mindless moans from her lungs with every twist of lips and tongue. Her mouth barely felt like her own anymore. An intoxicating lightness seeped into her every vein and nerve and sinew as he held her and kissed her, a freedom that made her feel like laughing and crying at once ...

He did not taste of rot.

He tasted of honey and orange and something smoky she couldn't quite name, tasted of warm summer nights and smouldering fires, and she came up on her toes and pressed herself closer against him, addicted to that sweet, addictive, masculine flavour from the very first glimpse of it. This time *he* was the one to moan. Something clenched below her navel at the sound, and she pressed her hips against him in a burst of primal instinct, ground along that hard bulge of his erection as she kissed him harder.

With a gasp, he tore away from her. '*Briannis.*'

She shrunk back, flustered, out of breath. 'Am I ... am I doing it wrong?'

'No.' His voice was hoarse and raw. 'You're perfectly, outrageously delicious, and I'm no longer used to *anything*. You'll make me spend in my trousers like some blustering youth if you're not careful.'

'Oh.' Her face heated. How could he just ... *speak* such indisputably improper words, stand there half-dressed and ruffled and mesmerising, and look so damnably royal at the same time? Hands still pressed to his chest, she didn't manage to draw her gaze away from his lips – firm and red and moist on one side, and even the paler, tighter side looked pinker than before.

As if she'd kissed the life right back into him.

She'd never felt so powerful in her life.

A shiver shook down her spine as she met the burning intensity of his gaze – those same eyes that had regarded her with so much distant coldness a few minutes ago. 'I think I would like to do that again.'

There was just a hint of cruelty to the familiar smile that slid around his lips, and even that sight made her knees tremble with relief. 'Do what?'

'You know what I mean!' Her blush heated to a bonfire. 'I ... You ...'

'Tell me.' Fingertips brushed over her nape, stealing her breath with their merciless tenderness. 'What is it you'd like to do again?'

Her lips formed the shapes of the word, more or less. No sound came out.

'Briannis?' he murmured.

The sound of her name on his lips was a caress she felt all the way to that burning core beneath her navel – the sound of an *encouragement*, not a reproach, not a demand. She was not going to shock or infuriate him this way, she realised with an odd pang of relief. She could not make him gasp or faint or call her a little barbarian, because whatever she said or did or wanted, he was a thousand times worse, and however many vices he may possess, he was not a hypocrite.

'I want to kiss you,' she blurted out hoarsely.

'You do?' His living eye crinkled at the corner. 'Well, we should be able to arrange that, shouldn't we?'

And perhaps it was courage, perhaps it was madness, perhaps it was both those things and a hundred others too ... but her hands moved themselves, sliding into the silk strands of his hair. Her heels lifted. Her head came up. And then *she* was kissing *him*, and sweet divines, it was even better this time, because his groan was gravelly with abandon and *she* was driving him to make those sounds and ...

Her knees buckled.

He caught her before she could plummet to the floor, hands around her waist, pulling her back against him. Chest shaking with laughter, he muttered, 'Are you that impatient to kneel before me?'

'You swine!' she squeaked.

His chuckle was a warm caress against the crown of her head. 'You're trembling like a leaf, my little murderess. Perhaps I should be tucking you back into bed.'

'Into ...' She opened one eye, head swimming. 'Into *your* bed.'

'Yes?' How was it possible for a voice so sensual, so seductive, to sound that innocent at the same time? 'Unless you'd prefer for me to carry you to the Starlit Room, of course, which would offer you more quiet and solitude but also less potential for being kissed awake. Just say the word. Your choice is my command.'

Her heart gave a little stutter. Being *kissed awake*? While she was barely dressed and half-asleep and already *in a bed*? Impossible – absolutely, utterly impossible – except that when she tried to articulate why the concept was so perfectly laughable, all she could come up with was that a respectable lady simply did not do such things.

And that wasn't allowed to be a reason anymore.

So she'd have to tell him that she didn't want to sleep in his bed ... but that would be a lie. It was too reassuring, the new softness in his gaze. Too soothing. All she wanted was to stay close to it, and the Starlit Room was far, far too many doors away.

Did it matter if she went along with the madness? It was all just temporary insanity anyway. Sooner or later, she would find a way back home. She'd leave the Keep and its king behind and become herself again, and no one would ever know about the unimaginable wickedness of her days in Faerie.

With no neighbours to shriek at her anywhere near, she might as well allow herself to let go.

'I'll stay here,' she whispered.

He swept her off her feet and installed her back between the pillows without another word – as if he feared that one more joke or innuendo would be enough to change her mind.

She did no such thing. Sinking into the mattress was like sinking into a hot bath of exactly the right temperature, plush blankets murmuring at her trembling limbs to relax. She was *exhausted*, she realised only as her eyes fluttered shut, her near-death and the nerve-wrecking argument still taking its toll on her body, the lingering aftereffects of the foxglove all too noticeable as the thrill of wickedness wore off. Why in the world was she kissing fae kings if she just needed to sleep?

Although sleep would never taste so heavenly. She craved his touch the moment he released her, feeling strangely lonely in this big, lush bed.

It was in that moment of drowsiness that she abruptly re-alised her brilliant plan of action had one serious, glaring flaw.

'Moridyr?' It was strange to call him by his name, and even stranger to do it from his bed, the taste of his lips still on hers. 'I ... I just thought of something.'

He was still standing beside her as she blinked open her eyes, expression cautious, but not in a hostile way. 'You did?'

'If I return to the city to open the gates and I don't manage immediately ...' She swallowed nervously. 'Then you'll still be alone in the meantime, won't you?'

Was that a brief moment of hesitation?

But his smile grew onto his face with all its usual sardonic wryness; she must have imagined the pause. 'Ah. You're worried I'll spend the next three years tormented by lovesickness, staring longingly out of the tower windows every moment of the day?'

Her cheeks heated again. 'I just ...'

'I know.' He gave a small shrug as he turned away and sauntered towards the comfortable chair by the window, tidying his ruffled shirt. 'You shouldn't be worrying about me. I've been on my own for fourteen years – I've learned to do without the company. So as much as I appreciate your presence ...'

He didn't finish the sentence.

'You don't need me?' she suggested, her nausea flaring out of nowhere.

He sighed, sinking into his seat and meeting her eyes again. 'Needing people has proven itself rather dangerous in the past. Amuse yourself while you're here, but don't make the mistake of expecting grand romantic sentiments from me.'

Which was just as well. Of course she wasn't looking for anything of the kind. Grand romantic sentiments sounded like the opposite of temporary, and either way, he was the least suitable man she could possibly imagine attracting. If she was going to be sane and rational about this, wasn't it immensely helpful of him to do the same?

'Ah,' she muttered, forcing herself to nod. 'Good. We agree, then.'

And yet she couldn't help but notice, as she snuggled into the pillows and pulled the blankets tighter around herself, that the relief did once again not feel like relief at all.

Chapter 9

One should never sacrifice sincerity for a misguided notion of politeness or kindness. Instead, if your intimacy will allow it, you should strive to deliver an unpleasant truth in the gentlest manner possible.
Lady Lockwell's Handbook of Etiquette

MORIDYR MADE HIS WAY down the broad central stairs with heavy feet and a nagging headache building behind his dead eye.

Lack of sleep, he tried to tell himself, but he knew there was little substance to that explanation; with no one to expect him to rise or sleep at the usual times of the day, his diurnal rhythm had known odder patterns over these lonely years at Rosethorn Keep. It was rather that one little sentence that sung through his mind like an unwelcome lullaby, all the more sharp-teethed for the sincerity with which she'd spoken it.

I'm not sure I could forgive you.

And so, like the coward he was, he'd caved.

She deserved to know. She *had* to know. It was cruel madness to allow her to hold hope while he already knew her plan would come to naught. But he knew damn well the roses wouldn't be so easily assuaged, not after he'd looked for the solution to the same damn problem for decades, and as long as neither of them could leave the Keep ... well, she wouldn't find out how unwelcome she was in Elidian, either.

Which meant that, in theory, she might as well not know.

He muttered a curse, rubbing his temple. The theory so rarely matched reality, he'd found over the course of the centuries.

But he might still be able to redeem himself; it was that realisation that had eventually sent him out of his chair and down through the silent, Briannis-less halls of Rosethorn Keep. Her return to the city might not be as utterly impossible as he'd thought based on the mirror's information of the previous day. Cyril did not *intend* to let her in again, but what if there was some magic that could smuggle her through the gates without him noticing? Some fae trick to give her the money she needed without the Princeps' permission? If something could still be done, it wouldn't be so bad that he hadn't told her yet. After all, the conditions she'd set in order to stop trying to kill him – the conditions he'd agreed to – could still be met.

If the roses ever retreated, through whatever unexpected change of circumstances, she *could* still return to the city as planned. It would just require a little extra effort to circumvent Cyril's devious intentions.

He nonetheless descended the stairs to Mirror Hall more slowly than usual.

It was as if he saw the Keep with entirely new eyes as he made his way down – the mosaic floors, the luminescent mushrooms, the twinkling lights hiding between the leaves and flowers. What did she see when she walked these enchanting corridors? A prison? A trap? A strange and temporary fever dream?

Not home. Perhaps that was all he needed to know.

I'm not sure I could forgive you.

The doors to the hall swung open with too much force as he approached, as if they sensed his desire to burst through and slam them into the walls. Behind them, the mirror abruptly ceased its monotone humming. Moridyr caught a glimpse of himself in the silver surface and wished he hadn't; the sight of his dead half made him wonder just how poison-drugged she must have been to kiss him the way she had.

He should probably have kept his hands off her altogether.

Which would have been easier if she hadn't pouted so furiously at him with that little rosebud mouth, and if she hadn't so passionately sworn to never betray him again, and if she hadn't clung to him as if he was her last hope in a world of darkness.

Feeling a little conflicted, Your Majesty? the mirror purred.

It took an inhuman effort not to swing one of the heavy antler candelabras at the smooth surface. 'What are the exact measures Cyril took to make sure Briannis would not be able to return to Elidian? Can they be evaded?'

Those are two questions, the mirror pointed out. It sounded unusually cautious. Perhaps it had belatedly sensed just how close it was to being reduced to a pile of silver shards. *Which of them do you want me to answer?*

Moridyr bit down another curse. 'The first.'

Lord Cyril has sent a group of his personal executioners after Miss Iavi to follow her into Faerie and kill her the moment she emerges from Rosethorn Keep or tries to return before reaching the Keep. The mirror sounded even more cautious as it rattled off the answer. *In the unlikely case she manages to escape them, guards at the northern city gate have been instructed to stop any woman matching her description. Marsh dwellers living near the city have been promised a bounty for her head, whether they kill her on the Faerie side or the human side of the marshes.*

The soft, droning voice broke off. Moridyr imagined, in that moment of absolute silence, that he could hear the mirror whimpering quietly to itself.

Fuck's sake. Just *how* fearsome had Briannis's reputation grown, for the Princeps to take such drastic measures?

Or, more likely, it was the news of her last mission the bastard wanted to stifle. Moridyr closed his eyes, seeing the scheme unfold before him. Just like Cyril had never claimed responsibility for Tal's death, he would probably wait to observe the consequences of this crime before he decided whether he wanted his name linked to it. And so Briannis Iavi had to disappear forever – by whatever means necessary.

He'd even roused the fucking *marsh dwellers*. As much as those rogues ruled themselves, they all answered to the authority of coin: if promised sufficient reward, Moridyr suspected they'd happily chase their target to the other side of the world.

Which meant he wouldn't be able to save her from Cyril's schemes. Not all the way from Rosethorn Keep, at least, and leaving the Keep would never be an option.

Moridyr III, the last king of Faerie.

So she truly couldn't leave.

So he had to tell her.

Is that the sort of company you want? she'd snapped. *A resentful prisoner?*

Didn't matter. Better a prisoner than a woman chasing an impossible hope. Better resentful because of the truth than resentful for having been lied to.

But he climbed the stairs to his bedroom more slowly than he ever had in his life, and when he found her still asleep in the bed they'd shared, it was relief he felt more than anything else.

***

She woke around the fall of dusk, with a small, fragile groan that made his heart constrict in his chest. But her eyes were clear when she turned around in her pillows and found him sitting in the chair where he'd spent the last few hours, and she was no longer as mortally pale as that morning.

For a few moments she merely blinked at him, as if he was some memory she was trying to piece together. Then, abruptly, she blushed – a bright, rosy blush that spread across her cheeks and made her look innocent and tantalising at the same time, drawing his attention straight back to the moist pinkness of her parted lips, the soft curves of her body beneath her chemise. His cock eagerly stirred in his trousers, as if to remind him of the host of things he'd rather be doing to her than starting the conversation they were about to have.

Fuck's sake – he truly had been on his own for too long.

He managed a smile, swallowing every tempting proposal welling up in him. Until he'd gotten the hard truths over his lips, he should probably attempt to appear at least the slightest bit trustworthy and respectable.

'Good afternoon,' he said. Bland but safe. 'Or evening, probably.'

'Did I sleep all day?' Her gaze flicked to the window and back to him, still in the same shirt she'd clung to that morning, still coat-less and cravat-less. 'And did you sit here all day?'

'I take your safety seriously,' he said, which was not an answer to her question, but a truth he knew she'd interpret as one. 'How are you feeling?'

Her tousled hair tumbled over her shoulders as she sat up and pulled the sheets back around her hips, failing to cover the soft swell of her breast below her flimsy chemise. Another rush of blood flowed to his loins. Modest little Briannis Iavi looked like she'd spent the past few hours gasping and moaning in his arms, and that thought alone was enough to make him wonder what it would be like to sink into her, the way her eyes would grow wide as he filled her, the way her lips would part into a cry of shocked pleasure. Soft skin and tight warmth and—

Fuck. Something else to think about – *anything* else to think about. Dying mountain slopes. Closed gates. Murderers and marsh dwellers hunting for her head. He focused on the small frown that drew her brows together, the thoughtful expression that he hoped was a sign of sensible words to come. As long as she started talking about poisoning symptoms, he probably wouldn't get carried away by glimpses of pale skin and pebbling nipples.

Not too much, anyway.

'I'm a little ...' She paused, eyes narrowing a fraction as she surveyed him from his bed. As if she was assessing risks. As if *he* was the one to be diagnosed. 'A little disappointed.'

His heart skipped a beat.

Did she know? Had she somehow heard his questions and the mirror's answers all the way from here, some trickery bit of Keep magic he'd been unaware of so far? Had he done, said, thought anything to betray the secret and his own cowardice, the impossible deal they'd made?

'Oh?' he managed to croak out.

'I was promised the pleasure of being kissed awake,' she continued, a frighteningly effective imitation of a lady dissatisfied with her maid's treatment of her best silk gown. 'Instead, all I get is you ogling me from ten feet away. Did you decide to be a virtuous gentleman after all while I was sleeping? Because that would be some *spectacularly* bad thinking on your part.'

Moridyr stared at her.

A smile trembled around the corners of her lips, a smile he'd never seen before – revealing brand new dimples in her cheeks and making her brown eyes shine like polished gold. It was a smile that *teased*, that promised mischief and bewitching delights. It told him two things, both of them exhilarating and alarming in equal amounts.

First of all, Briannis Iavi would always be deeply, desperately unhappy in the life of a well-mannered lady.

And second of all, he had once again underestimated her.

A swift kick of longing drove him to his feet before he could regain his senses. It was Cyril they should be talking about, assassins on her heels and a price on her head ... but he found himself stepping towards the bed as if her words were now steering *his* body, the corners of his lips unable to stay down as he met her gaze.

How in the world was he supposed to resist that smile? How could he *not* attempt to lure it onto her lips again?

'Your humble servant begs your forgiveness, my lady.' He swept into a dramatic bow by the side of the bed, his voice just a fraction hoarse. 'Please allow me to make up for the grave error I unwittingly committed. I desperately await your commands.'

Her delighted giggle made his heart soar. 'Kiss me.'

He raised an eyebrow, unable to help himself. He shouldn't, he really shouldn't, but ... 'Where?'

'What do you— *Oh*.' She turned a bright purple, eyes widening. 'You *degenerate*!'

'I thought we had an agreement,' he muttered as he sank down on the edge of the bed, pushing away the nagging awareness that his part of the agreement was little more than a wishful fairy tale. She'd asked for this, hadn't she? It would be rude to refuse her. 'No more proper manners here. Where do you want me to kiss you?'

Her breath came too fast, small breasts heaving temptingly against her chemise. Her pupils had swallowed all but a narrow ring of golden brown as she gawked at him. Even as her lips twitched and trembled, no sound came out – as if the mere thought of such wickedness had rendered her vocal chords numb.

Moridyr lifted his right hand. She stiffened but remained in place as he brushed a fingertip down her throat, savouring the smoothness of her flawless skin and the rapid pulse beating through her veins.

'Here?' he murmured.

She gasped in a sharp breath. 'Yes.'

He bent over and trailed his lips down her neck, nibbling softly on her shoulder. At the graze of his teeth, she squirmed, then moaned when he did it again.

'And here?' He let his fingers wander with his lips still against her skin, stroking down along her collarbone until he met the linen of her chemise and held still. 'Here?'

'Yes,' she whispered again.

Following the line his fingers had drawn, he kissed a slow trail down her body, focusing on the tender skin of her neck, collarbone, and shoulder. The pulse at the hollow of her throat was frantic under his lips. He flicked his tongue against it, then resumed his languid way down, licking and nuzzling and nibbling. Briannis's breathing grew more ragged with each kiss, her skin soon flushed with warmth, her hands fisted in the blankets. When he pressed a last kiss just above the neckline of her shift and looked up, her eyes had glazed over.

'Am I forgiven yet?' he said softly.

She let out a breathy, throaty laugh. 'Almost.'

His cock was throbbing, pulsating iron in his breeches now, aching for her warmth, screaming at him to flip her over in the blankets and take her until his name was the only thing left on her mind. Somehow, he restrained himself. Somehow, he managed to kiss the rim of her ear without laying a finger on her and mutter, 'Do you want me to continue, then?'

'Yes.' It was little more than a breath. '*Yes.*'

Slowly, ever so slowly, he allowed his fingers to trail down.

Over the first swell of her breast. Past a pert nipple, making her breath hitch. And down, farther down, ribs and side and hip and thigh, until he slipped below her blankets and found the hitched up hem of her chemise just above her knee. Kissing her neck, her shoulder, he slid the fabric higher, revealing a willowy leg, the skin pale and smooth.

'Moridyr ...' she breathed.

He brushed his lips over hers.

She half-gasped, half-moaned into his kiss, and then she was kissing him back with passionate, almost desperate vigour, nails digging into his shoulders, mouth opening to allow him access. He curled one hand around her nape as his other travelled a path back up her leg. Over the sensitive inside of her thigh. Beneath her chemise. She was so gods-dammed warm and so velvety soft, and her body trembled so very eagerly wherever he went, pleasure and anticipation building below every inch of skin he touched ...

If she so much as *looked* at his crotch a moment too long, he feared he might explode.

But she was in too deep now to do anything but what his hands and lips made her do; her hips bucked towards him, her fingers tangled in his hair, her mouth turned greedy and wild as if she'd waited her whole life to be kissed like this. He slid his hand the last few inches up her thighs. There, finally, were soft curls and damp warmth and ... Divines help him, she was *drenched*, the perfect, glorious slickness of a woman who'd been starved of every bit of passion she deserved.

'Is this what you want?' he rasped. 'Do you want me to touch you here?'

Her eyes fluttered closed. She nodded, breath short.

He slid a finger into her.

Her gasp was a revelation, shock and wonder and pleasure as he slowly entered her sweet, soft tightness. Dropping her head back, she arched into him, thighs spreading wider to allow him access. He probed deeper, and again she gasped, lips parting in desperate abandon.

'How does that feel?' he murmured against the hollow of her neck, retracting, then pushing his finger back into her. 'Do you want me to do it again?

'Yes,' she breathed. 'Yes. *Moridyr* ...'

His name, sweet on her lips, sent a shudder down his spine. He gently began to thrust back and forth, thumb stroking the sensitive little bud between her slick lips until she was panting with each stroke. She was so incredibly, impossibly tight around him, and fuck, he wanted her undone and unbridled in his arms – wanted her so utterly overcome she'd never spend another thought on Elidian etiquette. He wanted her to moan his name again. He wanted her begging for his cock.

More than anything else, he wanted her to stay – *happily*.

Her thighs shook against his wrist. He lowered his head and kissed her throat as he fucked her with his fingers, sliding a second digit into her. Her moans turned into mewls. She was straining under his hands, that slow-building tension just before eruption, and again he grazed his teeth down the expanse of her neck ...

'Stop,' she breathed.

Had her command held magic, he couldn't have frozen more abruptly.

The wrong word. A word that cut through the delightful symphony of her moans like a sudden hailstorm through a warm summer's day. What was wrong? Had he miscalculated? Hurt her? Even worse – *scared* her?

He slid his fingers out of her, arousal seeping away in the blink of an eye. She let out a shaking breath but didn't move for three, four heartbeats, frozen in the blankets like a terrified little mouse. Around them, the room had becoming frighteningly quiet, as if even the Keep itself was holding its breath in confusion.

Stop.

He had heard her say it, hadn't he?

'Briannis?' he said quietly.

'I ... I ...' She wouldn't meet his gaze as he shifted back to look at her, messy chestnut curls hiding most of her face from view. Her hands fidgeted with her chemise, pulling the linen back in place. 'I'm sorry. I'm *sorry*. I ... I don't think I can ...'

The garbled flow of her words drifted off, leaving only heavy, panting breaths behind. Her eyes were wide open when he gently nudged up her head to meet his gaze. They had glazed over, but lust had mingled with something close to panic in the dark of her pupils; she gaped at him like a rabbit at a wolf about to devour it, paralysed, anticipating the worst.

Fuck.

He reflexively yanked back his hand, feeling suddenly filthy in every place that had touched her. 'If I did anything you didn't want me—'

'It's not that!' She almost sobbed the words – and yet he couldn't catch a shred of insincerity in that brusque interruption, in the pleading look in her eyes. 'I *did* want— I mean, I *do* want— Oh, I'm not making any sense at all! I'm so sorry, I ...'

'There's nothing you need to be sorry for.' He'd rarely been so glad for the forced truth of his words. At least she'd know he meant it, sitting small and trembling on his bed, looking nothing like the woman who had calmly and easily driven a knife into his liver two nights ago. 'And I strongly suspect you're making perfect sense. What is the matter?'

'I just don't think I can forget this.' Her throat – that pale, soft throat he'd kissed – bobbed dangerously. 'I don't think I can pretend it never happened.'

When she was back home.

Which she would never be.

He had to tell her – had to tell her *now*, before it became a betrayal no matter how he phrased the news. 'Briannis …'

'It shouldn't feel so *good!*' she burst out, as if she hadn't even heard him, her voice shrill to a point far beyond ladylike distress. A tear rolled down her cheek. 'It doesn't make sense! I'm not supposed to want this, any of this – I don't *want* to want it! Why do I have to feel so terrible about feeling so wonderful? Why can't I just be … be …'

Her outburst died away. Her dewy eyes found him, begging for answers, imploring him to save her – bitter irony, given that he was the last man to be her hero in this story. What in hell could he tell her? That it was to be expected? That burying your true nature below rules upon rules was always bound to go wrong in the end, that all of Elidian was a den of sinners below the sparkling, sophisticated façade?

You're rotten by nature; you're as bad as the rakes and lightskirts you despise. He knew how she would hear the words.

'Respectability,' he said, choosing his words with painstaking care, 'is a curse in itself, I'm afraid.'

She hiccupped a little sob.

Carefully, he sat back and reached for one of her hands. She averted her eyes but entwined their fingers nonetheless, as if she was afraid to break the contact yet afraid to accept the comfort at the same time.

Whatever was left of his heart cracked a little.

Damn the bad news, then – he couldn't distress her even more, not when she was clinging to his hand like this. He'd tell her later. Soon.

After she'd stopped crying.

'Briannis,' he said again.

She sniffled. 'Yes?'

'Why does it matter so much? Being prim and proper every minute of your life?'

'Because the alternative is worse,' she stammered, eyes determinedly focused on the ruffled blankets between them. 'Because ... because ...'

He waited.

'He tried so *hard*,' she finally blurted out, and now the tears were welling in her eyes in earnest, dripping onto her chemise. She clung to his hand as if she were drowning in the memories. 'My father. He fled Kraaled when I was little. My mother was a niece of a member of the Twelve, and when he was killed, they took half his family with him. Father just managed to get away with me after she died. So he came to Elidian – you know what they say, the Free City, no class laws, no nobility above the law ... He thought we'd have a future there.'

The Free City. Moridyr clenched his jaw, swallowing the bitter words on their way to his lips. Elidian *had* been free, yes, until Cyril had claimed the Princeps' seat – until the bastard had slowly, methodically, started stripping away those hard-won freedoms and called them necessary measurements against the evil of the fae.

'But Father didn't understand the city,' Briannis whispered, wiping her cheek. She still didn't look up at him. 'He didn't learn the language well. He didn't understand that when people can be anything they want to be, they'll find other ways to make each other outsiders. In Kraaled, he could be as eccentric as he wanted, because he was a learned man and good at what he did. But in Elidian, everyone can write. Everyone with money can attend university. So what you need to distinguish yourself from all the others who are just as good as you are is social grace ... and he just *couldn't* comprehend that.'

Moridyr let out a slow breath. 'I see.'

'And he had no idea how to raise a child. Let alone a daughter. I ...' She let out a strangled sound, sob and laugh at once. 'I was *such* an aberrant girl. I proudly told people I knew the name of every human bone by heart and read treatises on anatomy before bedtime and ... and dissected caterpillars for fun—'

'*Caterpillars?*' Not the moment to laugh, but the grin growing on his lips wasn't so easily discouraged. It was such an oddly charming image, the vision of her bent over a table, apron over her dress and scalpels in her hands – so much more genuine than the cramped, forced version of her that had slipped into his home a few days ago.

'They're immensely interesting!' She reared up, forgetting to cry for a moment as she yanked back her hand in an animated gesture. 'You see, when they go into metamorphosis, their whole body melts into goo – even their *brain* becomes this strange sort of liquid in their cocoon – and still, if you give them enough time, they'll turn into butterflies. Isn't that ridiculous? And— Oh.' Her hands froze mid-swing, sank back into her lap. 'I ... I'm sorry. You probably didn't want to know about caterpillars.'

'What I would like to know,' he said as he crossed his legs in the blankets, 'is who told you that you shouldn't be talking about caterpillars.'

Her face darkened. 'Everyone.'

He could admittedly see that, from what he remembered about Elidian's middle class. There was a reason he'd generally avoided that particular segment of the population.

'It started when the neighbour's dog was giving birth,' she added quietly. 'I heard her whining in the shed behind their house. She'd been having contractions for hours, no puppies to be seen – turned out the birth canal was way too narrow to let them through. So I helped – I *did* get them all out alive – but then Mrs. Bartlett found me there, covered in blood, and ...' A deep, shivery breath. 'I tried to explain! I tried to tell her what the problem was and how I'd solved it, but she only screamed at me and called me a little barbarian and told me a good girl would just have called for help.'

For fuck's sake. 'How old were you?'

'Eleven.' She rubbed her face, looked away. 'After that I started to notice. How people whispered when I walked down the street with my hair in tangles and a basket of preserved organs in my hands. How the other children were called inside when I tried to make friends. How people looked at me when I talked about marsh fever and infections while they tried to chat about the weather. So I cried and I cried and eventually Father found me a governess and told her to deal with the issue.'

It took an effort not to swear out loud this time. 'I don't suppose she was in favour of dissecting caterpillars?'

Briannis let out a blubbering laugh. 'She informed me ladies did not talk about insects. Or about bones. Or about exotic diseases and their symptoms – actually, not about common diseases either. And she got me new dresses and taught me to do my hair and to curtsy at the right times and ... *everything.*'

'And your father ...'

'Oh, Father loved it once he saw how well I could play the game.' A sad, wistful smile crept up on her lips. 'He kept telling me I was going to get what he never got. I was going to find my home in the city. I was going to belong there. Only when he was dying did I discover how much he'd spent on Mrs. Sedgewick and the dresses and all of it – it was far too much. We didn't even *have* that money. But he was so sure I would find my way in the end ...'

She became silent, staring at the far wall with melancholic, unseeing eyes.

'When did he die?' Moridyr asked cautiously.

'I was seventeen.' She seemed to jolt back into the present time and place with a little shock. 'And utterly destitute, since it turned out he'd spent all we had. But Mrs. Sedgewick referred me to a friend of a friend of a friend and I got a position as a lady's companion. Daughter of the Viscount Templeton. And for a while I believed I was' – she swallowed – 'getting there.'

There being that elusive yet coveted state of acceptability – of being one of *them*, rather than one of those *they* looked down on. She was taking shape in his mind, seventeen-year-old Briannis, perpetually almost there, choosing her steps with the caution of a traveller traversing the treacherous marshes around the city ...

And yet never fully at home

'What changed?' he said.

'Marjorie – the lady I worked for ...' Her jaw twitched. 'She was ... assaulted.'

He knew the tone in which she spoke that word, and his stomach sank an inch. 'Ah.'

'And then she ended up being pregnant. So her father decided she'd have to *marry* the monster.'

There was a tremble of fury in her voice – something far darker, far more dangerous than the glares she'd aimed at him even when he'd threatened her and toyed with her and forced her to speak and eat. This, he realised, was not the Briannis Iavi he'd come to know in those first hours, well-mannered and disapproving of his nonsense. This was Briannis Iavi, healer and saviour of innocent dogs, who would gladly murder a fae king to avenge the ruined women of Elidian.

A new piece of the puzzle fell into place.

'You killed him,' he said.

She met his gaze for the first time since he'd released her, lips tight, head held high, her whole bearing strangely majestic for a woman sitting half-naked in bed with tousled hair tumbling down her shoulders. There was no regret in her eyes. No burning conscience catching up with her. Just plain, simple facts as she said, 'Yes.'

Ruthless – *frighteningly* ruthless, really, if he remembered that he'd been the next victim on her list – and yet he hadn't yet wanted to kiss her as desperately as in that moment.

Instead, he said, 'Was it your idea?'

'Lady Phyllis – Marjorie's mother – mused out loud one morning that it would be very helpful if the wretch would just die. So I told her that may not be as complicated as it seemed.' A faint smile played on her lips, and he wondered if she knew how clear the hint of pride in it was. 'That's the thing about human bodies, you see. If you know how they work, it becomes rather easy to make them stop working, too.'

'Hairpins and poisons?'

Her smile turned wry. 'I didn't even need the poison. Stuck a pin into his eye while he was sleeping, and they never even figured out it was murder. Unexpected death in his sleep, they called it, and that was the end of it – or at least I thought it would be the end of it.'

Moridyr cocked his head. 'I don't suppose he rose from the grave with a pin lodged in his brain?'

'Oh, no.' She looked affronted at the suggestion of having delivered shoddy work. 'Of course not. That pin was lodged firmly in place, His Lordship was dead, and the Viscount couldn't make Marjorie marry him. That was all just as it should be. Except that a year later, a friend of Lady Phyllis was being blackmailed by a fellow who knew her lady-in-waiting was a little more than just a lady-in-waiting to her, and the friend was quite desperate to get rid of her blackmailer. So Lady Phyllis told her she had *just* the solution, and ...'

'You killed another one.'

'I killed another one.' She sighed, tucking a chestnut curl behind her ear as she hesitated for a moment. 'I thought it would just be a little extra money. But then Marjorie caught wind of it and sent me off, because she didn't want to risk involvement if I were to be found out, and then suddenly I *needed* the money.'

Almost there. And then, suddenly, not even close at all.

'I kept it so quiet for such a long time,' she said, her voice strangely distant. 'It was just noble ladies whispering among each other for years. And they never knew it was me – when I met with them, I told them I was just the messenger, that I would pass on their payment and instructions to the real killer. I kept thinking I could find a respectable job soon. But in the end the gossip rags picked up on it, and *then* ...' A joyless little laugh. 'Then it all became even *worse*.'

'The gossip rags are hardly known for their discretion,' Moridyr said dryly.

'They kept giving me these ridiculous nicknames!' She spread her arms, voice taking the loud, dramatic tone of a newspaper boy trying to sell his wares. 'The Widowmaker has struck again! The Lady in Black! The Butcher of Baker's Lane! The Evening Star! The—'

'Wait, wait, wait.' He covered his mouth with his dead hand, unable to suppress the grin creeping up on him. 'The *Evening Star*?'

'Yes.' She glared at him. 'You see, Moridyr, the mysterious murderess rumoured to be an exotic Issian beauty was the last thing the victims saw before the darkness of eternal night engulfed— *Don't* laugh!'

Too late; his amusement was bursting out of him like water breaking through a dam, loud and unstoppable and oddly freeing. Briannis followed after a moment of hesitation – sour, joyless chuckles, but they left her shoulders shaking all the same.

'They are creative,' he managed. 'You have to give them that.'

'It was *terrible!*' She wiped her eyes, suppressing another peal of laughter. 'I'd taken up residence with a landlady who housed half a dozen unmarried young women, and they'd all be discussing it at the breakfast table! I had to look innocent and say things like "Would you please pass me the marmalade, Christabel?" while they were talking about my supposed exotic beauty and how they would *never* involve themselves with murderers. And then at dinner they would ask me what I did all day and I could hardly tell them they'd read it in the papers tomorrow!'

'The Widowmaker and her scalpels,' he said dryly, 'striking again.'

She scoffed. 'Those widows were usually the ones who hired me in the first place. And then one of the idiots betrayed me when she was arrested for the murder of her husband. You should have seen the landlady's face when the city guards dragged me out of the house.'

His chuckle sounded unnatural to his own ears this time. 'And yet you want to take the risk of returning?'

'I miss the parks at springtime,' she said, abruptly quiet again. 'And the cherry waffles they sell in that little stand on East Avenue. And the bookshops on Broad Street and the alleys with the seamstresses' workshops and the sounds of the book presses in the university district. And ...'

She hesitated, hands twisting together nervously. Moridyr stared at her, heart in his throat and stomach heavy like lead – knowing damn well that she would never see or hear or taste any of those things again, and unable to force the words over his lips.

'And Father wanted me to manage,' she whispered, stumbling through the syllables. 'I promised him I would. So really, I need to try. I wouldn't be able to forgive myself if I didn't.'

I'm not sure I could forgive you.

For the first time in three decades, his tongue felt truly dead in his mouth.

If he told her now that there was no going back, she'd loathe staying with him. It was no longer a faint, headache-inducing fear. It was a *certainty*, a fact he could read in the wistful tremble of her smile and the longing in her eyes. She'd hate Faerie. She'd hate the Keep.

In the end, she may grow to hate him, too.

And he would be alone again – might be worse off than when he'd been alone before.

Whereas if he didn't tell her ...

His heart seemed to be beating too slow and too fast at the same time. Was it such a mad idea to keep the secret? He'd sown the first seeds to show her what life could be like here, far away from the city. With enough time, he *could* make her enjoy it. And if she simply decided she wanted to stay in the end, of her own volition, no threats or ultimatums needed ... well, he'd never even need to tell her the truth. He'd never need to break her heart.

So all he had to do was convince her.

All he had to do was be someone she could want.

'Then we'll try,' he heard himself say – not a lie, not when he was fully willing to try, even knowing perfectly well that the roses would not let go of them so easily. 'But first we're going to get you something to eat. Then I suggest you sleep some more. If you feel better tomorrow morning, we can get started on the actual work.'

The gratefulness in her watery smile cut straight through his heart, or through whatever rotten remnant of it was left in his chest. 'Thank you,' she whispered.

For listening? For understanding? For kissing her, or for not kissing her again? For being a selfish bastard and lying to her for his own shallow benefit?

'At your service, morning star,' he said, shoving those doubts aside and holding out his hand to help her out of bed.

Chapter 10

I cannot overstate my disapproval of those who, for their own indelicate amusement, employ sentences which admit a double meaning. This is a distinctive mark of low breeding, and a lady would do well to avoid such persons.

Lady Lockwell's Handbook of Etiquette

BRIANNIS AWOKE TO AN empty bed.

He must have slept beside her, if the dented pillows and the messy blankets could be trusted as witnesses ... but the sun was only just rising, the first orange light peeking in between the ever-present rose vines over the windows, and the king of Faerie was nowhere to be seen. As if he'd made an effort to sneak out without notice. As if he'd tried to avoid her.

Once again, he had not stayed to kiss her awake.

Which should not bother her – which, truly, should do the *opposite* of bother her. And yet she had to admit she was feeling decidedly displeased as she sat up and threw a glance around the room, finding the chairs and windowsills empty as well. After the way he'd listened to her rambling yesterday – after the way he'd fed her dinner and then carried her back to bed – leaving her to wake alone seemed uncourteous to the point of rudeness.

Then again, had she *told* him to stay? Perhaps he'd thought he'd do her a favour, allowing her a few minutes to gather her thoughts after ...

Yesterday.

Yesterday.

She glanced down at her own body as she swung her legs out of bed and felt the heat crawl back onto her cheeks at the memory alone. Eyes making her insides swim. Lips setting her skin on fire. Soft, nimble fingers brushing up her knees and thighs and ...

And *there.*

She'd known the body parts existed, knew the names the books had bestowed upon every bone and muscle and joint in their vicinity, and yet none of those familiar scientific terms seemed in the least sufficient to describe what she'd felt. It was as if he'd taught her a whole new language, one that existed only between the two of them, and had used it to draw every drop of pleasure from her body until she was trembling and gasping and pleading for more. Already she felt like something had shifted inside her. It was small but unspeakably significant all the same – something she hadn't understood before and could never stop understanding now.

What if they don't want to be respectable?

She pushed that thought aside with a shake of her head and stepped out of bed. A question for later. *She* still knew what she wanted, and spending whole days in the pillows wasn't going to bring her any closer to that goal. It was about time she set to work in earnest and found out how to get rid of these blasted roses for long enough to slip out.

When she opened the nearest closet, she found not the coats and breeches she'd expected, but three brand new dresses she hadn't seen before. She picked the one in cornflower blue, adorned with silvery threads that shimmered in the early sunlight. As all the other dresses in this place, it fit like it had been made to her measurements.

A shame she couldn't bring the Keep and its impeccable sense of fashion with her when she returned home.

She shoved that thought from her mind, too.

'I'd like to find the breakfast room,' she said out loud, running her fingers through her hair to smooth out the worst of the tangles. She really ought to pin it into a more appropriate style, but it was oddly liberating to wear it loose. And who would care? Not Moridyr, surely. 'Would you show me the way, please?'

The bedroom door opened itself.

She made her way down the hallway, following the directions the castle provided, her footsteps echoing against the polished quartz floors. To her own surprise, she recognised at least half of the rooms she passed – the one with the wisteria flowers dripping from the ceiling, the one with the cosy reading corner tucked into the back wall, and there was the staircase that led to the dining hall ... Perhaps the Keep wasn't the impossible labyrinth she'd supposed it to be at first. Who knew; if she was forced to stay here long enough, she might just learn to find her own bedroom without getting lost.

The breakfast room was as she'd remembered it from her last visit. Even the poisoned teapot still stood ominously at the centre of the table, as if to ungently remind her of the vial of foxglove she'd emptied into it.

She couldn't suppress a wince at the memory.

But Moridyr was alive and well in his usual chair – or at least as alive as she'd ever known him to be – and his familiar barbed smile showed no trace of renewed resentment. 'I see you've woken early, too?'

'Most unpleasantly, yes,' she informed him, sinking down in the chair she'd occupied at their previous shared breakfast. Somehow, the mere sight of him sent her belly fluttering all over again, brewing a heat at her core that made it disturbingly difficult to form full sentences. 'You once again seem to have forgotten about your promise to kiss me awake in the mornings. I'm almost starting to worry the centuries damaged your memory.'

The small tremor at the living corner of his mouth told her he hadn't forgotten anything. 'Last time I kissed you, you told me to stop.'

'You weren't exactly ...' Her head caught fire again. 'You weren't just *kissing* me.'

'I recall, thank you,' he said dryly. 'Still, I'd rather resist the temptation of your eminently kissable face a few hours longer than run the risk of hurting you. Something to eat? I'd recommend the strawberries – they're quite sweet today.'

'The ...' She blinked at him, then at the plump red fruits beside his plate, trying desperately to drag her thoughts back into the line with this new subject. 'Strawberries?'

He chuckled. 'I do suppose you've heard of them?'

'You know perfectly well that's not the point!' she protested, blushing impossibly harder. 'How can you possibly chat about breakfast and pretend nothing has happened when you ... you ...'

'When I what?' His voice slid back into its most honeyed, most infuriating territory. 'Please tell me what I've done to deserve your ire, morning star.'

It was that nickname that broke the last of her well-mannered resistance, the way it sent shivers into the deepest, most shadowy parts of her. 'You can't just act like you didn't have your *fingers inside me* a few hours ago! That's not something you talk about over strawberries!'

He took a sip of tea. 'You've had your knife inside me too.'

'That,' she said exasperatedly, 'is something *extremely* different.'

'In the sense that I'd be happy to repeat one incident and not the other, yes.' He smiled at her over his teacup, shameless proposals in every flutter of his lashes, in every twitch of his lips. 'In the sense that both murder and sex tend to change one's household dynamics, no. That said, if you'd prefer for me to forget breakfast and reminiscence poetically on the delightful softness of your slit instead, I'll be happy to oblige, of course.'

Heat exploded within her, so violently she forgot how to breathe for a heartbeat or two. 'You ... you ...'

'So,' he said, flicking an elegant gesture at the table, 'strawberries?'

'I'll never be able to look at strawberries the same way again,' she said weakly, plucking the bowl out of the air as it obediently hovered towards her.

'Excellent.' He leaned back in his chair, raising his cup to his lips. 'May they brighten your breakfasts for many years to come.'

Ladies did not roll their eyes at kings, but Briannis very much did. Somehow, the rich, golden sound of his laughter made everything worse and better at the same time.

'So,' she said with as much dignity as she could muster, stabbing her fork into a strawberry with the force she'd used, years ago, to slide a razor-thin blade between a man's vertebrae and skull, 'about those roses.'

He sobered immediately, more swiftly than she'd expected. Surely he had known she would bring up the topic sooner or later?

'Ah. The roses.' The lightness in his voice seemed forced, all of a sudden. 'Please tell me what innovative ideas you've come up with. None of mine have proven to be very valuable over the years.'

'I'm not sure I've been very innovative yet,' Briannis said slowly, 'but it seems to me there are roughly two ways to go about this. You said the roses defend the Keep when they sense the presence of someone capable of harming you, yes?'

He nodded, lips pressed into a firm line.

'So then we need to either make me weak enough to not be a danger or make you strong enough to not be *in* danger. And considering that you already broke my neck to the point of leaving me unconscious and unable to move my limbs, I'm guessing that first strategy won't be terribly effective.'

'Impeccable logic.' There was no whiff of mockery, of that light edge of sarcasm that hovered below most of his words. If anything, he sounded vaguely ... impressed? 'So your proposal is to somehow restore my powers?'

She swallowed. 'It may be ridiculous, but—'

'Briannis,' he interrupted, abruptly sitting straighter, 'if you're saying something ridiculous, I promise you I'll be more than happy to tell you. There's no need to do it yourself before that point. What have you been thinking?'

'It's just that I know so little of your magic and how it works,' she said, turning her fork and the strawberry skewered onto it around between her fingers. 'But the one thought I had was ... Look, you're the physical embodiment of fae magic, aren't you? Your powers are waning, so you are dying. But if that's a true equalisation, shouldn't it work both ways? Shouldn't you

161

regain some of your powers if you're in better physical shape, too?'

He stared at her, teacup hanging motionless in his fingers halfway between his lips and the table.

'Feel free to tell me if it's a nonsensical thought,' she added nervously, sticking the strawberry into her mouth just so she'd have an excuse to look down. It was sinfully sweet as the juices exploded on her tongue. 'I just—'

'It's not a nonsensical thought.' He sounded almost curt. 'It's very much a healer's thought, I suppose. I never considered looking at it that way.'

'Do you think ...' She swallowed the fruit, fighting the desperate spark of hope in her chest. 'Do you think it might work?'

'No,' he said wryly.

The spark sizzled out. She numbly said, 'Oh.'

'But you may have noticed I'm not the greatest of optimists,' he added, a bitter twist to his smile now. 'So don't despair yet. We may as well spend a while trying.'

'Oh.' It came out a little less pathetic this time. 'Well, if you don't mind ...'

'The worst that could happen is that I'll feel a little less dead by the time you're done,' he said, raising an eyebrow at her. 'Speaking of which, you weren't finished experimenting on me with your lavender brew. I'm afraid that between your near-death and several more pleasant developments, I haven't had the mind to pay much attention to my pain levels, but if we were to continue our testing for a few more days ...'

She snorted before she could stop herself. 'You expect me to apply it for you again, don't you?'

The glance he gave her was about as innocent as any corpse's glance could be. 'Well, if you happened to volunteer, I wouldn't *stop* you, of course.'

'How very magnanimous of you.' She popped another strawberry into her cheek, then crossed her arms. 'And what is in it for me, if I may ask?'

'Oh,' he said smugly, 'I'm confident I can make the work very much worth your while if you let me, morning star.'

It was so easy, this game – so alarmingly easy. 'Grand words for a man incapable of lying.'

'I'm still capable of being mistaken, of course,' he said, clearly not expecting to be from the way he quirked his eyebrow at her. 'We'll never know if we don't try. Aren't you excited about this opportunity to prove me a vain, arrogant bastard?'

'Ah,' Briannis said, pointing her fork at him. 'You're saying this is really just ... research.'

'Nothing but research.' Even the dead half of his face looked alive in the brightening morning light, the brittle skin crinkling at his eye, the curve of his leathery lips almost mischievous. 'Are you willing to take the risk for the sake of science?'

'With a heavy heart.' She sighed, butchering another strawberry. 'Truly, a very heavy heart.'

She did not get a lot of research done that day.

Covering Moridyr in her salve of beeswax and lavender was a thoroughly distracting endeavour, from the involuntary moans he didn't manage to suppress to the far more deliberate innuendos he muttered in between breaths. By the time she was done with him, her skin was glowing with the warmth of a thousand fires, and she couldn't produce even the thinnest of objections when he pulled her into his lap and kissed her.

Somehow, they wasted a day making salves and feeding each other strawberries. She crawled into his bed that evening with the dutiful resolve to spend her time on more fruitful tasks tomorrow.

Except that his dead skin needed tending to all over the next day, and rubbing the lavender mixture onto his lean back and chest and shoulders was far too enjoyable to allow him to take care of the task himself. Still, she managed an earnest proposal to look for afflictions similar to his in the grand libraries of the Keep afterwards, and even made it halfway to the room in question. After that promising start, however, she made the mistake of answering just a challenge or two too many and suddenly found herself deep into a competitive game of lawn bowls on the plush carpet of the Purple Salon. She won the game three times in a row, and somehow that seemed far more significant than the undeniable fact she had still not made any noteworthy progress by the time evening fell.

It was alright, she comforted herself as she lay curled up in Moridyr's bed that night, his arm around her but not touching any skin below the safe shield of her chemise. Healing was slow work; Father had repeated it to her so many times. There was only so much she could do while she tried new medicines and waited for them to take effect.

And if all of this was temporary anyway, she might as well enjoy the time she had left in the Keep.

She made it to the library on the third day, and even found a book on magical afflictions – which was, unfortunately, so utterly riveting that she did not make it out of the first chapter without needing three more handbooks and encyclopaedias to elaborate on every word she read. Evening fell without warning while she was still trying to figure out how much a fae disease called *trahaër* had to do with the Elidian marsh fever. Of her three full pages of scribbled notes, not a single word concerned the mystery of half-dead fae kings and how to heal them.

'See,' she told Moridyr over dinner, forgetting to use the right knives and forks in between her gesticulations, 'if they are somehow related, of *course* we're unable to find a cure for the issue with simple mortal medicine. Not that I think we'll easily convince the Elidian burghers to accept fae medicines instead, but—'

'If you wish to find yourself outlawed a second time,' he said dryly, 'this would probably be an excellent place to start. Cyril isn't going to allow any positive news on magic to spread.'

She stabbed the tender piece of meat on her plate, pulling a face. 'If His Excellence wants to stand between me and a cure for marsh fever, he'll have to keep a very good eye on his neck for the years to come.'

'At times,' Moridyr said, looking amused, 'I'm quite happy I'm at least locked up with you *here*, morning star. I would be far more nervous anywhere else.'

The fact that it couldn't be a lie was the most bewildering part of that remark. 'Because you can still stop me here?'

'Exactly.' His smile turned sour. 'Imagine: outside you could throw as many knives at me as you wished, and I would only have my considerable charms at my disposal to stop you.'

Reasonably, Briannis flipped her knife around in her hand and threw it at him. It missed him by at least two feet and hit one of the antler candelabras behind his head instead, clattering to the floor with a noise that could have woken a slumbering mountain. A week ago, she would have flinched. Now, somehow, it felt tremendously satisfying to be loud and utterly unashamed – to not make herself small and vulnerable once again.

Moridyr threw his head back and laughed, and that felt even better.

'Knife-throwing isn't exactly part of the average surgeon's repertoire,' she said mournfully, asking the Keep for a new knife in her thoughts. It appeared next to her plate with a flicker of hesitation, as if the castle warned her not to aim any projectiles at its lord again. 'I think you're safe for now.'

He chuckled. 'Want to learn?'

'Learn ... what?'

'How to throw a knife more decently?' He pressed his long fingers together, his smile a devilish challenge. 'We do have some portraits I'm not all that eager to keep unharmed, and frankly, I feel any assassin worth her salt should be able to at least hit an elephant with a knife.'

She narrowed her eyes at him – a frightening vision at the opposite head of the table, but frightening in an elegant, sophisticated way, radiating the threat of words and magic rather than brawn and muscle. 'Are you saying *you* could hit an elephant with a knife?'

He held out a dead-fingered hand with a gesture so graceful it blurred the lines of affected, beckoning at the knife she'd just launched into the grand room beyond him. The weapon obediently flew into his grip.

He swung once.

The blade whizzed over the table, past Briannis, and landed with a visceral smack in the wall behind her back. When she whipped around, she found it buried two inches between the eyes of the imposing portrait that hung between the primroses and white acacias.

'Great-uncle Nerion,' Moridyr said dryly. 'Never liked him much anyway.'

And so Briannis spent most of the fourth day in one of the Keep's broad galleries, throwing daggers at the pompous face of the last Issian king before the Alchemists' Revolution while Moridyr delivered a continuous stream of commentary on foot positioning and the angle of her elbow. The fifth morning, she woke with hurting muscles all over her arms and torso, and this time Moridyr was the one to play the healer's role, rubbing coneflower oil into her skin until the pain subsided.

One thing led to another. They spent most of the day on the broad royal bed, laughing and teasing, exchanging caresses and kisses as if the roses weren't still crawling ominously over the windows.

It shouldn't be so easy to start feeling at home in a place that could, by definition, never be hers – a place that belonged to another people, to a magic she didn't possess, to a world she could never be part of. She barely *knew* Moridyr, for goodness' sake. Not in the way she knew Elidian, where her feet avoided every protruding cobblestone instinctively, where she could tell her location by the smells of the restaurants and the sounds of the workplaces even with her eyes closed. The Keep may be beautiful, and intriguing, and filled with a luxury she'd never imagined in her life ... but it still had doors she wasn't allowed to open.

And its lord might laugh with her, might kiss her and appreciate her company, but he'd told her blunt and simple that he'd never love her.

She wasn't considering settling for that, was she?

She climbed to the highest tower of the castle on the sixth day, winding staircase after winding staircase, until even the flowers no longer grew over the walls and only thick layers of cobwebs covered the ceiling. In nothing but a thin silk dress, the world was icily cold there, half a mile above the mountaintops themselves. But even in the top room, a bleak cell barely six feet in all directions, the roses still circled the windows, ready to stop her if she tried to stick so much as a hand outside.

If she squinted, she could just make out the drab green of the marshes at the horizon. The place where Father's body lay cold in the ground, waiting for her.

She'd promised him.

Her fists clenched by her side, the memory so much more tangible away from the glitter and splendour of Rosethorn Keep.

Father *did* love her. He'd wanted her to be happy. He'd wanted her to succeed in his place. So she'd damn well show them, the people who had laughed at him and ridiculed him, who had left him to die on that ratty straw mattress after all the lives he'd saved – she'd prove them wrong about the Iavi name, about little barbarian girls destined for the gutter. They'd wanted her to be powerless? Then she'd return and be the most powerful of them all, the woman who'd looked into the eyes of death and returned, who understood a world the masses of Elidian still cowered from.

She'd figure out the riddle of the blasted roses. She'd say her goodbyes to this wondrous prison, to the curses and blessings of magic, to the man who was still little more than a stranger below the dangerous, dazzling allure.

And then she'd go home.

Chapter 11

In the face of a friend's grief, a lady must exhibit heart-felt consideration and sympathy, offering every possible comfort to the best of her ability.
Lady Lockwell's Handbook of Etiquette

IN THE DAYS THAT followed, Briannis finally found a steadier rhythm within the confines of Rosethorn Keep.

She spent her mornings poring over ancient manuscripts, trying to decipher the vernacular and illustrations of a science she knew only from the human perspective, looking for any information on magic-induced diseases. At the midday meal, they discussed her findings. Her afternoons were the designated time for knife training and exploration of the Keep, so that after a second week, she was finally capable of finding her way from one side of the castle to the other without asking the building itself for help. Treating Moridyr's dead skin with an ever more complicated salve of herbs and infused oils, finally, was a task she'd scheduled for the evenings: she'd soon learned it was the last sensible thing she'd do for the day no matter the hour. Something about him made it utterly impossible to stop touching him once she'd started.

And then he'd sweep her into his arms and carry her to his bed and, sweet divines, *kiss* her – kiss her every night as if it was the very first time all over again, as if he'd hungered for her lips all day the way he'd hungered for her touch for fourteen long years. Minutes melted into hours under his mouth and finger-tips. And *she* melted with them, turned into some creature of fire and desire under his clever hands – found herself craving every breath, every caress, every murmured word of admiration as if there was nothing in the world but him.

She learned the sensitive spots beneath his jaw and collar-bones. She learned the little moan he'd grant her when she nipped at his earlobe just so. She learned the silky feel of his long red hair around her fingers and the leathery softness of dead lips against her thumb, the scrape of his nails along her spine and the taste of his skin on her tongue ... as if he was untrodden land to be charted and she was his own chosen ex-plorer, finding treasures wherever she went.

He'd unpin her hair. He'd take off her dress. He'd wrap her in his arms and nuzzle her shoulder, stroke her belly, and hold her until she fell asleep.

Not once did he try to resume what they'd started that first time in his bed, fingers sliding into places she'd never even *dreamed* of before.

'I have my pride, morning star,' he dryly said when she asked him one night, drowsy from the heat of his kisses. 'It's no fun performing for an unappreciative audience. If you're not beg-ging me, I'm waiting.'

'You and your fun,' she grumbled.

He'd laughed and pulled her closer to his chest, kissing her cheek and neck and shoulders until she couldn't help herself and moaned.

Days grew into weeks. The weeks grew into half a month and then a full month, occasions she marked with an oddly detached sense of resignation. Her salve began to yield results and soothe the dry ache of Moridyr's skin; her literature study, on the other hand, was frustratingly useless. The roses stayed in place. The Keep remained a lavish, glittering prison.

It was two days after the first month mark that she woke up in the middle of the night alone.

He always woke early in the mornings; she was accustomed to finding the bed empty at dawn. But at night? She sat up, her own tiredness abruptly gone – at night he was *always* there, a mere twitch of her hand away, ready to pull her back into his arms every time she stirred. Where had he gone? The bathroom?

But the door to the bathroom was open, and she didn't hear a sound.

'Moridyr?' she whispered.

No answer.

'Moridyr?' She swung her feet out of bed, all traces of her dreams evaporating as the first tendrils of concern got hold of her. 'Are you here?'

Once again, the room remained silent. And only then did she see his boots, black and meticulously polished, still neatly in their place beside the nightstand.

Had he walked out into the castle barefoot?

But he *never* left his bedroom half-dressed. No matter how hard she tried to muss him up in the mornings, she'd never seen him walk into the open castle without boots and coat and cravat, hair brushed and preferably bound together. A rule he'd set for himself in the first lonely days at the Keep, he'd told her: the only way to make sure he wouldn't end up neglecting himself within weeks.

And yet ... his boots.

Briannis hurried to the door and peered out into the corridor. No sign of life to be seen. So what was she supposed to do, then – go out and find him? He was a grown man. He'd survived half her lifetime in solitary confinement, and several centuries before that time. Surely he didn't need a little human assassin running after him to drag him back into bed if he might just be taking a walk to shake off the sleepless thoughts?

But to crawl back beneath the covers now, with the pangs of worry twinging in her guts ...

She drew in a deep breath and slipped into the moonlit castle. Around her, the familiar outlines of the Keep played strange games with shadows, turning rooms she knew into haunted versions of themselves. A cold draft slid below her chemise, and she shivered, cursing herself for not bringing a shawl along.

She barely knew the castle well enough to find him by day. How in the world was she going to locate him in the dark of night?

'Could you lead me to him?' she whispered at the ceiling. 'I'm worried.'

Nothing happened for an excruciating heartbeat or two.

Then the door on the far side of the room inched open.

As she rushed forward, she imagined for a moment that she felt a pulse of some almost human emotion oozing from the walls around her – as if the Keep was answering her plea with a plea in return, the worry of an old but powerless friend slipping into her veins. Just a moment, and then it was gone, brief enough to make her wonder if it hadn't merely been her own concern clouding her thoughts.

But she wouldn't feel so possessively protective of the king of Faerie himself, would she?

Questions for later. She shook them away, slipping through the chink of the door and hurrying towards the next one opening on the other side of the corridor. To the left, past the lamp in the giant snail shell. Through the tunnel of branches and up the winding stairs that circled around the majestic statue of a winged wyvern. It was then that she realised, with a jolt, where the castle was taking her.

The locked door.

The maimed bodies of my dead wives.

That had been a joke, hadn't it? He hadn't stated it as a fact, just as a question; it did not have to be true. It *couldn't* be true. He wasn't that sort of man.

And yet her feet faltered. Because there had to be a reason he wouldn't tell her what lay beyond the door, and reasonably speaking, it could hardly be a flattering one. If he *was* hiding some gruesome secret, some shadowy part of his past ... did she even want to know?

Again that strange, foreign sensation of worry vibrated through her.

And then she was running, damn the jokes and the ominous truths, because he'd held her and kissed her and now he was wandering through a pitch-dark castle on bare feet ... Chemise fluttering around her knees, she whirled around corners, jumped down flights of stairs, bit away the cold of an open window. There it was, that wooden door with the black rose burned into its surface—

Open.

And behind it ...

There were no corpses. No captive princesses. Not even any exotic or forbidden flowers.

As she stumbled to a standstill in the narrow corridor, all the saw in the silvery light of the waxing moon was a small, simple bed, neatly made with many-coloured pillows. A wooden sword. A knitted, cat-sized dragon. A desk full of books she recognised with a single glance – schoolbooks, the standard works on history and language Father had owned since his own childhood.

The realisation rose in her like a cresting ice-cold wave.

A child's room.

It was a *child's* room Moridyr was sitting in, cross-legged on the plush, worn carpet, his slender back to the door. A child that must have lived at Rosethorn Keep. A child she'd never heard him as much as breathe about, who wasn't currently here with him – who couldn't have been here in a long time.

A child he must have loved.

Something started crumbling in the back of her mind.

He didn't want her here. What was she doing, intruding on this little sanctuary, a place of memories he hadn't chosen to share with her? If it wasn't guilt that had closed this door to her but rather pain and grief, she should be sneaking back into bed and hoping he hadn't noticed—

'Briannis?' he said.

In the unmoving darkness, even his voice did not sound like his own – too quiet, too fragile. She froze where she stood, heart hammering wildly against her ribs.

'I'm sorry,' she breathed. 'I was worried. If you want me to leave ...'

'Please ...' The word cracked a little. 'Please don't leave.'

The pit in her stomach gaped wider.

He seemed so unusually frail in the moonlight, shoulders slumped and red locks tangling around his bent head, his frame covered by nothing but a loose black dressing gown. Where was the unbreakable armour of his wry sarcasm? The sharp wit, the unwavering control? She risked one step closer, as if he were a wounded animal that might bite at any moment – then another step when he didn't object, and another, until she stood in the doorway of that small room, breathing in the smell of coarse wool and parchment. There was no grand magic splendour here. No royal lustre created to impress. Just a safe, cosy place, a room where a child might find solace from the world outside.

'It's his birthday,' Moridyr added on a whisper, as if he'd heard the questions she didn't speak. 'It's always worst on his birthday.'

Her heart was brittle glass, cracking further at every word. 'Was he ... was he yours?'

'My nephew.' It came out flatly, heavily. 'But I raised him since he was a little boy. Couldn't have loved him more if he was my own.'

Past tense. She clawed her nails into her palms in the silence that fell, fighting the words crowding her tongue. Could she ask? She *had* to ask, and yet the question felt too harsh, too brusque, when she finally managed to get it past her lips. 'What happened to him?'

'He left,' Moridyr said quietly. 'To save the world. Like young boys do, I suppose.'

Her shoulders sagged in premature relief. Then the rest of his answer hit, the self-reproach and the bitterness, and once again the breath caught in her throat as understanding dawned.

'You let him go to the city.' It wasn't a question this time. 'To Elidian.'

He swallowed audibly. 'Yes.'

Into the viper's nest. Into the place that tried its hardest to wipe out every trace of Faerie within its walls, the city where the Mirror Queen's spies roamed the streets and where the Princeps' guards wouldn't hesitate to draw their swords at even the faintest rumour of magic. She imagined a small, red-haired fae boy trekking across the marches, bag on his shoulders and steely resolve in his heart ...

That had to be at least fourteen years ago. It had been fourteen years since the last inhabitant of Rosethorn Keep had left. And the world hadn't yet been saved.

'He's careful,' Moridyr muttered, sounding as if he was trying to convince himself more than her. 'And damn clever. And ... not actually a child anymore, I suppose. But he's in terrible danger all the same, and I'm sitting here in this fucking palace and there's *nothing* I can do to help, *nothing* I can do to save him—'

She moved instinctively, a reflex of the heart more than muscles. Two steps forward. To her knees. Moridyr abruptly went quiet as she wrapped her arms around his shoulders and pressed him against her chest, burying her face in the silky warmth of his hair. His long fingers clutched her wrists, as if the mere touch could bring back that little boy of decades ago.

The sound that struggled from his throat was half-sigh, half-sob, a whimper of utter helplessness.

It was in that moment that Briannis knew she'd been a fool.

A stubborn, delusional fool, to deny what she should have known the first moment he'd pressed his lips to hers: that there would be no forgetting this man. That she didn't *want* to forget him. That his weaponised smiles and tender touches had become a part of her as essential as Father's books and Mrs. Sedgewick's rules, and that a few dozen miles between them would change nothing about that – that she could go home, but she could never return to the woman she'd been before.

Most of all, that she couldn't stand to watch him suffer in her arms for a single heartbeat more.

'Moridyr,' she whispered, holding him tighter. 'Come back to bed with me.'

She didn't know what she'd have done if he had refused, but to her relief, he moved the moment the words left her mouth – as if he'd been waiting for that little nudge, for *anything* to tear him away from his memories. He rose with familiar ease when she released him. Somehow, even weary and grieving, even barefoot and dressed in nothing but a simple silk dressing gown, he managed to look unbearably regal, his unkempt long hair falling over his dead shoulder like a cascade of pure copper. Only as he turned did she see his face. The lost gleam in his green eye and the haunted hollowness of the other, and—

And the traces of tears glistening on his living cheek in the moonlight.

Tears. From the man who'd rather turn himself into a villain than suffer the role of the victim in her story. From the beautiful, beautiful monster who'd told her he'd never love or need her.

She held out her hand, and he grabbed it like a lifeline.

'Come,' she whispered.

He followed her in silence through the dark castle, the only sound the soft padding of their feet on the marble floors. Briannis's heart was fluttering in the very tips of her fingers. In the soles of her feet. Her skin prickled below the flimsy caresses of her chemise, warm and cold at once – not a feeling of fear or nervousness, bur rather the sensation of being about to pull a door shut she'd never be able to open again.

The bedroom waited, unchanged. She sensed the Keep again as she stepped over the threshold, sure now that it wasn't her own mind nuzzling at her consciousness like a shy but curious dog. It was not a sensation of worry, this time, but rather of wary caution.

It's alright, she told the castle, hoping it was true. *I have him, now. You can look away.*

The feeling vanished.

She pulled Moridyr to the bed, settling him on the edge with what felt like healer's firmness more than seductress's charm. Then she knelt before him.

177

And started to pry open the knots of his robe with quick, trembling fingers.

His eyes widened, surprise breaking through the haze of grief and fatigue. 'What are you—'

'Hush,' she told him, pulling apart ribbons of black silk. The motions came so mind-bogglingly easily – as if *this* was what she was born to do, not healing, not killing, but comforting fae kings in the dead of night. It didn't leave room for doubt, this strange sense of rightness. It left room only for that desolate void in his eyes, and for all she wanted him, *needed* him to feel instead. 'I'm taking care of you. Let me take this off.'

'But I'm not wearing—'

'I suspected that.' She felt almost giddy as she tugged at his hand, the last thing keeping the dark cloth in place. 'Utterly scandalous. Absolutely unheard of. Are *you* going to make a fuss about propriety now?'

He didn't move his arm, blinking at her, pinning his dressing gown firmly against his chest. 'I'm trying to make a fuss about your wishes, Briannis.'

'Which is very gallant,' she muttered, 'but as you told me, wishes can change.'

He froze.

For an instant, he sat motionless on the edge of the mattress, staring at her as if he had never seen her before – as if she was some delicate flower, destined to wilt as soon as he touched its fragile petals. Thoughts visibly spun behind his eyes, turning her words over and over in his mind. Trying to find another meaning. Another implication. Anything but what the burning warmth of her body was telling her – that message she'd ignored so stubbornly for weeks and weeks on end.

'You said you didn't want to remember,' he finally managed, his voice rough. 'So if this is an attempt to distract me, I suggest you find another method – because if you continue like this, I'll make very damn sure you remember every single minute of this night for the rest of your life, morning star.'

Heat flared hotter at her core, so violently she almost gasped. 'Good.'

Eyes narrowing, he lowered his head towards her. Something sharpened in the air around him with that motion – a flicker of the beast below his skin, something that wasn't cruelty but rather a promise of raw, ruthless pleasure. It was a sharpening that did away with all grief and fear and helplessness. A sharpening that was nothing but the pure, undiluted thrill of the hunt.

'Good?' he said softly.

'I've realised a thing or two,' she whispered, and she couldn't tell whether the smile that rose upon her face was wistful or joyful – only that it may be the most genuine smile her lips had shaped in her life. 'The first of which is that I don't want to forget you.'

In the depths of his eyes, she could see the exact moment her words landed, the exact moment he realized the gravity of what she was saying. His lips parted, but no sound escaped. She could feel his hot breath on her skin now, their faces a mere few inches apart.

A mere few inches to the point of no return.

'And the second?' he murmured, his hand holding his dressing gown tight enough to turn even the living knuckles white.

She let go of his forearm, reaching up instead to wrap her fingers around his collar. Below his ribs, his heart was a frantic rattle, echoing the dizzying pulse of her blood in her veins.

'The second ...' She ran a fingertip down his neck, the spot that never failed to make him squirm. He let out a choked groan, every muscle straining with need as she made her way down to his shoulder. 'The second realisation is that I really don't want you capable of thinking for the rest of the night.'

He didn't move, but his breath came in short, shallow gasps now.

'I promise you I'm not doing this for you,' she added with a breathless chuckle. '*I* want to learn. *I* want to feel. So if you want me to stop, just say the word – but if it's only my innocence you're worried about, I'm all yours.'

His eyes fluttered shut, jaw twitching. 'Please say that again.'

'I'm all yours,' she breathed.

'And if I tell you ...' His voice lowered to a dark, ominous purr, a warning as much as a promise. 'If I tell you that I've been thinking about that delicious little body of yours for weeks on end, that I've dreamed up a thousand different ways to make you come screaming in my arms, and that I'm not sure I'll let you out of my sight before I've tried and tested every single one of them – would you say it again?'

Her hands were shaking – her knees were shaking – she was quite sure even her heart itself was shaking – but her whispered words came out level and without hesitation. 'Still all yours.'

'Then by all means,' he murmured, finally releasing the silk he'd held pressed to his chest, 'go on and wipe every gods-damned thought from this gods-damned mind of mine, morning star.'

She brushed the dressing gown off his shoulders.

This part of him she knew all too well, angular shoulders and sharply drawn ribs, skin she'd had under her hands more often than she could count now. Still kneeling between his thighs, she let her hands run down over his chest, his stomach, slowing down as she passed his navel and the asymmetric trail of hair below. The silk pooled in his lap and around his hips. Uncharted territory. *Dangerous* territory.

Or so she'd thought.

She leaned forward and pressed her lips to the line between firm abdominal muscles and pale, gaunt skin. He tasted of salt and luscious sin, a flavour that could rival every delicious dish she'd ever eaten.

His moan made her belly clench so tight it hurt.

She trailed her lips down an inch, kissed him again, and drank in the sound of his catching breath. Another inch down; this time, her lips grazed the red trail of hair below his navel. On either side of her, his hands had fisted in the blankets, shaking with restraint, but a small moan was all that escaped him as she sank even lower.

She flicked out her tongue, tasting him, making him gasp. 'You're holding back.'

'I'm trying not to scare you,' he ground out through gritted teeth. 'You do realise I'm half-dead *all over*, don't you? It would be ...' His breath caught again. 'It would be most unfortunate for my self-esteem if you got the vapours at the sight of me.'

With a laugh, she moved farther down.

Through smooth, ink-black silk, her mouth found the hard length below his dressing gown, bulging against the cloth like a prisoner desperate to escape. Moridyr cursed. His erection twitched towards her. And then his fingers were in her hair, pressing her down, grabbing the strands so tightly that tears welled in her eyes ... She barely felt the pain. The surge of power washed out everything else she could feel – power and the over-whelming, all-encompassing feeling of being exactly where she ought to be.

In a burst of courage, she pulled his robe away.

The silk slid off him like a slithering serpent, revealing his body in all its grotesque glory for the very first time – the mus-culature of his thighs, the skin-over-bone of his dead hip, and at the very centre of it all ...

The imposing length jutting up from a wreath of coppery curls, begging for her attention.

For one moment, it wasn't just lust that made her wrap her fingers around him.

Sweet divines, but it was such a *fascinating* instrument, these six inches of rock-hard flesh twitching and trembling in her palm ... She gave it a little squeeze, delighted by the way it jolted back in response. One side of it was ruddy and throbbing with life, closest to the descriptions she'd found in Father's books. But the other was mortally pale, almost translucent, so that the veins below its surface stood out like marble veins – just a little colder, she noted reflexively, although no less turgid than the living side. Would it be numb to the touch? But when she ran a finger along the rim of the living half, then the dead half, she received two very similar strangled moans in return.

'Not numb, then,' she concluded out loud.

His laugh was more growl than laugh. 'I can assure you neither side is anywhere near numb, Briannis.'

'Well, that's good news.' She bent over, studying the object in her hand from up close in the near-dark. The small red hairs at the base. The slightly ridged skin, the smooth head. Moisture was leaking from the little slit at the top, just waiting to be tasted – so taste him she did, flicking her tongue over the gleaming skin, lapping up the salty, briny flavour.

He let out a throaty groan, the sound more animal than fae, as his fingers pulled tighter in her hair.

'Not numb,' she repeated with a giggle and kissed him again.

There was so much to discover here, so much to explore – the warm, velvety texture against her tongue. The taste of him, salty at the tip and muskier at the base. The way his veins pulsed under her fingers as she gingerly brushed along the hard shaft, and sweet divines, the *sounds* he was making, the involuntary shudders of his hips shifting towards her ... She kissed. She licked. She nuzzled and sucked and stroked, cataloguing his every response and reaction, revelling in the glorious power of it.

'Briannis.' His fingers tightened in her hair. And his *voice* ... Oh, her body turned scorching hot and soft at the sound of it, all rasp and gravel, all unravelling restraint. 'Briannis, unless you want me to spend all over you ...'

She looked up, lips swollen and sensitive, her fingers still wrapped around his girth. He sat watching her with eyes that shone like molten onyx and emerald, his chest heaving, his teeth clenched on his lower lip. His skin seemed too small for the power straining below. Like a cage about to snap. Like a predator about to break free.

'It's probably not very ladylike,' she suggested hoarsely, smoothing the pad of her thumb over the throbbing red vein that ran along the topmost side of his shaft. 'Getting spent all over yourself, I mean.'

He sucked in a sharp breath. 'Briannis.'

She laughed and took him back into her mouth.

As deep as she could, this time, tongue twisting around his slick head, fingers cradling the base of his length ... Something tightened under her touch. She sucked hard, and he cursed, and that wonderful tightening sensation of his hardness deepened. His fingers wrapped around the back of her nape, keeping her in place as his hips began to buck towards her – deeper and deeper and ...

His cry was a surrender. A liberation.

Waves and waves of hot, sticky seed pulsed into her mouth as he convulsed around her, thighs clenching tight, nails clawing into her nape and shoulders. She swallowed. She swallowed again. The sweet-bitter taste filled her throat until she didn't think she'd ever taste anything else again – the, glorious unmistakable flavour of victory.

'*Briannis*,' he groaned again, and the sound of her name made her toes curl against the floor.

The fingers in her hair pulled back her head, forcing her to let go of his hard flesh in her mouth. She didn't want to release him. She wanted to play with him until night turned into day, wanted to discover every little thing that made him howl and squirm and curse ... But his shaking fingers slid from her hair to her waist and lifted her off the floor, into his lap, against the rapid rise and fall of his muscular chest.

She rested her forehead against his dead shoulder, pressing quick kisses to every rib she could reach.

'I hope you know,' he murmured, lips brushing over her earlobe, 'how much I'm going to enjoy taking my revenge for that, sweetheart.'

Her skin seemed to have laid itself bare in a way it never had before, the merest touch enough to make her shudder violently. She felt every shift of his thighs beneath her bottom. Every whisper of cloth over her back and shoulders. Every brush of his fingers as they travelled down along her spine, to where the hem of her chemise had skirted itself up around her hips.

A moan escaped her as he stripped the flimsy fabric off her, finally baring all of her body to the silver moonlight.

And then his mouth was on hers, conquering and demanding, fingers tightening around her neck to lock her against him. Whatever words she'd dreamed of saying turned to mush in her mind. He claimed her mouth with a hunger that banished all rational thought, reducing her to instinct and primal sensations – to lips and tongue and this burning, melting need between her thighs, places where she *needed* to feel his fingers again ... She wrapped her legs around his hips instinctively, grinding herself against him. Her reward was his growl against her mouth, the hot shudder of his cock jolting back to life.

'Please,' she gasped, barely knowing what she was begging for.

'Patience, morning star.' His fingers slid along her inner thigh, squeezing and teasing, until they reached that fiery spot where she was hungering, *hurting* for him. His first stroke between her inner lips was torturous relief, winding her even tighter. 'I'm going to fuck you soon, I promise. Good and hard and deep. But you're so gods-damned tight and I don't want to hurt you ... So you're going to come for me first, do you understand?'

'Yes,' she breathed. It was a miracle she managed to get even a single word out; her body was throbbing with a need that left little room for speech. *'Please.'*

'Should have known you would be so very polite,' he murmured against her neck. His fingers slid through the wetness pooling between her thighs, found her entrance, and dipped in. A moan wrestled free from her lungs, and he chuckled. 'Do you want more of that?'

'Yes.' She was clinging to the last edges of her sanity, nails into his shoulders. 'Yes, yes, *yes.*'

He paused. 'You're forgetting something, sweetheart.'

'Please,' she got out. 'Please, I need—'

'I know what you need.' One finger slid deeper, and she squeezed her eyes shut and clung to that sensation, that perfect, slick invasion as he moved into her. His voice was the last steady rock in her spinning world, a little light guiding her through the storm. 'You need me to take you until you can't remember your own name. You need to feel my cock stretching you open, need it so deep inside you that you can barely breathe anymore. Don't worry. It's coming soon.'

Soon wasn't enough, she wanted to tell him. Didn't he know how she was *burning* – how he was only making it worse, teasing his finger in and out of her, fanning the ache for the raw abandon he promised? But she could no longer find the words to argue. A guttural moan was all that left her mouth, containing everything she craved, things she'd never felt but recognised the moment he whispered the words into her ear.

'You're so beautiful, Briannis.' His thumb rubbed the spot that made her frantic, adding to the symphony of sizzling nerves. 'I've dreamed of you for weeks, and somehow you're still more beautiful than I ever thought you could be ...'

Blindly, she found his mouth and kissed him, gasping, pleading wordlessly for relief. He slid a second finger into her, and then a third, stretching her open for him as his thumb continued to stroke that sensitive bud between her lips.

She was lost. She was ruined. She didn't give a damn anymore.

Release found her suddenly and devastatingly. Like a shattering glass, the bubble of tension broke, and pleasure washed over her as she clenched around his fingers – waning only slowly while she slumped against his shoulder, moaned his name again and again and again. He held her as she sobbed with bliss in his embrace. Held her as the world spun violently around her. Held her, still whispering precious words into her ear, as he lifted her from his lap and eased her down in the blankets.

'More?' he murmured, settling himself over her.

He was already hard again – sweet divines, she could have sworn he'd somehow grown *larger* in these few minutes. The pale half of him seemed hewn from marble, resting against her wet, sticky thigh as she looked down her body.

'More,' she whispered.

He took himself in hand as he supported himself on his other elbow, sliding the smooth head of his erection between her thighs. Back and forth. Back and forth. Her entrance clenched around that silken friction every time he passed, and she no longer cared how large he was – just that he had to be inside her *now* and that he was nowhere near yet ... She grabbed for him, trying to make him hold still as her own hips bucked up. He laughed, moving away.

'*Damn* you!' she panted, dropping her hand.

'Did you just swear at me, morning star?' He tilted his hips so that the length of his shaft slid between her lips. Long, red hair tickled her shoulder and breast as he lowered his head to kiss her. 'I must be better at this than I thought. Anything else I can make you say while the madness lasts?'

'You said ...' She barely had breath enough to shape the words. 'You said you were going to ... to ...'

For one moment she thought it was enough. He slid between her legs again, then found her entrance and pushed inside – just a little. Just the barest tip. Just enough to make every muscle in her body clench and spasm around the invasion.

Then he pulled back.

'What did I say?' he muttered sweetly, trailing his lips along her jaw.

'You said you'd fuck me!' she burst out – and oh, it felt *good*, the unforgivable vulgarity of that word on her lips. It felt like wrestling free. It felt like sinking a knife between Mrs. Bartlett's third and fourth rib in that little shed behind the neighbours' house. So she came up on her elbows and kissed him and said it again, in little gasps against his lips. 'I want you to fuck me. I need you to fuck me. I'm going to kill you if you don't—'

His laughter was like sunlight, warming every inch of her skin. 'In that case, my fearsome little dagger ...'

He pressed into her again.

And this time he didn't stop.

He sank into her slowly, so slowly, until she was sure there couldn't possibly be more of him and yet he kept going, filling her until she thought she would burst around him. It wasn't pain, the sensation that flooded her. It was fullness. It was *completeness*. It was him, so much of him that she could weep with it ... But he was all the way in now, and slowly her body adjusted around his girth, preparing for what was to come.

Then he moved.

Fullness morphed into friction, a long, slick slide out of her followed by – *oh* – another intrusion, another wondrous thrust into her body. She cried out. He thrust again. And then he was truly fucking her, deep, lazy strokes that began to build a whole new wave of tension inside her, driving moans from her lips with every motion. His ...

His cock?

Could she call it a cock?

But it *was* a cock, to the blazes with it – not a *length* or a *member* or even a *manhood*, just a proud, powerful cock thrusting into her over and over and over again. Gasping, she clenched her thighs around his hips again, pressing herself closer. His hiss of pleasure was the only approval she needed. Her hands tangled in his hair, wrapping long strands of pure silk around her fingers, and divines help her, he was kissing her again ...

It was too much – not nearly enough, and yet far too much. His mouth was hot and demanding, his tongue sliding and suckling against hers. His free hand cupped her bottom, squeezing the sensitive flesh, tilting her towards him. And through it all, the sensation so new and yet so perfectly, brilliantly right, his cock was claiming every inch of her for itself, pounding into her as if it were staking a claim on her soul.

On her heart.

Teetering on the precipice of insanity, there was no alarm, no panic in even that thought.

She clung to him, lost to the assault of sensations. His lips moved to her throat. His thrusts were deeper, faster now, filling her with abandon, and she knew the wave that rose inside her, surrendered to it gladly. Once more he slammed into her, so deep she thought she might lose her mind. Once more ...

'Briannis,' he growled, teeth scraping her neck. 'Come for me.'

Was it the overwhelming pleasure? Was it the magic of his command? Was it everything at once, the touch and taste and smell of him, the heat of his body against hers?

She obeyed without thinking.

Like a breaking wave, ecstasy crashed over her and pulled her under – into a deep, dark place she'd never known existed before. The Keep ceased to be. So did the world outside. There was just his roar as he thrust into her one last time and every single muscle and nerve in her body clenched around him, as hot wetness flooded her, as he pressed his lips against her forehead and moaned through his own release.

For a moment, there was no sound at all. Just him. Just perfection.

Then he rolled over and tucked her into his arms, seed spilling over her thighs and the blankets as she moved. His hands caressed her hair. His voice was thick with wonder and disbelief when he whispered her name, the syllables sounding brand new on his lips.

'So,' she murmured groggily into his shoulder, 'what were the other nine hundred and ninety-eight ways you were talking about?'

She could listen to his laughter for days. Perhaps this was all she wanted to do for the rest of his life – fuck him and make him laugh and threaten to kill him every now and then.

'Give me a minute to catch my breath, morning star,' he said, still chuckling as he sank back into the pillows. 'Maybe two.'

Already his cock was hardening against her belly, twitching back to life before it had fully softened. She glared at it between their bodies. Covered in glistening juices, the dead, marble-veined side looked even more otherworldly.

'Is it even supposed to recover that fast?' she said, looking back up at his face. 'The books suggested otherwise.'

He pulled up an eyebrow. 'You're a rather inspiring presence, apparently.'

'Flatterer.' She scoffed. 'I'm beginning to think you're congratulating yourself on plain old rigor mortis rather than virility.'

'Complaints?' he said dryly.

She would have liked to argue, just because she was starting to find she enjoyed arguing more than she'd ever thought she could. It would have been so satisfying to get that smug little smile off his face for a few moments, if only for the principle of it.

But that also meant she'd have to keep her hands off him for a few moments longer, and she wasn't quite ready to make such sacrifices yet.

'No complaints,' she said, crawling from his arms so she could climb over him and straddle him in the blankets. 'Just curiosity. Tell me about the next point on your list.'

He grinned. 'For research?'

'For research,' she agreed, and kissed him.

Chapter 12

A lady should always exercise prudence and refrain from acting hastily.
                    Lady Lockwell's Handbook of Etiquette

DAWN WAS TOO BRIGHT.

Briannis woke slowly, drowsily, wrestling free of her dreams the way one might drag herself out of stubborn quicksand. Sleep was warm and safe and comfortable. Reality, on the other hand, was glaringly sunny and sore and also oddly ... sticky?

Oh.

Oh.

Her eyes flew open.

The king of Faerie lay sleeping next to her, sinfully naked, his copper-red hair a blanket over his side and back and shoulders – looking strangely innocent in the golden sunlight that flooded the room and the canopy bed. The decaying side of his face lay buried in his pillow. Staring only at his living side, every trace of bitterness mellowed from his features, Briannis could imagine for the first time who he must have been before the Princeps closed the gates through the Elidian marshes – unspeakably beautiful, unspeakably powerful, a proud yet dutiful ruler to the magic of the world.

Her fingers itched to touch him. To brush a strand of hair from his face, to kiss those lush lips again. To make a start on item number ... something. She'd rather lost count over the course of the night.

She was sore and filthy and bruised in places she'd never been before, yet a smile found its way to her lips all the same. Best to let him sleep, she decided, slipping her legs out of bed. Divines knew he'd need his strength, next time she got her hands on him. In the meantime, she could take a bath and find breakfast for the both of—

She froze.

Only now did she understand why the sunlight had seemed so intolerably bright the moment she opened her eyes.

There was nothing covering the windows.

No vines. No roses. Not the tiniest, most innocent petal. In the space where she'd only seen flowers and thorns as long as she'd known this room, she now looked out over a stark blue morning sky and mountains as far as the eye could see.

Only after several heartbeats did she realise her mouth had sagged open.

This had to be a joke, hadn't it? A misunderstanding? In other rooms, the roses had sometimes retreated as long as she didn't come too close to the windows. Granted, here at the heart of the castle, so close to the sanctuary of the man they were protecting, she'd never seen that happen – but perhaps today was a first? Perhaps they had finally realised *she* would be here to keep him safe even if their protection failed?

But she stepped towards the light, and the vines did not creep back over the glass.

Holding her breath, she nudged open the frame just a hair's breadth. Fresh air, clear and bitterly cold, slipped into the room, sending her bare skin pebbling. No roses. No vines. As if they'd never even been there, keeping her prisoner for over a full month.

She opened the window entirely and risked the briefest glimpse outside. The grey granite stretched out on all sides of the frame, interrupted here and there by more glass or pillars or turrets jutting from the main structure of the building. The roses were there, too, basking in the morning light – unmoving.

Like normal, innocent flowers.

They become activated when anyone capable of harming me approaches the Keep ...

Capable of harming him.

Oh, divines have mercy.

Her heart was pounding in her ears as she stepped back from the window and turned, feeling as if she was watching someone else go through the motions, as if it was barely *her* standing naked in a royal fae bedroom, looking at the sleeping king in the bed they'd shared. Harming him. His exquisite, disfigured body in the blankets. The soft lines around his living lips. The traces of tears she'd seen glimmering in the moonlight, memories of the child he'd raised and loved.

She imagined drawing a knife on him. Hands around the worn leather of the hilt. The smooth, balanced weight of the blade as she'd aim it and ...

She felt like gagging.

This wasn't just about not *wanting* to kill him. Her guts rebelled at the mere thought of the blood on his skin, the fear and betrayal in his eyes. Her muscles resisted the slightest imitation of the motions. Even if someone tried to force her at knifepoint ...

Her blade might end up in her own chest before she'd let it touch him.

She pushed the window shut, staggered two steps towards the bed. Still Moridyr did not wake up. Her heart felt too large, looking at him, as if something was pressing on the inside of her ribs, yearning to burst out – spurring her to crawl back into his arms, clutch him to her chest with every ounce of strength she possessed, and tell him ...

Tell him ...

She forgot to breathe as the realisation dawned.

That she *loved* him?

No. *No.* This was impossible. He was ... an ally. A friend, perhaps. A deadly, vicious, temporary friend whose sole role was to get her *out* of his home again, to become a pleasant memory while she lived the rest of her life in the city. And fine, perhaps he'd held her at night and listened to her ramblings on ulcers and intestinal infections, perhaps he'd taught her to throw knives and how to be improper at times ... but that was all part of his own game, wasn't it? Just his slow and successful attempt at seduction? Just for his own amusement?

Wasn't it?

I dreamed of you for weeks ...

Was it?

Her hands had started trembling. Her heartbeat was a drum in her ears, turning the harrowing silence of the Keep into a cacophony of panic.

She couldn't *think* here, looking at his unspeakably beautiful face, at the lips that had kissed her in places she hadn't even thought possible and murmured her name over and over again as she finally fell asleep. Her feet moved themselves, frantically. Chemise. Stockings. Dress. Shoes. She needed out of this room, out of his presence ...

Something pulsed past her consciousness, a faint throb of concern.

The Keep. She'd have cursed out loud if she hadn't been afraid to wake Moridyr. How was she supposed to think with the metaphysical equivalent of a worried dog turning around her ankles, staring up at her with pleading eyes?

Out. Sweet divines, she needed *out*.

Silk skirts snapped around her legs as she fled the room, feeling like she was leaving her heart behind to beat on its own beneath the blankets. How could she not have seen this coming? How, *how* had she been foolish enough to get herself caught up in this brand new prison just as she was making her way out of the last one?

And what the blazes was she supposed to do now?

Stay here? Betray Father and everything she'd ever worked for, in favour of a world that wasn't her own and would never be her own? Accept she'd never see the mills and the canals and the tea shops of Elidian again? Wait for some nameless fae boy to save all of Faerie, or if he failed, for Moridyr to die slowly and irrevocably as the power drained further and further from his land?

Or return to Elidian to slit Cyril's throat and do the saving herself?

That last option made sense; rationally, she knew it. She *wanted* to see the city again, didn't she? Returning home for the sake of Faerie would fulfil her dreams. It would save Moridyr's life. It would give him what he needed – not *her*, a single powerless human running through his home, but a reunion with the people on whose behalf he'd suffered for so long, a restoration of his magic. That was what she'd promised him when they decided to work together; that was what she owed him.

But she would have to leave him behind. His kisses, his smiles, his nettling remarks. And once she'd finished her work in Elidian, once his people had returned to his court and he could have every single fae woman he wanted ... would he even remember her?

What if she became a mere pleasant memory to him, the very thing she'd intended for him to be to her?

Her breath was ragged in her throat as she ran down the corridors, down the stairs, past every room and corner she'd gotten to know so well in these weeks. And there it was again, that strange, otherworldly presence, the emotions of the Keep pushing themselves at her ...

No, they were more than just emotions, this time, coming at her so fast she didn't even have time to brace herself. Her feet were still standing in the middle of a shadowy, window-less corridor full of ambrosias and bellflowers. She still saw the fossils in the floor tiles, still smelled the dusty walls, still heard her own uneven breath. But part of her was back in the sun-streaked abundance of Moridyr's bedroom, *knowing* the shape of the room without truly seeing or hearing a thing – she'd become the walls, the curving ceiling, the window she hadn't fully closed. Through a new sense that was neither hers nor his, she felt the empty space where she'd been in the bed, the weight of his body still in it. Could feel the yearning that radiated off it, too, a feeling that far too closely matched the sound of his voice last night.

Briannis ...

'Stop!' she burst out at the flower-covered walls.

The sensation vanished.

She stood panting and trembling in the empty corridor, clutching her chest as if she could still feel the weight of Moridyr's desire pressing on her heart. It was too deep, that longing. Too all-consuming. Not what he should be feeling, the man who had so easily told her he'd never need her to stay around.

Slivers of the Keep's awareness slid along the edges of her mind, poking and prodding, as if testing whether its little show of magic had yielded the desired effect.

Was the damn castle trying to keep her here?

A cold shiver crept up her arms as she glanced at the walls surrounding her, locking her in. Rosethorn Keep, with its uncanny mind magic and its undying loyalty to its king and ruler ... What if it hadn't been fully her own decision last night, to take down the walls she'd kept up between them? What if it wasn't her own heart beating in her chest with so much warmth it hurt?

Could it be just fae magic and trickery, after all?

She wobbled two steps forward, almost expecting the doors of the room to slam shut around her. Nothing moved.

Not *yet*.

She started running.

Out. *Out*. Her heart pounded in her chest, her breaths coming in jagged gasps as she sprinted down the twisting halls of the Keep. Away from Moridyr's bedroom. Away from the temptation and the confusion that lingered within it. She needed to clear her head, to figure out what was hers and what was nothing but enchanted emotion – needed to remember what the world felt like outside these gilded walls. There, finally, was the corridor she knew from the very first morning she'd slipped into the castle, an eternity ago ...

And the gate.

The *gate*.

The smooth handle was heavy in her hand – heavier than she remembered it to be. She was fully prepared for the roses to reappear as she pulled the low door open an inch, just enough to suck in another deep lungful of icy air ... but nothing happened even as she warily stuck her head outside, thorny vines dangling innocently from the arches above her.

No snares lashing out. Not even the smallest, tiniest motion. Which meant ...

She was *free*.

Her skin hungrily soaked up the sunlight as she stepped out into the grand, *glorious* openness of the world outside – nothing but empty air and more empty air as far as the eye could see, no wall or window to stop her. The cutting mountain breeze snatched at her skirts and hair. The cold crept below her dress in an instant, evaporating the sweat between her shoulder blades. She closed her eyes and smelled the fresh earth again, heard the howl of the wind, felt the warmth of the sun on her face ...

And thought of Moridyr.

Hurting, dying Moridyr, who lay sleeping in his bed within the self-imposed confines of his prison – who hadn't felt the wind on his skin for decades, who might wither away with the rest of Faerie before he'd ever have the sun on his face again. What if he'd woken up by now? What if the Keep woke him and warned him?

What would he think she'd done – left forever?

And sweet divines, why was she worrying about him when it was *her* future on the line?

Love. Or fae enchantments. There was no way to tell the difference until she'd excluded one of them. How far did she have to be away from the Keep to nullify any influence it may have on her sanity – just a few steps outside the gate? She didn't feel particularly saner here on the bare terrace, although those throbs of the castle's attention had vanished from her mind as far as she could tell.

Would she be safe from its magic down the cliff?

That was what she would do, she decided, firmly stepping forward. She'd climb down the way she'd come and find the bags she'd left behind in the cave where she'd spent her last night outside; it seemed bad form to leave those lying about anyway. And there, safely away from the magic of the castle and its king, she'd think. She'd make her decision. She'd climb back up and inform Moridyr of what she'd do.

A solid, sensible plan ... But she found her feet dragging within moments, and it had nothing to do with the gaping depths that opened up before her.

Would he have woken up already?

He'd know, wouldn't he, that she wouldn't leave forever without a word of goodbye? Not in a silk dress and these elegant shoes that would never survive two weeks of traversing mountain paths?

Of course he'd know. She pushed herself back into motion, shuffling down the uneven path with her breath held. He wasn't some hysterical child, and this unnecessary dread she felt – this sense of doom turning her stomach and weighing down her feet – was all the more reason to get away from him before she tried to make her decisions. She couldn't decide her fate and potentially the future of Faerie based on nothing but sentimentality.

So she walked.

Down and down and down and down, until her knees were objecting every time she set down another foot onto the rocky earth, until her thighs were screaming with exhaustion and sweat was defying the wintry cold to roll down her back. She didn't dare to stop moving. Whenever she glanced up, she could see the castle perched high above her on the rock – like a beckoning finger, tempting her to return. And she *couldn't* go back, not yet – not until she'd sorted out these conflicting thoughts and emotions that were tearing her apart.

She had to go home. Hadn't that been the only thing she'd wanted, all these weeks?

But going home might mean losing him forever. Going home might break his heart. And no matter how fast she walked, no matter how hard she tried to numb the ache in her chest below the far more urgent hurt of her overtaxed limbs, that did not feel remotely like something she wanted.

So what was she supposed to do, then? Stay here? Betray Father and all he had sacrificed for her to find her place in the city, for her to be ...

Happy?

She stumbled to a standstill on the path, closer to the foot of the cliff already than she had realised.

Father had wanted her to be *happy*.

She barely even saw the steep slopes anymore. Cold mountain wind stung her hands, her face, and she welcomed the provocation without feeling the pain, watching her own thoughts with a clarity unrivalled by any insight she'd had in her life. It was like sitting in the Nightingale Theatre again, tucked away on the highest balcony, and watching the heavy red curtains part to reveal a whole new world – to delight and surprise her with every twist and turn of the play unfolding before her ...

Except she was the play now. Her world, her mind, her memories.

Had Father wanted her to fit in with the Elidian nobles, all those times he'd told her to work hard and find her place in life? Or had he just wanted her to fit in *somewhere*? To be safe and joyful and content in whichever way she could manage, in whatever place she wanted?

He *had* led a pleasant and prosperous life in Kraaled, before it all collapsed. If he could see her now, standing in the heart of Faerie, holding the heart of its ruler in her hands ... would he really tell her to leave? To turn her back on a king so she could go back to vying for the attention of dukes and earls?

You'll melt your brain someday, Bri, thinking so hard ...

Had she been making this endlessly more complicated than it needed to be?

She no longer felt her sore knees and thighs, walking down the last bends of the path to where the valley opened up before her. She no longer felt *anything.* Weeks and weeks of trying to escape her prison ... yet had she ever felt impatient to leave since her last, near-fatal attempt to poison her target? Had she ever truly missed her old life, rather than the dream of it, the hope of what she one day might have?

But right here she *had* pretty dresses and ballrooms and a castle to do her chores for her. How could even the richest noblewoman's life in mortal lands compare?

She all but floated down the sunlit path, feeling lighter than a bubble of soap, oddly tempted to burst out laughing at the flood of relief. Even the barren mountain slopes no longer looked so grim around her. She didn't *have* to leave. She could just grab her luggage and climb back up, inform Moridyr she'd changed her mind, and start figuring out how they would save Faerie from certain doom without leaving Rosethorn Keep. She could still kiss him and make him laugh and—

'Look at *that,*' a male voice drawled behind her, the words loud in the serene silence of the mountains. 'Our little murderess has finally returned!'

She could not have frozen more abruptly if she'd tried.

Thinking fast was an assassin's skill – one that had saved her life more than a handful of times in the narrow alleys of Elidian, confronted with an inconveniently nosy guard or a sharp-eyed servant. But here, in the early morning sun of the Faerie mountains, her mind went blank for three crucial heartbeats as a chorus of eager and surprised male voices cried out behind her.

People?

In these dying mountains?

'Do you think she will be as happy to see us, gentlemen?' another voice yelled, and roaring laughter rose from – sweet divines, from how many mouths?

Only then did she spin around, disoriented mind wrestling to make sense of the sight before her. People, indeed. *Humans.* Five, six, no, *eight* of them, strolling up towards her along the path she'd just so blindly walked. Unshaven faces, unwashed clothes. Wrapped in patched-up fur and leather. The look of men who had been on the road for a while – who had been on the road for much longer than they'd intended to be.

Finally returned.

Had they ... had they been waiting for her?

'That's a surprise, isn't it, Miss?' the first of them grunted, and there was something in his yellow-toothed grin that sent her stumbling two steps away from him. 'Didn't the Princeps tell you about the little welcoming committee that would be awaiting your return?'

Lord Cyril.

Who had killed the previous Princeps, and quite possibly the rest of the family too, including the wife he'd just wed ... She stared at the eight of them, sauntering towards her with muffled sniggers and leers, and truly felt the icy mountain wind for the first time since she'd stepped outside the gates of the Keep.

They *had* been waiting for her.

Why in the world had she continued to believe she could trust Elidian's ruler? Why hadn't she wondered for even a second what a man of his methods would reasonably do to the assassin he'd needed once and would never need again?

She wasn't sure if she was still breathing. She wasn't quite sure how to breathe.

'I ... I'm quite surprised, indeed.' It didn't sound like her own anymore, that meek, frightened voice she heard speaking the words. 'Should I optimistically presume you are here to safely accompany me back to the city, perhaps?'

They roared with laughter at that.

'We'll *accompany* you for a while, don't worry,' the broadest of them informed her with a smirk, to be rewarded for his cleverness with another round of howling amusement. 'You kept us waiting a while, ladybird. Next time the Princeps gives orders to trail anyone however long it takes, I'll make the fucker pay more for my frozen balls, let me tell you.'

No. *No.* Her feet staggered another few steps back. No use – they'd be faster and stronger, and she did not even have a single knife on her body. No poisons, either, and she'd never manage to strangle all eight of them with her stockings. What else could she do? If she screamed as long and loud as she could, would Moridyr hear it?

But even if he did ...

What could he do?

He wouldn't leave the Keep. He couldn't risk his life and the magic of his people, and walking into a circle of Cyril's murderers was the *last* thing he would do. She'd wandered into this trap all by herself, and all by herself she'd have to find a way out of it – that, or—

No.

No.

But her heartbeat wouldn't slow, a nauseating rattle choking the breath from her lungs. Playing for time was all she could do. And even then ... what was she waiting for?

'If ... if you followed me all the way here,' she choked out, voice quavering, 'then why didn't the Princeps just send the lot of you to do the job?'

'Oh, he did,' one of them groused. 'We couldn't figure out how to get into that fucking castle. You walked in without trouble, though, didn't you, love?'

'To be fair,' the tall one said with a snicker, 'I'd let her in too if she showed up on my doorstep looking like that.'

Oh, sweet mother Eostre, she *was* looking like a harlot, wasn't she? No gloves. Hair a loose mess.

Then again ...

What fucking right did that give them to treat her this way?

'If you'd let me in looking like this,' she said sharply, and suddenly she sounded a lot more like herself, 'you may end up regretting it, sir. Go on like this, and you'll regret it, too. I'm not sure if you're fully aware who you're speaking to.'

Their chuckles grew louder. 'Getting mouthy, Miss?'

'Merely trying to be polite and warn you,' she retorted icily. One last glance up at the mountain ridges hiding Rosethorn Keep from view, and she made her decision. However this ended, at least there was one person she could keep safe for the years to come. 'I just killed a fae king. Perhaps you should worry about your own mortality before threatening me.'

'Oh, I'm sure he was distracted enough when you ended him,' the closest one said, sending her that yellow grin again. His nose was too red. His hands were too large, and too close to the three knives hanging on his belt. 'But you're not dealing with some pretty king here, sweet. We know how to use our' – a chuckle – 'swords.'

She did not step back as he came forward. The stench of sweat and fire around him was suffocating, but damn it all, she couldn't run forever. 'Do you, now?'

'Nothing but the best for you.' His wink aimed for saucy, yet landed close to predatory. 'And trust me – after a month and a fucking half of waiting, we'll take our time for you. So ...' He spread his arms, stepping closer. 'Shall we get started?'

She should, presumably, have cried.

Begged, perhaps. Prayed. Fainted, in good ladylike fashion. But she was not some frail, meek victim, she was *not* going to primly simper her way to the grave, and so she jutted up her chin and coldly said, 'Please do. If you dawdled any longer, I might suspect some of your attributes have indeed frozen off in the night.'

'Little bitch,' he growled and stepped forward.

She moved without thinking.

It was all instinct, her lurch forward. All instinct, to dodge the bastard's outstretched hand, wrap her fingers around the rough hilt of his largest knife, and yank it from its sheath.

And nothing but habit to slide it into his widening left eye with a savage twist of her wrist.

The blade sank in with a sickening squelch, sending out a spray of blood as it punctured through to the brain. He had time for one last roar, loud and sharp with agony, before collapsing onto the uneven rocks and twitching all the way to eternal stillness.

Briannis was already moving.

The bloody knife clutched in her hand, she spun, took stock of her opponents with a single glance around, and aimed. It was Moridyr's voice in her ear, now, phantom fingers lifting her elbow, correcting her grip on the knife. *With a bit of luck, I'm sure you could hit an elephant now, morning star ...*

The blade whizzed from her hands and slammed into the tallest man's forehead, just above his right eyebrow. He stood for one last moment, staring at her with unseeing eyes before tumbling backwards with an undignified thud.

The men around them were no longer laughing.

'I warned you,' she said as she knelt down, her voice gloriously cold and gloriously unladylike. With calm fingers, she pried two knives from her first victim's belt. 'Who is next?'

They were shuffling back. Out of throwing distance, back to wherever they'd set up camp for this past month and a half ... But knives and swords had appeared in their hands, too. And by the looks in their eyes, they weren't fleeing – rather, the opposite.

She had just been a pretty piece of prey. A means to a doubtlessly sizeable reward. Now, she'd killed their friends.

And there were still six of them left.

She saw the small, travel-sized crossbow just in time, in the hands of the broad-shouldered man who'd lingered at the back of the group – cocked and loaded and coming up to aim at her. Her feet reacted before her mind could. A sprint of maybe ten steps and she dove into the small cave in which she'd spent her last night outside. Hidden in the shadows, her bags lay against the back wall, although they'd clearly searched them to take every last bit of food. The daisy soap was still there, too, white and flowery.

Thank every holy power in the world these weren't the sort of men to appreciate cleanliness on the road.

Trying to gather her breath, she ducked against the rough granite wall of the cave, squeezing her eyes shut to better hear the sound of their movements outside. Footsteps. Muffled voices, discussing strategies she couldn't make out. The impatient tapping of steel against stone.

The two knives in her hand felt small and pathetic in comparison, her silk dress a laughable piece of armour.

Six of them. And there was only her, in this barren land of dying magic.

So how in the world was she going to get herself out of this trap?

Chapter 13

Always shut the door behind you.
Lady Lockwell's Handbook of Etiquette

MORIDYR AWOKE FEELING ... wrong.

Which did not make sense at all – what in the world could be the matter, on this sweet, sun-streaked morning? His bed was warm. The sky was bright and blue. And Briannis ...

Sweet divines, *Briannis.*

He made a valiant yet doomed attempt to return to the dream he'd been dreaming, a fading string of impressions of hot breath and desperate moans and warm, slick, living skin. But the sense of wrongness persisted, trickling into those pleasant images like poison – the nonsensical yet bone-deep realisation that somewhere, something was about to go catastrophically wrong.

A long, drowsy groan escaped him as he shifted beneath his blankets, racking his brain for any reasonable answer. Was

Faerie in danger? Had the roses noticed a new threat? But how could anything be threatening him if Briannis was here and ...

If Briannis was here.

His eyes flew open as the unease abruptly took a physical shape – or rather, the absence of one.

That was what his senses had subconsciously noted, long before he was awake enough to remember he had eyes and ears – his room was too silent, too motionless, no quiet rustle of blankets or breaths. The bed beside him was empty. Only the hairs on her pillow and the tousled mess of the blankets remained as evidence that his heated memories were not merely dreams, that he *had* held her, taken her, made her come again and again and again in his arms.

Where was she – the bathroom? The breakfast table? But there, behind the sparkling veil of the canopy ...

The window was a wide open square of stark blue, no rose or thorn to be seen.

The uncanny sensation of wrongness solidified into a bitter weight in his stomach.

The roses were gone? But that didn't make sense: this part of the castle, his own bedroom, was always the very last place where they retreated and the first place where they returned at the approach of danger. So if they were no longer covering the windows *here* ...

He closed his eyes, consciousness blurring with that of the Keep. And it was in that moment that he knew it wasn't merely his own worry he'd been feeling, that it wasn't his own heart pounding spurts of alarm through his veins – it was the castle.

Screaming at him, insofar as a castle could scream.

Because Briannis ... she was gone.

Not just from his bed. Not just from the room. He couldn't find the weight of her presence *anywhere* in the sprawling halls and corridors of Rosethorn Keep – an empty, desolate pile of walls and floors and glass and stone gaping back at him, devoid of any life or sound. Devoid of her heartbeat, that one little spark of light he'd never stopped reaching out to at irregular moments during the day because it still seemed too good to be true to have her here.

Gone.

He sat frozen in his bed as understanding finally dawned.

The roses had retreated. Which did not make any sense at all, which ought to be impossible – unless something far more impossible had happened. An option he hadn't even *thought* to consider until this moment, not while he was still little more than a rotting corpse, a selfish liar, a captor disguising himself as a fellow captive.

But the roses had never grown over the gates and windows for the boy either, even after he'd left his harmless childhood long behind and was very much able to kill and maim – because he had loved Moridyr. Not as a king or as a ruler to be served – as a father he wouldn't be able to harm even to save himself.

He'd thought it was a consequence of youthful innocence. Family and duty. The precious bond between child and ... well, as close to a father as the little brat had left, which was not much, but presumably still better than nothing. But if the roses had vanished for Briannis, too ...

Had she somehow fallen in love with him?

And then *fled* rather than told him?

The floor swayed beneath his feet as he scrambled out of bed, naked and helpless, heart cracking to shards in his chest. Around him, the Keep was still pulsing with dread, and he could no longer tell how much of it was his own. Hadn't she reminded him time and time again that all she wanted was to see Elidian again? Of *course* she would slip out the moment she found the windows empty. Of *course* she wouldn't let her feelings get in the way of that life-long goal – not Briannis, who had denied every wish and desire only to please the eternally disapproving burghers of the city.

His Briannis.

Who had just stepped out into a world where murderers and marsh dwellers were hunting for her.

Terror filled his throat, so thick he almost gagged on it. He grabbed for his clothes blindly, pulling the silk and linen onto his limbs with shaking hands. For fuck's sake, why hadn't he warned her the moment he found out about Cyril's treacherous promises? Was there any way to warn her *now*? But he had no idea how long she'd been gone, how far she'd already walked ...

If she had already run into them.

What if— Fuck, he didn't even want to *think* the thought that rose in him as the last bitter fragments of reality pierced through to his brain. What if he'd already killed her with his stupid, selfish secrecy?

He wanted to scream. He wanted to rip the curtains from the windows with his bare hands, wanted to slam his fists *through* the walls that bound him ... But what good would it do? Anger was useless. Grief was useless. He could only stand here, frozen in shock, powerless and shaken to the core, as the sun rose over an empty Rosethorn Keep and informed him of the ugly truth – that this was yet another battle he had lost.

Like that first morning from hell, when the news had arrived – the bloodbath in the city, Tal and Violet and the girls. Like the first whispers of the closed gates. Like the first time the roses had crowded over the walls and he'd exhausted himself to unconsciousness to make them abide for a few more days. Like the first courtiers leaving, grim and defeated, until no one was left but his boy.

Like that last gods-damned morning, fourteen years ago. *It's time for me to go.*

He'd staggered out of his bedroom much the same way the next day, lost and adrift in a castle that felt too empty, too light, too large for him alone – realising how much he'd relied on the awareness of nearby life only when the last flicker of it was gone. Life he didn't *need*, he'd told himself every single day since. Life he could perfectly well do without, for the sake of his people.

And then ...

Briannis.

He found himself floundering down the stairs now, feeling like a piece of him was shattering with every step he took. What was the sense in denying it? He'd been starving for a decade and a half, not for food but for the touch of skin on skin, for the simple delight of voices and laughter. And then ... then she'd walked in with a knife in her hand and become *everything*. His voice of reason. His untiring healer. His formidable, vehement opponent in every game he played. Like a ravenous man overstuffing himself at a loaded banquet table, it had been so stupidly easy to tell himself she wouldn't be going anywhere – that she was all his, regardless of when she'd accept that fact herself.

And now she was gone.

As always. Like everyone.

A roar ripped from his throat, echoing back at him through the empty stairwells. There was nothing but silence as the sound died away. No footsteps. No questions. Just the Keep still buzzing around him, that half-conscious presence that was both him and not him, company only in the way his own voice could break the silence.

He'd cracked and stitched himself back together so many times in this cell an eternity removed from the rest of the world, friends and family and every single fae who'd left Faerie and never returned ... People he hadn't needed. People he hadn't *allowed* himself to need. But Briannis had looked at him without seeing a monster, had cried in his arms and kissed him, had tended to his wounds and played his games and *won* them ...

And so he'd stepped right into the trap.

He could tell himself he didn't need her as often as he liked. He could tell *her* he didn't need her, and divines knew he'd done it, too, utter fool that he was – but all the pretty words in the world didn't change the slightest thing about the simple, ugly facts. That he was lost. That he loved her. That he couldn't do this without her anymore.

And that she was going to die.

Unless he could warn her in time. Unless—

What was he thinking? These were not the sort of thoughts he should be entertaining for even the briefest moment – too reckless, too treasonous. He couldn't start compromising everything he had built and stood for, the legacy of every king and queen who'd come before him, the safety of every single fae wandering over the surface of the earth ... And what for? The life of a single person?

The life of *his* single person.

Impossible. *Impossible*, and the height of selfishness, too. But his feet wouldn't stop moving, and only as he descended the last staircase did he realise that his seemingly aimless wandering had been aimed for a crystal-clear destination from the very first step.

The front gates.

The same gates he hadn't stepped through since the day his father drew his last breath, a hundred and eighty-seven years ago.

It was the first rule he'd been taught in his life, before he was old enough to know his flowers or any other law of his kingdom – *One of us must be here at all times, Moridyr.* Five thousand years of an unbroken lineage. There was no gambling away that sort of heritage. He might doom all of Faerie to extinction for nothing but a broken heart, for nothing but his own selfish wishes and desires ...

Moridyr III, last king of Faerie.

But he pulled handfuls of begonias from the walls as he passed them, and his fingers wrapped themselves about the bronze doorhandle without hesitation – the same handle Briannis must have held divines knew how many hours ago.

The outside air was so cold as he pulled open the door. Colder than he remembered.

He faltered in the doorway, the sun on his face but his back still shrouded in the castle's shadow – caught between heart and duty, between hope and despair. A fool's gambit, all of this. For all he knew, she didn't even *want* him to come after her. Hadn't she snuck away without a word, giving him no chance to even make an attempt at convincing her?

But if he'd been honest with her from the start, she'd never have walked out towards her own doom in the first place ...

It was then that he heard the sound – faint and distant, but clear as a blaring war horn against the dead silence of Faerie. The soft but unmistakable cry of a dying man.

And he was running.

Boots crunching over gravel, dead branches snapping underfoot, he sprinted towards the fight, all but throwing himself over the edge of the cliff in his hurry to make it into the valley below. Faerie wasn't going to kill him. The knives and arrows waiting for him at the foot of the mountain, on the other hand ...

Moridyr III, last king of Faerie.

The epithet he'd seen in his nightmares for years on end, and finally, the words no longer stung. If he had to be the last, at least he wouldn't wither away like a dying flame, starved of air and fuel until it finally surrendered to the darkness. Better to die fighting. Better to go down for love than to live without it.

His morning star needed him.

So damn it all, into the night he'd go.

Chapter 14

Selflessness lies at the heart of good manners: a well-bred lady knows when to make sacrifices for those she holds dear.

Lady Lockwell's Handbook of Etiquette

BRIANNIS WAS DOWN TO one knife and five opponents.

Crouched against the cold, moist wall of her hideaway, she could just see the feet of the last man she'd taken down, swinging her second knife into his throat the moment he'd snuck into view with his crossbow. Now she found herself clinging to her last weapon with trembling hands, like a lost child holding on to a stuffed animal, and tried to figure out if it was even worth it to kill a fourth of them.

Or if she should save that last blade for her own throat.

What an incomprehensible thought, that she'd lain sleeping in silk blankets an hour ago, dreaming of soft kisses in the safest place in the world. That if she'd just turned around and woken Moridyr ...

Moridyr.

Would he know she was gone by now? And if she didn't return, what would he be thinking? That she'd *deliberately* left forever?

That single thought hurt more than even the prospect of a knife to the chest. She ought to leave some message here, just in case someone found it and managed to deliver it to Rosethorn Keep – but outside, her attackers were moving again, and she couldn't afford to turn her attention away from them. If they showed any sign of vulnerability ... If they underestimated her for even a moment again ...

She wasn't a warrior. She killed cleanly and civilly, using brains rather than brawn. But for Moridyr's sake, she might be able to forget those rational objections for a moment.

No slitting her own throat yet, she decided, fingers tightening around the hilt. They'd find out what a little hellcat in silk and lace could do.

And so would she.

They were approaching as a group this time, worn boots thudding against the moss and pebbles as they warily moved to surround the cave. She watched their every move with eagle eyes, like the most malevolent of healers – looking not for a weakness to heal but for one to exploit. Was he limping a little, the bearded man with the woollen hat? A well-aimed kick to the side of his kneecap might render him as good as immobile. And the one on the right, swinging his sword with so much bravura ... His right eye was red and swollen and worryingly wet. Some infection? His sight would be impaired on that side: if she was quick enough, and he didn't have much depth perception anyway, would she be able to hit him?

It was as if she was back in the alleys and teashops of Elidian, spending hours observing patterns and finding the flaws in them – and sweet divines, even with the fear pulsing through her veins, she could not deny that she *did* enjoy it.

They strode closer, like hunters cornering a frightened animal. She let her eyes dart over them, determined not to let them guess the first target she'd chosen ...

Without warning, the limping, hat-wearing man faltered.

It was just a deepening of his uneven gait at the first step; at his second step, he came to a standstill entirely. His knife dropped to the rocky ground as he grabbed for his throat, steel clattering against stone.

'Hawk?' one of his companions snapped.

Hawk choked out a gasping sound, his face slowly turning purple.

A heart attack? His breakfast coming back up to bite him? Briannis didn't take the time to wait for answers, not with five pairs of eyes momentarily turned away from her. Lunging forward, out of the cave, she made a sprint for the swordfighter closest to her, the one with the infected eye and the blissfully unprotected throat – knife up, gaze on target ...

Hawk dropped twitching to the ground.

Her prospective victim jerked around as he noticed her, swinging his sword at her but miscalculating the distance between them. She avoided the honed edge by a few inches, heartbeat a thunderous roar in her ears. Down swung her weapon. This – *this* was familiar, the motion no different at the heart of Faerie than in the sparkling ballrooms or the narrow alleyways of Elidian. The blade sank through skin and jugular veins, abruptly cutting off the man's cry of alarm as she punctured his windpipe.

Someone else started screaming.

She didn't even hear it at first as she pulled back her bloodied knife, the alarm drowned out by the rush of blood in her ears and the familiar dying gurgle of the collapsing man before her.

But then the shrill shouts came through – 'Get back! Get *back*!' – and she turned despite herself, despite knowing her focus should be on these last three men who'd be more and more desperate to get their knives into her chest no matter the cost.

And there, sauntering down the last steps of the path along the cliff ...

Moridyr.

Moridyr?

She had to be dreaming. Hallucinating. How many times had he told her he wouldn't leave the Keep no matter how deep the silence, no matter how unbearable the loneliness? There was no sensible reason he would suddenly show up here, like some knight in shining black silk, ready to save her from her own stupid mistakes.

And yet ... could she possibly imagine something so frighteningly magnificent, something so wickedly powerful?

In the morning sun, his hair shone like red gold, framing the cadaver mask of his face, cascading down his back and shoulders. His coat billowed out around his body like the unfurling wings of a carrion bird. A small trail of flowers marked his steps, tansies and peonies springing from the earth wherever his feet had touched the barren rocks, and in his hand, clenched between skeletal fingers ...

The squashed petals of blood-red flowers.

Begonias. *Beware.*

On the pebble-strewn earth, Hawk let out one last wail, then became quiet forever.

'Moridyr?' she breathed.

He did not even look at her. Some of the crimson flowers turned to dust in his fingers, and behind her, a new voice choked on a scream as the magic came down. She let out a sob-like laugh and stumbled towards him, blade slipping from her trembling fingers – she was safe. *Safe*. She *would* return to the Keep and she *would* tell him she loved him and she *would*—

A furious scream rose behind her.

And before she had time to turn, to run, to even understand what was happening, two bulging, fur-covered arms hooked around her shoulders.

A knife settled against her throat, shaking with anger and colder than anything she'd felt in her life. The stench of old porridge and unwashed teeth washed over her as a cracking voice barked, 'No more magic! No more magic or our little lady here dies!'

The choking behind her eased.

No – no, no, *no* – but Moridyr's steps faltered with his magic, and the powerless fury and fear in his widening eyes almost sent her knees buckling. This couldn't be the end of it. He was the king of Faerie, wasn't he? There had to be *something* he could do? But his power was a shadow of its past potency, his commands held no power outside the Keep, and that knife against her throat ...

She knew a little too well how close she was to a gasping, gurgling end.

'As I thought,' the voice groused behind her as Moridyr remained unmoving; a chuckle followed, hoarse and joyless. 'So much for the Princeps' orders. Made some new friends, little bitch?'

A pit opened in her stomach as the full extent of her mistake sank in. She should never have run towards him so easily. Should never have let go of her weapon so eagerly. Should never have let his name pass her lips with so much relief. Now they knew just how much power it held, that blade by her throat.

Moridyr didn't move, the peonies blooming brighter around his feet.

'It's the flowers,' another voice panted behind her, hoarse with fear. 'He's doing something with those flowers.'

'Drop the fucking flowers!' the man holding her snapped, and something warm trickled down her throat from where his knife met her skin – blood. That was *blood*. She didn't even feel the pain. 'If you want Miss Iavi to live ...'

'No,' she croaked. 'No, please, I—'

'Not the most impressive of threats,' Moridyr coldly interrupted, every inch the bored, imperturbable fae king as his gaze brushed the small circle of Cyril's murderers. 'You don't give the impression you're planning to let Miss Iavi live regardless of my responses.'

A small silence fell as her captor contemplated that argument. Then, with a new waft of old porridge smells, he grunted, 'Well, we won't kill her *yet*.'

'Ah.' Moridyr's eyebrow snaked up. 'I understand you're offering me a fair fighting chance? Not really Cyril's style, but perhaps you will positively surprise me.'

'What?' the man holding her groused, sounding a little uncertain of himself now.

Moridyr sighed – that perfectly elegant, deeply disappointed sigh laced with a hint of cruel amusement. 'Let me put it in simpler terms. You will let Miss Iavi go the moment I drop these flowers. If you don't, if you harm even the slightest hair on her head, the three of you may prepare for a number of very unpleasant days.' He considered that, then thoughtfully corrected, 'Weeks.'

She'd forgotten how effortlessly frightening he could be, the little sneer on his lips, his dead eye gleaming with the steadfast promise of cruelty. No matter how tightly the man behind her held her, he couldn't hide the small tremble that shook him as he snapped, 'We have a deal.'

He, too, knew that he'd be out of cards to play the moment she *was* dead – that they might stand a better chance against a fae king without flowers than against an infuriated half-corpse with no reason to hold back. But Moridyr—

What was he going to do?

There were no knives within his reach, not the most pitiful rusted blade. The flowers around his feet were harmless. And the moment he let go of the ones he was holding, these men would be upon him – fighting not just for the price Cyril had set upon her head, but his, too.

'No,' she whispered again.

He wouldn't even look at her as the begonias dropped from his hand, petals whirling to the earth like flakes of blood-drenched snow.

'Step back,' one of the men said loudly, sounding as though he were biting *through* his teeth. 'Step away from those fucking flowers.'

Moridyr obeyed, his hands loosely along his sides, not a tremble of nervousness in the wry curve of his lips. 'Now let her go.' His voice was pure, deadly venom – not a threat, but sweet divines, it *sounded* like a threat.

Her captor turned the knife away from her throat, then hooked his foot around her ankle and shoved her onto the rugged ground.

For a moment she couldn't think – couldn't hear – couldn't see – as the world tilted around her and she landed sideways on the stone, sharp pebbles digging through silk and skin in pinpricks of agony. Footsteps slammed against the earth, past her, towards him. Shouts tore through the air, incoherent commands and panicked threats—

And then, unmistakably, cries of pain.

Briannis rolled over onto her belly, frantically blinking tears from her eyes, and lifted her head as far as she dared. Some fifty feet away, Moridyr still stood unmoving in the morning sun, head held high and hands clasped behind his back. But around him ...

Growing rapidly from the earth like ropes unreeling from their spools, thick, flowery vines were sprouting forward, forming a barrier between him and the men attacking. They writhed through the air like snakes about to strike, coiled around wrists and ankles, lashed out at eyes and ears and throats ... Iron-hard thorns grew on the leathery green surface before her very eyes, and wounds burst open wherever the vines met with bare skin, biting deep and viciously.

Thorns.

Again.

She almost laughed in hysterical triumph – and only then did she see his face.

Eyes closed, lips contorted in a grimace, he'd tilted his head towards the sky, as if pleading with the sun itself for power. In the stark light, the contrast between life and death was more striking than it had ever seemed within the dusky confines of Rosethorn Keep. Yet as she watched, as the vines grew taller and thicker and stronger ...

The living side of his face was paling.

White pallor crept up his right cheek. Shadows crowded around his eye socket, hollowing out the space above his cheekbone. Skin drew tighter on his sharp jaw, his chin, his temple.

'*No!*' She didn't even hear herself over the screams and cries. 'Moridyr, stop!'

His lips – those sweet, soft lips she'd kissed – were turning grey.

Life for life. *I am Faerie.* She gaped at the vines, wrapping around bloodied throats and faces – a land devoid of magic, a land unable to bear fruit or flowers, and he was pouring his very own life force into that barren earth. Sacrificing what little health he had left. Offering death in exchange for his protection.

No – for *her* protection.

'No,' she whispered again, clawing her hands into the earth. She barely felt the sharp edges of the stones cutting into her palms. 'No, please. *Please.* Don't let him do this. Don't ...'

The vines swept higher into the sky, elated, like prisoners breathing fresh air for the very first time. And Moridyr's right hand – that beautiful hand that had held hers as she cried, the hand that had touched her in places she'd never even dared to think about – was withering.

Life for life.

'Take mine,' she choked at the earth.

The bloodthirsty vines suddenly grew still – no longer than the blink of an eye – then descended onto their victims with even more ferocious vigour.

'Please.' She pressed her forehead against the cold granite, breathing in the old smell of mud and moss. Could she hear something rumbling in the depths beneath her? 'Take it from me – take it from *me*. I'll give you whatever you want if you stop him. I'll stay here as long as you need – I'll stay here forever if you need me to – but *please* ...'

The stone no longer seemed motionless below her. It was as if she was lying on the surface of a wild, churning sea – a sea that was as solid as rock, but no calmer for that fact. She could feel the currents and the eddies and the maelstroms below that deceptive surface. Could feel the cold of the water drawing into her palm, as if she was sinking her hand, her wrist, her forearm into the waves. She no longer felt the tips of her fingers. She no longer heard the screams. Just her own voice, muttering that word over and over again – 'Please, please, *please* ...'

The advance of the cold slowed, then halted halfway up her upper arm.

The world had gone icily quiet around her.

Her chest was heaving as if she'd been sprinting for hours. She tried to lift her head but didn't succeed on her first try; her arms were weak as twigs, bending under the weight of her body. With a parched groan, she rolled onto her side and tried again, managing this time to catch her first glimpse of the destruction the magic had left behind. Bloodied heaps of limbs, covered in vines and thorns. Moridyr, running towards her. And stretched out onto the earth before her ...

Her right arm.

Which had gone gaunt and grey up to the shoulder, flesh and muscle withered, hard bones pressing through the tight, dead skin of her hand and elbow.

Chapter 15

A proper gentleman never forces himself upon a lady's notice.

Lady Lockwell's Handbook of Etiquette

'No,' Moridyr was saying. 'Briannis. *Briannis.*'

His hands closed around her shoulders as he fell to his knees before her – his own hands, one dead, one perfectly, stunningly alive. Frantic fingers skimmed the dead flesh of her forearm, prodded her hollow wrist, rubbed over her numb palm. His words came in an accelerating chant. 'No, no, no, *no—*'

I'm fine, she wanted to say, but as she tried to speak, nothing but unintelligible syllables blubbered from her lips.

'How do I undo this?' She'd never heard his voice crack like that before. He wasn't talking to her, she numbly realised; his plea came tumbling out at the earth, at the mountains, at the thorns still crawling over the bodies of the men who had come so close to killing her. 'Please. *Please.* Tell me how I—'

This time she managed, 'I ... I'm fine.'

'For fuck's sake.' He pulled her upright, and there she sat, dazed and dizzy, as he clutched both his hands about her bony right wrist again. Below her, the sense of motion still vibrated through the rocks without ever moving so much as a pebble. 'What did you *do*, morning star? This wasn't supposed to—'

'Life for life,' she croaked. 'Was killing you.'

He stared at her.

'Told it to take mine.' She was gabbling, looking at him. His green eye was still so very green. So full of life. So full of heart. His cheek was pale, but a normal, *living* pale, all shock and no death, and although his jaw seemed a little sharper than before, that too may be nothing but panic. 'To give back yours and—'

'No,' he said again, his voice hollow. 'Briannis, no.'

'You ... saving me.' Her body wouldn't catch up with her mind, lips only releasing a fraction of what her heart was screaming at him. 'I left the Keep. If I hadn't—'

'You don't understand,' he hissed, and it turned out her dead forearm was not entirely numb by any means, because she could still feel the pain of his fingers digging into her skin. 'This was all my fault from the fucking start. I *knew* they'd be here. If I'd just told you ...'

His sentence drifted off.

She stared at him.

Knew they'd be here. Even echoing through her mind, the words wouldn't start making sense no matter how often she went over them. How could he possibly have guessed – how could *anyone* possibly have guessed ...

'What?' she said dazedly.

'The mirror,' he said, words spilling from his lips with bleak desperation. 'The mirror told me.'

This time nothing echoed.

Her thoughts had gone quiet. An unnatural, otherworldly stillness, like the stifling quiet of a lively city covered in midnight snow — every fibre of her mind holding its breath as it slowly, achingly, put the pieces together. The mirror. Cyril's betrayal. Those warnings — *It might not be possible for you to return* ...

But that was *weeks* ago.

'You ...' She sounded perfectly coherent all of a sudden. 'You didn't tell me? While you knew about it all this time?'

The look in his eyes was an answer before he even opened his mouth.

'What ... what else?' Her hands were trembling. Her *dead* hand was trembling, those skeletal fingers that had been perfectly soft and pink mere minutes ago, that would still have been her own healthy fingers if she hadn't so blindly walked into this trap. 'Is there anything else you kept from me? Anything else I need to know?'

His small hesitation didn't escape her. 'Perhaps we should get out of here before we—'

'They're all dead anyway!' she bit out, yanking her withered arm from his grip. 'What more do you know? I'm not going anywhere before I know exactly who is looking for me where — before I know if I can ... if I can ...'

Trust you.

She didn't get it past her lips, but he seemed to hear it all the same. 'Briannis—'

'*Tell* me!'

He closed his eyes, dead fingers tensing and loosening as if he was struggling not to reach out for her again. But his voice remained strangely composed, almost *businesslike*, as he hurriedly said, 'This should be the only group he's sent into Faerie. But he did instruct the watchers at the Elidian gates to look out for you, and there's a price on your head among the marsh dwellers. Those are the details I know. If you want to hear more, we should ask the mirror—'

'Hear *more*?' Her voice soared up. 'This isn't enough yet? You didn't at any point consider that I might have liked to know that every single plan I was making these weeks would lead straight to my damn grave?'

He drew in a deep breath, a small twitch in his living jaw. 'I did consider that, yes.'

'But?' she snapped.

'I didn't have the guts to tell you. I didn't know how you'd react.' The strain in his words betrayed just how desperately he was holding on to his unnatural calm, a flatness of tone that in no way resembled his usual effortless composure. 'And I supposed ... as long as the roses didn't move ...'

She would never need to know.

And then, against all his pessimistic expectations, they *had* moved.

Because she *loved* him – because she couldn't stop feeling it even now, the burning ache in her heart that threatened to engulf her every time her eyes slid over him. From his tousled hair to the pink blooming on his dead lips, from the sculpted edge of his jaw to the endlessly fascinating hollows of his left cheek ... Even terrified and in disarray, he was a sight she couldn't stop looking at, every inch of him beautiful and brimming with power and ...

Hers?

But would she ever have felt that way if he'd been honest from the start? If she had always known her choices were a blasted joke, no options but to surrender to her glittering prison or to fight herself to death?

'Briannis,' he said again, voice choked.

'You should go back inside.' Her lips felt as numb as her arm. 'It isn't safe for you to be out here so long.'

He didn't move. 'You're wounded. At least let me—'

'Take care of me?' she interrupted sharply. 'Like you tried to spare my fragile feminine feelings by hiding my own fucking *life* from me, Moridyr?'

She wasn't sure what shocked him more: her snapped interruption or the vulgarity in it. 'It wasn't my intention to—'

'No, of course it wasn't! But you did!' At long last, the tears were finding their way out, welling from her eyes like red-hot drops of poison. She furiously wiped them off with her good hand. 'I need time to think more than I need anyone's worry, thank you very much. Go home. I'm not going anywhere – *obviously.*'

For a single heartbeat she was sure he would object again, the way his lips parted in a clear prelude to protest. Then he caught the look in her eyes and wisely snapped his mouth shut again, producing nothing but a single tight nod instead.

She watched him rise to his feet and take his leave without another word. Even as he passed the heap of thorns and dead bodies beside the path, he didn't falter; the sound of boots against gravel died away behind her as he made his way up the cliff, back to the castle he had sworn never to leave in the first place.

She didn't move – she barely even *thought* – until at long last the world had become silent and only the wind howled between the jagged mountaintops of Faerie.

The land where she had so gladly decided to stay.

The land she couldn't have left even if she had decided otherwise.

Was that supposed to make a difference? She should be mortally relieved, having survived the confrontation with Cyril's men more or less unscathed. And Moridyr ... Sweet divines, Moridyr had left the *Keep* to save her. She ought to be elated, oughtn't she, at that crystal-clear evidence of his devotion?

But she stared at the strangely white hand in her lap, at the streaks of blood that marred the dead, pallid skin of her forearm, and felt ... wrung out.

I didn't have the guts to tell you.

But why? For her benefit? Because he was afraid to upset her, as if she was some delicate young lady who couldn't go a day without her smelling salts? Or was it *himself* he had worried about, his own lonely heart and whatever the reveal of Cyril's trickery might change between the two of them?

Ridiculous, she tried to tell herself as she sat there trembling in the cutting autumn winds. He hadn't even cared that much about her all those weeks ago. Why would he have lied for the sake of her affection if he'd *told* her he could do without her perfectly well?

Or at least he'd told her ...

What exactly had his words been?

She closed her eyes and tried to remember. *Needing people is dangerous* – well, that wasn't a lie, but it also told her nothing about what exactly he had wanted from her at that moment. *I've been on my own for fourteen years.* Very true, too, and equally meaningless. *Don't expect any grand romantic gestures from me.*

That was just a piece of advice. A command, perhaps, that she had promptly followed. He hadn't said he didn't *feel* any grand romantic sentiments.

So he might have.

Really, the fact he hadn't bluntly told her the opposite and taken away all doubt she might possibly feel ... Didn't that suggest he'd desired her even then?

But the leap of her heart at that thought didn't feel as blissful as it had done before; rather, it felt like the heavy iron chain the Princeps' guards had locked around her ankle as they tied her to the wall in her cell and told her to prepare for the gallows. If he had wanted her that badly all this time, why hadn't he told her?

You know exactly why, Miss Iavi.

Fourteen long years.

And so, instead of being honest – instead of confessing his feelings and giving her the opportunity to decide however she wished to respond – he had resorted to lies and seduction and trickery. Had chosen, really, to embrace every single fae method she'd feared from the day she first set foot in his home.

Had he saved her from Cyril's murderers because she'd been in danger? Or rather because *his* feelings were wounded at the prospect of having to spend divines-knew-how-many more years alone in the Keep?

She felt cheated.

She felt toyed with.

And damn it all, she still couldn't stop wanting him.

Moridyr knew the exact moment she entered the Keep. It was as if the castle abruptly released a breath it had held for hours.

Or perhaps it was his own breath, too.

He had known she would return, or at least he had been almost entirely certain; the bitter truth was, after all, that she didn't have anywhere else to go. And yet, pacing the Emerald Boudoir, he hadn't been able to *entirely* exclude the possibility that she would stubbornly decide to embark on some suicidal quest towards Elidian without even informing him of it – it was, after all, how she had left the castle that morning, too.

But she was back. From where he stood between the richly embroidered couch and the salon table carved with vine motifs, he could sense her trajectory through the halls and corridors as if it were his own, a little slow, but not otherwise unusual. No indication of injuries. No others, at least, than the one he was already aware of.

The one that shouldn't even have been possible.

His temples were throbbing with a venomous mixture of fear, confusion, and shame. He needed to find out what exactly she'd done. There *had* to be a way to reverse it, and hell, he could deal with a few more inches of dead skin – it was the least he could do after his own damn lies had almost been the end of her.

That, and ...

And more, probably. He wasn't quite sure how bad the damage was.

She was aiming for the Starlit Room, the movement of her presence through the castle told him; he abruptly interrupted his own aimless pacing to make for the same destination. But when he arrived two minutes later, slightly out of breath and nauseous with worry, the door of the room in question was closed and – as he discovered when he knocked and tried to open it – locked.

'Briannis?' Her name echoed ominously through the empty corridor.

No response came from inside.

She was there, barely ten feet away from him – he could *feel* her, the steady pulse of her beating heart, the weight of her living presence rippling through the Keep's awareness. But she wasn't moving, and she certainly wasn't answering him.

'Briannis.' Fuck. She had still been able to get inside; the roses hadn't stopped her. So that had to mean she didn't *hate* him, did it? He hadn't messed up that badly? 'Could we talk? Please?'

Silence.

He didn't make a habit of begging. His adage had always been that those who didn't want him could take their poor taste elsewhere; that simple rule of thumb had simplified his life vastly on numerous occasions. But his morning star ... Fuck, he would plead with her on his bare knees if that was what it took to make sure she was at least alive and well, that she wasn't hiding any injuries just to avoid him, that he had done anything he could do for her. Even if she'd been about to abandon him without a word of goodbye, even if he was not the man she'd wanted in the end ...

He owed her that much.

'Briannis, I'm sorry.' He rested his forehead against the wooden door, hearing nothing but his own pounding heart in response. 'I'm well aware I'm a bloody idiot, and you're more than welcome to throw as many daggers at me as you like – just allow me to help you. Please. I don't want you to be hurt on your own.'

He could feel her moving on the other side of the door. Away from him.

Fuck.

That was an answer too, presumably. An answer he might have overridden with a command, had she been anyone else – but as much of a fool as he might be, he was rather sure that magic was the last thing that would improve this situation.

'I'll be around my bedroom if you need me,' he managed. *Our bedroom.* More words he should probably swallow. 'Please take care of yourself.'

There was no response as he walked off, his footsteps dim and desolate in the gaping openness of the castle. Her presence remained in its place behind him like a flame in the night, unbearably bright no matter the distance between them.

He slept alone that night, or rather lay awake alone, clutching a spare pillow to his chest and breathing in the scent of her body that lingered on the fabric.

Life turned into a bitter game of hide and seek the next morning. She didn't show up at the breakfast table, and when he followed the awareness of her presence to the library where she appeared to have settled down, she was gone before he arrived. Over the next couple of hours, they cycled through the music room and the Emerald Boudoir and back to the library, like the circles of some slow and excruciating dance, until he concluded that this could not be a matter of sheer coincidence and that she was somehow – although he wasn't sure how – avoiding him despite his magical advantage.

He retreated to his empty bedroom at that and counted down the hours until sunset, hoping despite his better judgement that she might show up to join him in bed that night.

She did not.

A resentful prisoner, she'd warned him she'd be – but for the love of everything holy in the world, had the weeks since that day changed nothing for her? He had miscalculated and hurt her, that he was very much willing to acknowledge ... But *she* was the one who'd run out without so much as a word the moment the roses retreated. And even if she didn't care for the Keep, even if all she had wanted was to see Elidian again, even if she was furious at him and mourning the future she'd imagined for herself, then what was he supposed to do now that she continued to flee him like this?

You should ask another question, the mirror drawled when he consulted it the next morning. *This one doesn't appeal to me one bit.*

'You can't refuse to answer questions,' Moridyr said wearily, watching his own sleep-deprived face stare back at him from the silver surface. 'If I insist I want this one, you will have to answer it whether you like it or not.'

The grating laugh of the looking glass reverberated through his skull. *I'm trying to do you a favour, you idiot. I could tell you what you should be doing, but don't you think Miss Iavi might feel royally tricked if she figures out you were just following the instructions of a piece of furniture to woo her?*

Moridyr earnestly contemplated taking the damned thing from the wall and locking it in one of the cobwebbed attic rooms, between portraits of great-great-great-aunts no one had liked much and the expensive yet hideous glasswork that various Issian kings had sent north in previous centuries.

I see you agree, the mirror smugly added.

He turned and fled the hall before he could do anything he would regret.

Her unattainable presence on the other side of the castle grew more maddening by the day, like a persistent itch under his skin he *just* couldn't scratch – keeping him awake at night, haunting his every thought by day. Had he believed the starvation of loneliness unbearable before? This was a thousand times worse, hankering for just the smallest crumb while knowing a full lavish banquet lay just out of reach, making a mockery of him with all he could have had and had stupidly let slip through his fingers.

He missed her laugh as he sat staring at the flower-covered walls in silence, the book he'd attempted to read unopened in his lap.

He missed the way her eyes lit up at the mention of deadly afflictions or festering sores. He missed her little frown of concentration while she was aiming knives at his forefathers' portraits. He missed the way she'd argue or swear, blurting out the words almost giddy with excitement, like a freed bird still thrilled by the absence of a cage around her wings.

Most of all, he missed believing she wanted him.

How had he ever thought he could entice her to stay? She'd warned him time and time again that she'd made up her mind about her future long ago – a future that by definition could not take place in Rosethorn Keep. A future, too, for which she needed only one type of man: the sort who would marry her before even kissing her, the sort she could take to proper balls and dinners where boring arseholes talked about themselves for hours. The sort of man who wasn't magically rotting away.

She hadn't wanted to fall in love with him. She'd tried to flee it, and was probably wishing she could rinse the whole damned feeling from her veins. So shouldn't he at the very least do her the favour of staying far, far away from her while she tried to make her heart behave?

For six long days, he tried.

For six long days, he wandered the halls of the castle like a lost soul, haunted by his thoughts and the memories that clung to every room and corner. He read, or tried to. He spent long and dreary hours in the music room. He ate three lunches a day, just to have something to do. He emptied out his wardrobe – counting a grand total of one hundred and seventy-six coats – and spent hours sorting the clothes by colour and material, and still all he could think about was Briannis peeling those same coats from his shoulders.

It was the morning of the seventh day that something snapped inside him.

They couldn't continue like this. At least *he* couldn't, and he refused to let her wither away in self-inflicted isolation the way he had allowed himself to do – he'd closed the door to that existence the moment he'd opened the gates of the Keep and stepped back into the sunlight after a hundred and eighty-seven years.

Either she'd want him, or he'd get her wherever the hell she wanted to be. He just needed her to tell him which it would be.

Which meant he needed to make her talk to him.

Woo her, the mirror had said.

And if a proper Elidian gentleman was what she wanted, then damn it, he would do it properly.

Chapter 16

A lady never refuses a dance with a man she does not wish to slight; once introduced, only a previous engagement is reason to reject a gentleman's request.
Lady Lockwell's Handbook of Etiquette

BRIANNIS STARED AT THE folded sheet of cream-white paper that had been shoved beneath the door of the Starlit Room, somewhere in the minutes between her turning her back to brush her hair and her moving to make her way outside.

He'd been at her door again.

The Keep hadn't warned her this time, as it had so faithfully done over and over in the past days – which suggested it was really just that letter. No traps or fae tricks. No fae kings lying in wait for her if she were to exit the room in a few minutes.

Still she couldn't bring herself to pick it up.

She was *scared*, that was the simple truth of it – scared that whatever he had to say to her would shatter the already fragile bonds of her self-restraint and send her throwing herself back into his arms. Scared that he was trying to manipulate her once again. Scared that she would let him, most of all ... Scared that deep inside her heart, she *wanted* to let him.

But it was just a letter. She could stop reading at any point, couldn't she?

She tiptoed forward, picking it up from the plush dark carpet the way one might pluck a delicate flower from the earth. On the inside, she did not find the passionate and poetic declaration of feelings she had feared, but a message far shorter and more prosaic and—

And *familiar.*

COURT BALL

The company of Miss Briannis Iavi
is requested at Rosethorn Keep, the Gilded Hall,
23rd of Oak Month, at 8 bells past noon.

And that was all.

It wasn't signed. But below those four lines of text – a text so well-established in her memory that even reading it felt strangely like coming home – a single crimson rose petal had been sealed in a dollop of white wax, stamped with what she suspected was the official crest of the family.

A ball.

Sweet divines, a *ball?*

But ... but there would be no one else, would there? There *could* be no one else. Just the two of them. Which meant she would have to face him – would have to see him smile and speak and dance – and somehow still keep her wits about her without giving in to his charms. Was he counting on that? Was this just a next step in divines knew what fae game he was playing, luring her back into his bed?

She couldn't take that risk.

What she needed more than anything else was the freedom to make her own choices – to *knowingly* make her choices. So this should be a simple one. Declining the invitation was the surest way to know he wasn't manipulating her again; after all, he clearly wanted her to accept.

The problem ...

A *ball.*

Manipulation or not, she didn't want to decline at all.

She remembered the affairs she'd attended at Marjorie's side, all glitter and splendour, as close to the life of her dreams as she'd ever been – the exhilaration, the wine, the dizzying dances. This would not be the same, of course. There would be no friends to giggle with, no chaperones keeping a watchful eye, no gossiping debutantes eager to catch the eye of some eligible bachelor. Just the two of them. And yet ...

For the first time since she'd left the Keep, she felt that spark of excitement again, the sensation of living in a world where everything was possible.

She crumpled the invitation in her dead fist, drawing in a deep breath. Fine, then. She would go.

But for the sake of every sliver of pride she had left, she would not be easy prey.

She'd never heard a bell toll in Rosethorn Keep before, but this night it did, eight long, heavy strikes that echoed through the rooms and corridors and sent even the massive walls them-selves shaking ever so slightly.

She was ready by that time.

The dress the Keep had produced for her – after she had described the requested model in painstaking detail – was absolutely perfect, a soft yellow like the first rays of dawn, the silk skirts shimmering with ethereal elegance around her ankles as she moved. Short, puffed sleeves took the boniest sharpness from her dead upper arm, and the broad, square neckline was just alluring enough without being in any way inviting. And the embroidery ...

She couldn't stop smiling whenever her eyes ran over the intricate swirls adorning the bodice and the hems of the skirts.

Her hair she'd twisted into a simple bun, fixing it into place with common, disappointingly blunt pins. To make up for the lack of murderous intentions, she'd snuck out and found a handful of orange lilies to affix between her curls.

Hatred.

That should give him something to think about.

As the bells struck eight, she swept out of the room without allowing herself a moment more to think – she'd done enough of that over the course of the day. Around her, the Keep buzzed with an excitement she found hard to place. Was it glad to see her give up her seclusion? Or was it rather nervousness, the castle knowing as well as she did how much might be at stake in this single meeting?

Down the familiar corridors she went, doors opening before her at every corner. Past the young child's bedroom, past the salon where she'd beaten Moridyr in lawn bowls, past the stairs that would bring her to the music room where she'd first attacked him ... And finally down the grand staircase that led into the grand Gilded Hall, her soft footsteps echoing through the quiet of the castle, her dress gleaming with a pearlescent glow in the light of the candles waiting below.

And there he was.

It hit her just like that magic punch below the midriff, the sight of him – standing straight and tall at the bottom of the stairs in an elaborate emerald coat, the gold embroidery of bell-flowers twinkling in the candlelight. His cravat was perfectly starched and tied. If not for his hip-long hair – if not for the gaping hollow of his left eye socket and the bonelike frame of the cheek below – he could have been the perfect Elidian gentleman, waiting to escort his companion to the grand ballroom.

Bellflowers. *Unwavering love.*

Her knees had already started trembling.

His eyes found her in that moment, but she could not read the expression in them no matter how hard she tried – relief? Reproach? Or did they simply urge her to take another step closer, back into the lion's den?

She took another step down.

He didn't move until she'd reached him, the epitome of well-bred patience, his expression closer to the coveted Elidian ideal of perfect placidity than she'd ever seen it before. What in the world was happening? Where were his sardonic comments, his wry smiles, the ever-eloquent commentary of his eyebrow quirking up? *There you are,* he should have purred, drawing her into his arms. *You have not the faintest idea how I have suffered in your absence, morning star.* And then she'd have kissed him whether she liked it or not, because blazes take her, the mere sight of his lips still set fire to something far too deep within her.

But all he said, with a polite bow of acknowledgement, was, 'Miss Iavi.'

She curtsied reflexively – sweet divines, why was she *curtsying*? It was safe, somehow, this predictable shield of manners to hide behind ... but surely he couldn't have summoned her here to play the perfect gentleman all night?

'Your Majesty,' she murmured, picking the safe option.

His gaze trailed down the embroidery on her dress, and for one infinitesimal moment she thought he stiffened as he recognised the flowers. Yellow carnation – *disappointment*. Narcissus – *selfishness*. Yellow chrysanthemum – *slighted love*. Embroidered in yellow, gold, and silver, they swirled along the bodice as the world's prettiest declaration of war, countering his opening move of the bellflowers with his very own weapons.

Now he surely would have to say something? But he looked back up at her with not the faintest glimmer of feeling in his eyes and held out his right arm in a gesture that was both courteous and distant.

'May I accompany you?'

She wondered what he'd do if she told him no, but she took his arm, glad for the silk gloves between her and his sleeve. Even through muslin and silk, the living warmth of his body was palpable, an unwelcome reminder of the strength of his arms around her, the safety of his presence that even her snug bed in the Starlit Room couldn't replace. She didn't need him to know how long she had lain awake every night of the past week, cursing her own hungry skin.

He guided her into the hall without speaking, offering her a moment to take in the room – the flower wreaths and garlands between the gilded pillars, the crystal chandeliers floating below the frescoed ceiling. Along the walls, a table with refreshments stood waiting, glasses of sparkling wine and plates with elegant bites of food. On a small stage at the head of the room, her eyes found the instruments she knew from the music room: cello and violins, their bows motionless beside them.

An unwelcome thrill of excitement ran through her. Did he actually *dance*?

It sent her heart and stomach all aflutter, walking next to the man she knew so well yet feeling like she was holding a stranger's arm – as if this wasn't the same Moridyr who had kissed her for hours, who had made her feel such indescribable pleasure that last night before everything collapsed. As if this was, somehow, a clean slate. A chance to start over.

Was that his intention? He had to *know* she wouldn't forget his deceit so easily, hadn't he?

'As there's no one to properly introduce us to each other,' he said lightly, as if he'd read her thoughts, 'I'm afraid I have no choice but to consider us acquainted, Miss Iavi. May I have the pleasure of the next dance with you?'

Her stomach twisted. So he did dance. And he, too, knew what a slight it would be to refuse him – sweet divines, why did she care? They weren't in Elidian! And yet, the smooth pinewood dancefloor was beckoning her as much as any Elidian dancefloor had done ...

'I'd be delighted,' she said, taking care not to let any actual delight shimmer through. She was *not* easy prey. She was *not* accepting any of this for the sake of his machinations, going along with whatever schemes he had in mind for her.

Just because she wanted it. That was all.

'The delight is mine entirely,' he returned, face still that impassive mask she had once admired in the most stoic of Elidian noblemen. Here ... it felt strange, that blandness, the absence of his natural humour and passion. It felt *wrong*.

She let go of his arm, turning to face him at the centre of the ballroom. No other dancers lined up on either side of them. No crowd along the walls, watching and gossiping and snapping their fans. Just the two of them, surrounded by gold and flowers, by the empty expanse of the smooth wooden floor.

Her heart hammered wildly in her chest. As guarded as his gaze was, it didn't leave her for a moment.

The instruments lifted themselves into position on the other side of the room, bows hovering promisingly over the strings.

For one moment, the silence hung heavy in the air between them.

Then the first notes drifted through the ballroom.

The dance came to her so easily, limbs moving without thought. Step forward. Gloved hand into his living hand. Turn, step, turn again. Oh, he *did* dance, gliding over the floor with a grace that made her breath catch in her throat, leading her through the steps with an ease that bordered on the mesmerising ... She tried to focus solely on the music, on the shapes her feet drew over the empty dancefloor, on the swirling of her dress around her ankles. But his hand was warm and strong whenever it touched hers. And his proximity was making it harder and harder to ignore the effortless elegance of his motions – that same effortless elegance with which he had, days ago, lifted her into his lap and ...

She should not be thinking about that.

Her belly warmed a little all the same.

Was this what he was after? Plain and simple seduction? She wasn't sure what offended her more: the notion that she would be docile enough to fall for that trick, or the snaking fear that it may not be entirely incorrect.

'I believe,' she said tersely – turn, step, turn – 'that we ought to have some conversation while dancing, Your Majesty. Why don't you tell me what game you're playing today?'

His answer was a little delayed, the distance between them opening and closing in time with the music. Then his warm hand wrapped around her waist, guiding her two steps forward as he muttered, 'Am I playing a game?'

'You're always playing a game.' She hated the twinge of her guts as he released her again, allowing her to twirl away from him in the next figure of the dance. As if to make up for it, her next words came out sharper – 'So what is it this time?

Soothing your own guilty conscience? Seducing the mortal of the month?'

Something twitched in his jaw even though his steps didn't falter. 'You are not the mortal of the month to me.'

It felt too good, provoking a reaction out of him. It felt like every crumb of power he'd denied her before. She whirled around with a sharp turn, sending her skirts swaying, and mockingly said, 'I'm beyond honoured, Your Majesty.'

'Briannis.' His fingers closed around hers too tightly as she stepped back into his hold, his voice as taut as his shoulders. 'Please. What do I need to tell you?'

'The truth?' she suggested with a small scoff.

He was silent for several turns, as if that simple request was too much to ask from a creature incapable of lying. The melody of the violins soared between them, taking her heart with it – an agonising nervousness she should *not* be feeling as he stepped back towards her, hand sliding around her waist to steer her through the next figure.

'I love you,' he said.

Damn her heart for skipping a beat even as her feet dutifully went through the motions. It was frustration at her own sentimental malleability more than anything else that made her whirl away from him too brusquely, her skin burning where he'd touched her. 'And this is the moment you decide to tell me that? Not when you first realised it? When you could have told me and given me a *choice*, rather than lied to me and strung me along in some twisted scheme?'

The violins sang their merry song on the other side of the room, a jarring contrast with the edge of her soaring voice.

He didn't meet her gaze as he turned back towards her. 'Briannis—'

'Yes, I know,' she said sharply. 'That would have been frightening. That would have made you vulnerable. That would have made it possible for me to reject you and leave you on your own again. That's the entire blasted *point*, you see.'

His sharp intake of breath didn't fit the composure of his words. 'Yes. I see.'

'So you can say you love me' – her voice should not have wobbled at those treacherous syllables – 'but in the end, you were perfectly happy to lie to me for your own benefit. And keeping me here no matter the price is not *love*, Moridyr. That's *possession*.'

She'd repeated it to herself so many times before. It had become close to a lullaby in the cold, silent bed in the Starlit Room, words she whispered over and over again until the urge to find him and slip back into his arms became bearable again. It was *true*, she was really quite sure of that – so why did it sound not nearly so convincing at the sight of his slumping shoulders, his downcast eyes?

He should have defended himself. It would have been so much easier if he'd tried to defend himself.

But all he said, stepping towards her in the empty, candlelit hall, was, 'Would you go back, then?'

That hurt – not a punch but rather a stab in the guts this time. She bit out a laugh, whirling away from him. 'Are you going to pretend I have choices *now*? Now that we both know I don't?'

'It's an honest question.' There was an urgency in his voice she didn't fully understand. 'Would you?'

No. No, I wouldn't.

Did he know? Did he have any idea of the decisions she had made on those barren slopes outside, just before everything had gone catastrophically wrong?

'Does it matter?' she said tersely. 'An answer to a hypothetical choice is not—'

'I'm not speaking in hypotheticals, Briannis.' He took her hand with too much strength as he turned back towards her, pulling her into his arms with such speed she almost cried out. His lips were tight with agitation – a tension she could feel mirrored, somehow, in her own guts. 'Cyril expects you to return on your own. For all his measures, I doubt he's prepared for a fae king to show up at his gates.'

Her feet tangled up.

She almost stumbled face-first against the floor as her body went rigid for the shortest of moments. Long enough for him to grab her, pull her against him, and whirl her back onto her feet with a motion as fluent as it was improper. Only then did her mind catch up, the ridiculous suggestion below those words – at the *gates*?

'You're joking,' she managed, out of breath.

'Not at all.' He held her close now, leading her effortlessly through whatever this dance had become – seduction attempt or battlefield or something else entirely. His green eye was sparkling with a grim resolve she'd never seen before. 'So do you want to go? See if we can kill a Princeps together?'

'But ...' The music was picking up speed, as if to mimic the feverish spinning of her mind. 'But you don't *want* me to go.'

'No.'

'So is this some attempt to absolve yourself of your guilt?'

He let out a breathless laugh, twirling her around in his arm and pulling her back against him. Sweet divines, his hard body, moving with all that smooth predator grace ... 'It has nothing to do with my guilt. Or with missing you. It's about the damn fact that you're unhappy and I can't stand to see you this way.'

'But your people!' she desperately objected in between shallow breaths. Her body was burning, and she didn't know whether his nearness or the whirling motions of the dance were to blame. 'You'd put yourself in danger again. You told me you wouldn't do that. You can't just ... ignore them, can you?'

The violins fell silent.

She stumbled to a standstill against him, panting, clutching his arms, unable to tear her gaze away from his. He was ... close. Far too close. If he so much as nodded – if she only came up on her toes – his lips would lie against hers again, those lips she knew so well, hot and hungry and demanding. Her heart was racing. Sweat prickled between her shoulder blades.

Something dangerous heated in the air between them – something that made her forget about secrets and traps and trickery for one heady moment.

'I'm not ignoring them,' he said, voice low and rough. 'I'm merely choosing not to let them determine my every move for once.'

She couldn't breathe.

'You make a terrible king out of me, Briannis Iavi.' There was no anger in the words. No defeat. Just plain, honest facts. 'But a better man. The only man I want to be, truly. So if you still want to return, if that is the choice you'd have made before I hid the truth from you, I will be more than honoured to escort you back to Elidian and get you every single reward the bastard promised you. Say the word. I'm ready to leave.'

The floor was swaying beneath her feet, as if the mountain itself had started shaking, reeling under the weight of his treason. 'Moridyr—'

'Do you want to go?' he interrupted, voice hoarse. 'Yes or no.'

The hall hadn't seemed so empty until now – candle flames shimmering on the gilded walls and the crystal chandeliers in two heartbeats of deep, expectant silence. A small muscle trembled at the hinge of his living jaw. It was the only outward trace of agitation, the only sign that his warm, unmoving hand on her waist was a lie.

If she just said the word, that little tremor told her, he'd let her go.

No traps. No trickery.

'No,' she whispered.

For one more moment, he stood frozen. Only then did he blink, slowly and emphatically, like a man waking up from a persistent nightmare.

'No?' he repeated, voice suddenly not as steady.

She swallowed. 'No. I don't want to go back.'

'You ... you *don't?*' There was a touch of concern to his gaze flicking over her body, down to the carnations and the chrysanthemums, as if she might be coming down with a mind-clouding fever. 'Are you very sure? There's no need to be polite if you—'

'I'm not being polite!' A trembling laugh escaped her. 'I have no intention at all of being polite to you!'

'But ...' he started, and the crack in his voice radiated straight to her heart, straight into something even deeper inside her, twinging so violently she almost winced. 'You wanted to return. Didn't you? Why else did you run out the very moment you could?'

She gaped at him. 'In silk slippers?'

'What?'

'You ... you thought I was running for good? In that slip of a dress? Without even a bag on my shoulders?' Her voice grew louder, higher. Something was fracturing inside her – her composure, perhaps. Her walls. Her safe and guarded intentions. 'I'm not *that* much of a fool, Moridyr.'

His eyes were growing wide. 'Then why—'

'I just wanted to be sure everything I was feeling was my own!' she burst out, shaking fingers digging into his upper arms. 'I've spent enough time bending to the wishes of others. For all I knew this was some accidental command of yours, or the Keep messing with my head even more than it's already doing, or—'

'Wait.' There was a new edge in his voice. 'You can feel the *Keep*?'

She tried to scoff but managed poorly. 'How else did you think I could avoid you so easily?'

'Ah.' His shaky inhalation told her he hadn't considered that explanation yet. 'Divines help me. I see. That is ... interesting.'

'Do you mean *problematic*?'

'No,' he said, wary and bewildered. 'Not exactly. But it's not supposed to open its mind to anyone except family members. Which ...'

He didn't finish that sentence.

'Oh,' she stammered.

'Yes,' he said weakly, and cleared his throat. 'So ... Yes.'

They were both silent for a single, strung-out moment.

There was something very close to panic in his eyes as he met her gaze – something that was at once a plea and an apology, fear and the smallest, most desperate spark of hope. *I love you.* He must have meant that. *Say the word. I'm ready to leave.*

Which had to be true, every single word of it – which meant that he would have let her go. If she changed her mind in two days, he likely still would.

No traps.

No trickery.

But that meant ... that meant she was *free*, didn't it?

Free to love him all by herself. Free to be happy. Free to live the life she *wanted* to live, without having to feel like she'd been tricked into it. She felt as if she could float from his arms, so great was the sudden weight falling from her shoulders; her laugh came bubbling out of her like the sparkles of fizzy wine, so utterly irrepressible she felt it in her toes.

'Briannis,' he said, voice choked. 'Are you—'

'Staying?' She giggled – she couldn't help herself. Had the candlelight always been this bright? The weight of her skirts so feathery light? 'Assuming you don't mind me running around your house for a few more years ...'

'*Mind?*' His laugh was almost a snarl as he pulled her closer, fingers clawing into the small of her back. 'I'd rather chop off my last living limbs than let you go, morning star. I may not be able to offer you a life of respectability, but if you'll have me anyway ...' His throat bobbed. 'I'll damn well do everything in my power to offer you happiness.'

That left her no choice but to kiss him.

If his words had left even the dimmest spark of doubt in her heart, the first touch of his lips extinguished it entirely. He welcomed her without hesitation, gentle yet fierce, kissing her as though he could not decide whether to worship or devour her – a kiss that said, *I'll gladly fight every blade and crown in the world for you.*

But to you, I'll surrender.

She tangled her fingers in his hair, the smooth strands gleaming coppery around her white gloves, and allowed herself to drown in him. To lose herself in the first sweep of his tongue into her mouth. To deliver herself to the wicked games of his fingers on her waist, her hips, her bottom, skin lighting up under his touches in vivid memory of that last night in his bed ... He kissed hungrily, pleading for more. She obeyed without thinking, pressing herself closer to his chest until he moaned her name against her lips.

Her body lit up like a bonfire. Without thinking, she let go of his hair and lowered her fingers to the intricate knots of his cravat. More, she needed *more* ...

His breath caught. 'Briannis?'

She began untangling the stiff white cloth.

'Briannis,' he said again, and this time she recognised the warning in those familiar syllables of her name. It was a warning that made her belly clench in delicious ways, elation as much as something far, far deeper. 'Are you really very sure—'

'Do I look unsure?' she giddily interrupted, pulling the starched cloth off his neck. Sweet divines, the *scent* of him ... She came up on her toes to press her nose into the hollow of his shoulder, nuzzling the dry skin of his dead side. 'I can't imagine. I'm frankly feeling surer by the heartbeat.'

Again his breath hitched, fingers tightening on her hips. 'We're standing in the middle of a ballroom. We ...'

'Oh, how *shockingly* inappropriate,' she retorted with an eye-roll, fingers slipping to the first buttons of his coat and quickly working down from there. 'Just think of what the violins will be whispering about us.'

'That's not what I was trying to—'

'No,' she said, yanking open his last two buttons because damn it all, this was taking ages and she still had two layers of clothing to go. 'What you're trying to say is that I'm being too hasty and I should first pledge my undying love to you a few dozen times and then perhaps we could try to exchange a single chaste kiss to the cheek before bedtime. And what *I'm* trying to say is that you're a coward and quite possibly a hypocrite, too. I'm not running from you again.'

A desperate burst of laughter escaped him. 'How did you get so wise all of a sudden when I'm still such an idiot?'

'Someone took my knives,' she murmured, continuing her handiwork on his vest. A delicate white shirt appeared below, the contours of his body shimmering through – half dead, but half living, too, and that sight turned even the greyish flesh of her right arm into a wry triumph. 'I had to find myself another weapon.'

'Someone,' he said sourly, 'had no idea what they were getting themselves into.'

She laughed. 'Good or bad?'

'Perfect,' he muttered, trailing his gaze up over her withered arm, the embroidered neckline of her dress, her suddenly dry mouth. 'Absolutely flawless.'

She kissed him again.

His fingers slid around her jaw in response, and there was no hesitation in his movements now, none of that ill-advised restraint that had him vacillating before ... He pulled her flush against him, his mouth devouring hers with an almost savage intensity, claiming every gasp and moan that escaped her. She clutched at his unbuttoned coat as she pressed herself closer to his half-bared chest. Until she could no longer tell his heartbeat from her own. Until she could feel the warmth of his body seeping into every vein and nerve in her body.

Perfect ... And yet he would have let her go.

She drew him even closer.

His dead hand lowered over her back towards the lacing of her dress, and without thinking, she ground against him until the jolt of his erection answered her challenge. He hissed against her lips. She did it again, and this time he cursed, breaking from their kiss to meet her heavy, intoxicated gaze. Need and desire burned in both his eyes, stormy currents like the magic she'd felt deep below the surface of the earth.

I am Faerie.

And that may have been true, but blazes take her, he was hers before anything else.

Her last night in his bed had been a revelation. An exploration of unknown, forbidden lands, treasures and danger lurking around every corner. But *this* ... this felt like coming home. This was where she belonged, not flitting across some grand ballroom in the latest fashion of the year, but tangled up in his arms, his lips on hers, her heart pounding with feelings she'd never even known it was capable of containing.

This was where she stopped fighting.

This was where she just sincerely and wholeheartedly ... *was*.

'I have been told ...' Her voice came out husky as she moved her attention back to the last few buttons of his waistcoat, unfastening them with shaking fingers. 'I have been told a lady should not be too eager when it comes to bedroom matters.'

The skin crinkled at his living eye. 'Have you, now?'

'It's never been explained to me in much detail,' she muttered, finishing her work and moving on to his shirt, 'but from what I've understood, I don't think I'm supposed to undress my lord and master halfway through a ball, for a start.'

'Call me your lord and master one more time' – he suppressed a small moan as her fingers brushed down the bared skin of his chest – 'and I might have to put you over my knee to get that nonsense out of you, morning star.'

Even her shiver was somehow pleasant. 'I'm rather sure a lady would not feel excited about that prospect.'

'Absolutely not,' he agreed, looking undeniably pleased with himself.

'Hmm.' She tugged his coat off his shoulders, then his waistcoat, then his shirt. 'Noted. I also think unbuttoning your breeches because I really, *really* want your cock in my mouth might fall into the category of "too eager", don't you think?'

'Briannis.' A hint of strain had snuck into his smile. 'Did you just say *cock*?'

'Not very ladylike either,' she murmured mournfully, setting herself to work on his breeches. The instrument in question stirred vehemently at the first touch, then broke free like a caged bird, red and pale and throbbing all over. 'Do you think it's more ill-bred to *say* the word cock or to *kiss* one?'

'Hard to choose,' he managed, sounding a fraction breathless. 'I think you might need to do both, just to be safe.'

She laughed and knelt before him, studying her target. In the bright candlelight, it looked even more intimidating – like a weapon, but a weapon so beautifully crafted she could not help but tremble at the sight of it.

Canting her head a fraction, she leaned forward and planted the softest kiss onto the glistening head. His growl vibrated straight through to the aching spot between her thighs, making her body draw tight with need.

'I didn't know well-mannered had a taste,' she said and licked him again, just because it could never hurt to test twice, 'but I'm pretty sure your cock tastes like the very opposite of it. Very shocking. Very scandalous. I should probably be calling for the smelling salts.'

His laughter was laced with moans. 'I'm not sure you fully understand what that filthy mouth of yours is doing to me, morning star.'

'Oh, I'm sure a *lady* shouldn't understand,' she said, looking back up at him with an innocent pout as her fingers tugged at the lacing of her own dress. 'Just like a lady probably shouldn't entertain thoughts of kissing you here until you're crying. Or of fucking you right on this very floor. Or—'

He stretched out a hand with a laugh like a surrender, stroking his fingers down her dress. His voice was hoarse as he muttered, 'Get out of my way.'

Before she could wonder, the yellow silk vanished, leaving just her shift behind. He knelt too and lifted the flimsy fabric over her head easily, baring pale skin and the occasional bruise and the grotesque, strangely appealing monstrosity of her right arm.

'Oh, dear,' she said with a shivery laugh, bare skin pebbling as cold air brushed over her back, her shoulders. 'I suppose this is where I politely blush and tremble and lie down for you to have your way with me?'

He unceremoniously pulled her onto the floor with him in response, turning so that she landed sprawling over him, small breasts rubbing against his ribs and muscular chest. 'That sounds like something a proper lady would do, yes.'

'Well,' she whispered, pressing herself up to straddle him. Oh, to have him so powerlessly below her, to conquer him at the heart of his hall ... Red hair lay in a messy crown around his head. Even his dead cheek was flushed pink with desire, and from his open breeches, his cock rose as if to imitate the gilded pillars lining the walls, pulsing with need. 'In that case – considering that I'm very much climbing on top of you nonetheless, that I'm definitely going to fuck you, and that I'm not planning to stop feeling eager about this anytime soon ...'

She faltered as she settled over him, the feel of his head brushing past her slick flesh and making the breath hitch in her throat. He didn't move beneath her, although his hands tightened on the smooth pinewood.

'In that case?' His voice was thick with a tension she could feel as if it were something tangible.

'We'll have to conclude' – and saying it felt even better than speaking the most vulgar of words out loud – 'that I'm really not a lady.'

She sank down onto him before he could respond.

Would she ever get used to the sheer size of him, to the way he stretched her open as he filled her? She doubted it. She *hoped* she wouldn't. This, finally, was the raw, overwhelming sensation she'd needed, enough to satisfy for one blissful moment the insatiable cravings of her heart – every nerve ending sizzling to life around him, drinking in the feel of him.

Her eyes fluttered shut as she moved down. She opened them only once she'd fully lowered herself, all of his cock sheathed inside her. His lips had parted, his eyes darkened until they were almost identical in colour – but his hands hadn't moved, clenched into fists as if his life depended on it.

'Touch me,' she breathed.

He obeyed before the last word had left her lips. Strong, yearning hands cupped her breasts as she moved up and pressed herself back down, faster now, hard enough to draw a hiss of pleasure from his lips. His fingers pinched her nipples as she rose again, and this time *she* was the one to cry out in ecstasy, a deeply unladylike sound that burst from her lips like a battle cry.

'More?' he purred.

'Please.' His hands let go of her breasts, and she whimpered. *'Please.'*

He grabbed her hips and drew her down hard as he thrust up, entering her with so much force she could do nothing but throw back her head and moan. And again. And again. He fucked her as she rode him with the deep, triumphant strokes of a conqueror, each one harder, deeper, *better*. The slap of flesh on flesh filled her ears. The musk of their bodies became all she could smell. She could have died – she could have lost him – and yet here she was, savouring every wicked stroke, her body so utterly at his mercy she could be nothing but his.

And nothing but *alive*.

It started somewhere miles deep inside her, the newly familiar tightening of her body, ripples of pleasure building with each breath, with each thrust. She moaned, clinging to that looming release. So, so close, and yet trying to reach it was like swimming against the stream, her body refusing to set her free just yet ...

'Use your fingers, morning star,' he muttered.

She had no time to hesitate, no time to even gasp at the utter debauchery of the suggestion; his command took effect the moment he uttered the words, and her fingers pulled themselves from his slender shoulders, slipping down to the soaked flesh between her thighs instead. Places where she'd never dared to touch herself before, but they ached for more, and *oh,* it felt good to rub over that most sensitive spot as he fucked her, to add to the tidal wave of sensation of his hands and cock. The pressure built higher. Bigger. Looming closer, finally, as she rubbed the centre of her own pleasure with moans that threatened to become powerless sobs ...

'Very good, my love.' His voice seemed to come from miles away. 'This is how I want to see you – mad with pleasure and full of me ...'

She blew apart.

The first waves of that glorious, hot release broke upon her, crashing over her in a flood of incoherent cries. She sagged down onto him, convulsing. For one eternal moment, all she felt was the bliss roaring through her veins, sweeping her into some maelstrom of nothing but the purest, deepest pleasure.

Then his arms were around her.

Then his lips were on her forehead.

She sobbed his name and clung to him until the last waves finally subsided, until she was empty and crumpled, a spent heap of flesh and bone. Until she was sweetly, deliciously sated and almost drowsy in the warmth of his embrace.

'I love you,' she whispered. 'I love you so much.'

'And even though humans are liars and tricksters,' he muttered into the hollow of her neck, a breathless chuckle in his voice, 'I might just believe you this time.'

She was too exhausted to do more than laugh. She snuggled into his chest with her eyes closed and her arms around his torso, drowning herself in the rapid, steady rattle of his heart.

She was home.

Home.

She wasn't sure if minutes or hours had gone by when she finally opened her eyes again to find half of the candles no longer burning, the splendour of the room darkening. He hadn't moved below her. His eyes were closed, his hands cradling her against his chest as if she were all that lay between him and imminent demise.

It was that thought that sparked a sudden flutter of anxiety in her heart.

'Moridyr?' she whispered.

'Hmm?' He sounded content. Almost sleepy. Not at all like a man desperately standing his ground against a certain, looming death.

And yet ...

'If we're not returning to the city,' she said breathlessly, coming up on her elbows to meet his gaze, 'then what is going to happen to you? If the gate doesn't open, I mean? If no one else stops Cyril, then ... then ...'

'Then I'll die at some point.' His smile was joyless, but there was no fear in it – none of the panic that was setting its claws into her heart at the same moment. 'Don't look so frightened, morning star. We still have time.'

'How long.' She barely dared to ask. 'How long do you have?'

'A few years,' he said slowly, mulling over the words before he spoke them. 'At least five, I'd say. If we're lucky, it's closer to a decade. More than enough for certain people to finish the work they've been preparing for years.'

'Like your nephew.'

This time there was a flicker of true joy in his smile. 'Yes.'

'But ...' She didn't want to talk about it – didn't even want to *think* about it, in this golden room where he'd danced with her and held her and made love to her. But she needed to know what to expect. She needed to know what to prepare for. 'Moridyr, I know you trust him and I suppose he's trying hard enough, but ... but I must have spent fourteen years in the same city with him, and I never even heard of him in all that time. So are you really quite sure—' She broke off as he chuckled. 'What?'

'Something I still had to tell you.' He came up on his elbows, half-heartedly wiping seed from his breeches, then muttering a command for it to vanish. It did. Turning back to her, he added, 'Remember that soap?'

Her blink felt owlish. 'The daisy soap?'

'Yes. He was the one who left it with you.' Moridyr's smile turned wry. 'I wondered if it might have been his work from the moment you mentioned the daisies – as far as I know, he's the only one who knows about that particular trick, in case he'd ever need to return to the Keep. The mirror confirmed it a few weeks ago.'

'Your *nephew* sent an assassin after you?' she said dazedly. 'Are those common fae family traditions?'

Moridyr shrugged. 'I suppose he assumed I'd handle the situation.'

'The situation meaning ... *me*.' Something occurred to her – something roughly as alarming as it was ludicrous. 'You're not saying he helped me get into the Keep because he thought you might *like* me, are you?'

'I'm quite sure that's exactly what he did.' A skewed grin. 'It does sound like him.'

'It does sound like an enormous risk!' she protested, voice rising.

'Yes,' Moridyr said, grin broadening. 'As I said, sounds like him. He probably amused himself thoroughly, coming up with the whole idea.'

She climbed off him with a dramatic snort. 'Divines have mercy on me. Is this where I conclude madness and manipulative tendencies run in the family, then?'

'I'm the last to doubt your diagnosis,' he said dryly, sitting up and crossing his arms over his knees. 'Don't worry too much, morning star. If the boy got that soap into your cell, he would have been perfectly able to get *you* out of that cell too, had he wanted to. Since he didn't, I'm going to assume he's not in dire need of your services and will handle Cyril just fine on his own.'

That seemed to Briannis a lot of faith in the sort of person who considered assassination attempts a proper form of matchmaking, but then again ... She *had* made it into the Keep. Moridyr *had* handled the situation. And the divines knew that she *had* fallen in love with him, deeply and senselessly.

So perhaps the little madman was at least the convenient type of mad.

'I'll try not to worry,' she said, drawing a finger down the jutting ridges of his left ribs until his breath caught. 'But if no one has ended Cyril in eight years or so, you have to promise you won't stop me from walking back to the city and doing it myself.'

'That is a compromise I can live with.' He smiled at her, that wicked fae smile dazzling with terrible intentions – the smile that could make her feel like a pearl-clutching saint even sitting naked on a seed-stained dancefloor. 'Until that time, however, I'm afraid we'll have to amuse ourselves.'

In this castle as large as a city, hundreds upon hundreds of rooms to discover, and as many corridors to explore. A library full of books. Rooms full of weapons. A kitchen that would never stop producing the most lavish of meals at the slightest request.

With him.

She had not known a heart could smile.

'A terrible fate,' she muttered, crawling back into his lap and running her fingers through his hair. 'Shall we get started, then?'

And his lips upon hers promised her she would not be bored for a minute of it.

The Wayfarer Fae series will continue with *Lies of the Ink Mage*, which is set to release in 2024.

Can't wait that long for more tormented fae men? Take a look at *Court of Blood and Bindings*, the first book of my Fae Isles series, which features another morally grey hero, a rebellious heroine, and a steamy enemies to lovers romance.

Acknowledgements

A WRITER WITHOUT FRIENDS is like... a garden without flowers, I suppose? (I'm trying to stick with the theme for this book.)

As with everything I write, *Curse of the Thorn King* would not have existed without the wonderful people who inspired me, believed in me, and guided me through my regular fits of writer's despair. In no particular order, I would like to thank: Steph for talking about sarcastic ginger heroes for long enough to make me write one; Amber for all the iddy brainstorm sessions that helped shape this world; Colleen for the *heeeeeees* and other invaluable words of encouragement; Vela for the epic and always helpful Walls Of Text; and Elsie for the ever-amusing supply of both useful and less useful animal facts. A special thanks to Erin, who managed once again not to strangle me when this book ended up twice as long as intended – your work has been flawless as always.

And, as always, all my love to W., who was no longer even surprised when I had to confess I accidentally wrote another book. You know me so well.

About the Author

Lisette Marshall is a fantasy romance author, language nerd and cartography enthusiast. Having grown up on a steady diet of epic fantasy, regency romance and cosy mysteries, she now writes steamy, swoony stories with a generous sprinkle of murder.

Lisette lives in the Netherlands (yes, below sea level) with her boyfriend and the few house plants that miraculously survive her highly irregular watering regime. When she's not reading or writing, she can usually be found drawing fantasy maps, baking and eating too many chocolate cookies, or geeking out over Ancient Greek.

To get in touch, visit www.lisettemarshall.com, or follow @authorlisettemarshall on Instagram, where she spends way too much time looking at pretty book pictures.

Printed in Great Britain
by Amazon

27388131R00155